Anne of Green Gables Has A Plan!

"Theodora," said Anne coaxingly, "I'm going to be curious and impertinent. You can snub me if you like. Why don't you and Ludovic Speed get married?"

Theodora laughed comfortably. "That's a question folks have been asking for quite a while. Well, I'd have no objection to marrying Ludovic. That's frank enough for you, isn't it? But Ludovic has never asked me."

"Is he too shy?" persisted Anne.

Theodora dropped her sewing and looked meditatively out over the green slopes of the summer world. "No, I don't think it is that. It's just his way. He never hurried in his life. He's fond of me, and he means to ask me to have him sometime. The only question is—will the time ever come?"

"Why don't you hurry him up?" asked Anne impatiently.

"If Ludovic could be hurried up, I'm not the one to do it. I'm too shy. Of course, I know it's the only way any Speed ever did make out to get married."

"Theodora," cried Anne. "I have a plan!"

Lucy Maud Montgomery fans will also enjoy these other
Bantam Books by the author

ANNE OF AVONLEA
ANNE OF GREEN GABLES
ANNE'S HOUSE OF DREAMS
ANNE OF THE ISLAND
ANNE OF WINDY POPLARS
ANNE OF INGLESIDE
EMILY CLIMBS
EMILY OF NEW MOON
EMILY'S QUEST
RAINBOW VALLEY
RILLA OF INGLESIDE

CHRONICLES
OF
AVONLEA

L.M. Montgomery

BANTAM BOOKS
TORONTO · NEW YORK · LONDON · SYDNEY · AUCKLAND

RL 7, IL age 12 and up

CHRONICLES OF AVONLEA

*A Bantam Starfire Book / published by arrangement with
the author's estate*

PRINTING HISTORY
First Canadian edition published September 1943.

Bantam edition / September 1988

*The Starfire logo is a registered trademark of Bantam Books, a division of
Bantam Doubleday Dell Publishing Group, Inc. Registered in U.S. Patent and
Trademark Office and elsewhere.*

ISBN 0-553-27534-8

Published simultaneously in the United States and Canada

---

*Bantam Books are published by Bantam Books, a division of Bantam Doubleday
Dell Publishing Group, Inc. Its trademark, consisting of the words ''Bantam
Books'' and the portrayal of a rooster, is Registered in U.S. Patent and Trademark
Office and in other countries. Marca Registrada. Bantam Books, 666 Fifth Avenue,
New York, New York 10103.*

PRINTED IN CANADA

COVER PRINTED IN U.S.A.

U   0 9 8 7 6 5 4 3 2 1

TO THE MEMORY OF

𝔐𝔯𝔰. 𝔚𝔦𝔩𝔩𝔦𝔞𝔪 𝔄. 𝔥𝔬𝔲𝔰𝔱𝔬𝔫

A DEAR FRIEND, WHO HAS GONE BEYOND

Contents

The unsung beauty hid
life's common things below:
                                        —Whittier.

1

The Hurrying of Ludovic

ANNE SHIRLEY was curled up on the window seat of Theodora Dix's sitting-room one Saturday evening, looking dreamily afar at some fair starland beyond the hills of sunset. Anne was visiting for a fortnight of her vacation at Echo Lodge, where Mr. and Mrs. Stephen Irving were spending the summer, and she often ran over to the old Dix homestead to chat for awhile with Theodora. They had had their chat out, on this particular evening, and Anne was giving herself over to the delight of building an air-castle. She leaned her shapely head, with its braided coronet of dark red hair, against the window-casing, and her gray eyes were like the moonlight gleam of shadowy pools.

Then she saw Ludovic Speed coming down the lane. He was yet far from the house, for the Dix lane was a long one, but Ludovic could be recognized as far as he could be seen. No one else in Middle Grafton had such a tall, gently stooping, placidly moving figure. In every kink and turn of it there was an individuality all Ludovic's own.

Anne roused herself from her dreams, thinking it would only be tactful to take her departure. Ludovic was courting Theodora. Everyone in Grafton knew that, or, if anyone were in ignorance of the fact, it was not because he had not had time to find out. Ludovic had been coming down that lane to see Theodora, in the same ruminating, unhastening fashion, for fifteen years!

When Anne, who was slim and girlish and romantic, rose to go, Theodora, who was plump and middle-aged and practical, said, with a twinkle in her eye:

1

"There isn't any hurry, child. Sit down and have your call out. You've seen Ludovic coming down the lane, and, I suppose, you think you'll be a crowd. But you won't. Ludovic rather likes a third person around, and so do I. It spurs up the conversation, as it were. When a man has been coming to see you straight along, twice a week for fifteen years, you get rather talked out by spells."

Theodora never pretended to bashfulness where Ludovic was concerned. She was not at all shy of referring to him and his dilatory courtship. Indeed, it seemed to amuse her.

Anne sat down again and together they watched Ludovic coming down the lane, gazing calmly about him at the lush clover fields and the blue loops of the river winding in and out of the misty valley below.

Anne looked at Theodora's placid, finely moulded face and tried to imagine what she herself would feel like if she were sitting there, waiting for an elderly lover who had, seemingly, taken so long to make up his mind. But even Anne's imagination failed her for this.

"Anyway," she thought, impatiently, "if I wanted him I think I'd find some way of hurrying him up. Ludovic *Speed!* Was there ever such a misfit of a name? Such a name for such a man is a delusion and a snare."

Presently Ludovic got to the house, but stood so long on the doorstep in a brown study, gazing into the tangled green boskage of the cherry orchard, that Theodora finally went and opened the door before he knocked. As she brought him into the sitting-room she made a comical grimace at Anne over his shoulder.

Ludovic smiled pleasantly at Anne. He liked her; she was the only young girl he knew, for he generally avoided young girls—they made him feel awkward and out of place. But Anne did not affect him in this fashion. She had a way of getting on with all sorts of people, and, although they had not known her very long, both Ludovic and Theodora looked upon her as an old friend.

Ludovic was tall and somewhat ungainly, but his unhesitating placidity gave him the appearance of a dignity that did not otherwise pertain to him. He had a drooping, silky, brown moustache, and a little curly tuft of imperial—a fashion which was regarded as eccentric in Grafton, where men had clean-shaven chins or went full-bearded. His eyes were dreamy and pleasant, with a touch of melancholy in their blue depths.

He sat down in the big bulgy old armchair that had belonged to Theodora's father. Ludovic always sat there, and Anne declared that the chair had come to look like him.

The conversation soon grew animated enough. Ludovic was a good talker when he had somebody to draw him out. He was well-read, and frequently surprised Anne by his shrewd comments on men and matters out in the world, of which only the faint echoes reached Grafton. He had also a liking for religious arguments with Theodora, who did not care much for politics or the making of history, but was avid of doctrines, and read everything pertaining thereto. When the conversation drifted into an eddy of friendly wrangling between Ludovic and Theodora over Christian Science, Anne understood that her usefulness was ended for the time being, and that she would not be missed.

"It's star time and good-night time," she said, and went away quietly.

But she had to stop to laugh when she was well out of sight of the house, in a green meadow be-starred with the white and gold of daisies. A wind, odour-freighted, blew daintily across it. Anne leaned against a white birch tree in the corner and laughed heartily, as she was apt to do whenever she thought of Ludovic and Theodora. To her eager youth, this courtship of theirs seemed a very amusing thing. She liked Ludovic, but allowed herself to be provoked with him.

"The dear, big, irritating goose!" she said aloud. "There never was such a lovable idiot before. He's just like the alligator in the old rhyme, who wouldn't go along, and wouldn't keep still, but just kept bobbing up and down."

Two evenings later, when Anne went over to the Dix place, she and Theodora drifted into a conversation about Ludovic. Theodora, who was the most industrious soul alive, and had a mania for fancy work into the bargain, was busying her smooth, plump fingers with a very elaborate

Battenburg lace centrepiece. Anne was lying back in a little rocker, with her slim hands folded in her lap, watching Theodora. She realized that Theodora was very handsome, in a stately, Juno-like fashion of firm, white flesh, large, clearly chiselled outlines, and great, cowey, brown eyes. When Theodora was not smiling, she looked very imposing. Anne thought it likely that Ludovic held her in awe.

"Did you and Ludovic talk about Christian Science *all* Saturday evening?" she asked.

Theodora overflowed into a smile.

"Yes, and we even quarrelled over it. At least *I* did. Ludovic wouldn't quarrel with anyone. You have to fight air when you spar with him. I hate to square up to a person who won't hit back."

"Theodora," said Anne coaxingly, "I am going to be curious and impertinent. You can snub me if you like. Why don't you and Ludovic get married?"

Theodora laughed comfortably.

"That's a question Grafton folks have been asking for quite a while, I reckon, Anne. Well, I'd have no objection to marrying Ludovic. That's frank enough for you, isn't it? But it's not easy to marry a man unless he asks you. And Ludovic has never asked me."

"Is he too shy?" persisted Anne. Since Theodora was in the mood, she meant to sift this puzzling affair to the bottom.

Theodora dropped her work and looked meditatively out over the green slopes of the summer world.

"No, I don't think it is that Ludovic isn't shy. It's just his way—the Speed way. The Speeds are all dreadfully deliberate. They spend years thinking over a thing before they make up their minds to do it. Sometimes they get so much in the habit of thinking about it that they never get over it—like old Alder Speed, who was always talking of going to England to see his brother, but never went, though there was no earthly reason why he shouldn't. They're not lazy, you know, but they love to take their time."

"And Ludovic is just an aggravated case of Speedism," suggested Anne.

"Exactly. He never hurried in his life. Why, he has been thinking for the last six years of getting his house painted. He talks it over with me every little while, and picks out the colour, and there the matter stays. He's fond of me, and he means to ask me to have him sometime. The only question is—will the time ever come?"

"Why don't you hurry him up?" asked Anne impatiently.

Theodora went back to her stitches with another laugh.

"If Ludovic could be hurried up, I'm not the one to do it. I'm too shy. It sounds ridiculous to hear a woman of my age and inches say that, but it is true. Of course, I know it's the only way any Speed ever did make out to get married. For instance, there's a cousin of mine married to Ludovic's brother. I don't say she proposed to him out and out, but, mind you, Anne, it wasn't far from it. I couldn't do anything like that. I *did* try once. When I realized that I was getting sere and mellow, and all the girls of my generation were going off on either hand, I tried to give Ludovic a hint. But it stuck in my throat. And now I don't mind. If I don't change Dix to Speed until I take the initiative, it will be Dix to the end of life. Ludovic doesn't realize that we are growing old, you know. He thinks we are giddy young folks yet, with plenty of time before us. That's the Speed failing. They never find out they're alive until they're dead."

"You're fond of Ludovic, aren't you?" asked Anne, detecting a note of real bitterness among Theodora's paradoxes.

"Laws, yes," said Theodora candidly. She did not think it worth while to blush over so settled a fact. "I think the world and all of Ludovic. And he certainly does need somebody to look after him. He's neglected—he looks frayed. You can see that for yourself. That old aunt of his looks after his house in some fashion, but she doesn't look after *him*. And he's coming now to the age when a man needs to be looked after and coddled a bit. I'm lonesome here, and Ludovic is lonesome up there, and it does seem ridiculous, doesn't it? I don't wonder that we're the standing joke of Grafton. Goodness knows, I laugh at it enough myself. I've sometimes thought that if Ludovic could be made jealous it might spur him along. But I never could flirt and there's nobody to flirt with if I could. Everybody hereabouts looks upon me as Ludovic's property and nobody would dream of interfering with him."

"Theodora," cried Anne, "I have a plan!"

"Now, what are you going to do?" exclaimed Theodora.

Anne told her. At first Theodora laughed and protested. In the end, she yielded somewhat doubtfully, overborne by Anne's enthusiasm.

"Well, try it, then," she said, resignedly. "If Ludovic gets mad and leaves me, I'll be worse off than ever. But nothing venture, nothing win. And there is a fighting chance, I suppose. Besides, I must admit I'm tired of his dilly-dallying."

Anne went back to Echo Lodge tingling with delight in her plot. She hunted up Arnold Sherman, and told him what was required of him. Arnold Sherman listened and laughed. He was an elderly widower, an intimate friend of Stephen Irving, and had come down to spend part of the summer with him and his wife in Prince Edward Island. He was handsome in a mature style, and he had a dash of mischief in him still, so that he entered readily enough into Anne's plan. It amused him to think of hurrying Ludovic Speed, and he knew that Theodora Dix could be depended on to do her part. The comedy would not be dull, whatever its outcome.

The curtain rose on the first act after prayer meeting on the next Thursday night. It was bright moonlight when the people came out of church, and everybody saw it plainly. Arnold Sherman stood upon the steps close to the door, and Ludovic Speed leaned up against a corner of the graveyard fence, as he had done for years. The boys said he had worn the paint off that particular place. Ludovic knew of no reason why he should paste himself up against the church door. Theodora would come out as usual, and he would join her as she went past the corner.

This was what happened; Theodora came down the steps, her stately figure outlined in its darkness against the gush of lamplight from the porch. Arnold Sherman asked her if he might see her home. Theodora took his arm calmly, and together they swept past the stupefied Ludovic, who stood helplessly gazing after them as if unable to believe his eyes.

For a few moments he stood there limply; then he started down the road after his fickle lady and her new admirer. The boys and irresponsible young men crowded after, expecting some excitement, but they were disappointed. Ludovic strode on until he overtook Theodora and Arnold Sherman, and then fell meekly in behind them.

Theodora hardly enjoyed her walk home, although Arnold Sherman laid himself out to be especially entertaining. Her heart yearned after Ludovic, whose shuffling footsteps she heard behind her. She feared that she had been very cruel, but she was in for it now. She steeled herself by the reflection that it was all for his own good, and she talked to Arnold Sherman as if he were the one man in the world. Poor, deserted Ludovic, following humbly behind, heard her, and if Theodora had known how bitter the cup she was holding to his lips really was, she would never have been resolute enough to present it, no matter for what ultimate good.

When she and Arnold turned in at her gate, Ludovic had to stop. Theodora looked over her shoulder and saw him standing still on the road. His forlorn figure haunted her thoughts all night. If Anne had not run over the next day and bolstered up her convictions, she might have spoiled everything by prematurely relenting.

Ludovic, meanwhile, stood still on the road, quite oblivious to the hoots and comments of the vastly amused small boy contingent, until Theodora and his rival disappeared from his view under the firs in the hollow of her lane. Then he turned about and went home, not with his usual leisurely amble, but with a perturbed stride which proclaimed his inward disquiet.

He felt bewildered. If the world had come suddenly to an end or if the lazy, meandering Grafton River had turned about and flowed up hill, Ludovic could not have been more astonished. For fifteen years he had walked home from meetings with Theodora; and now this elderly stranger, with all the glamour of "the States" hanging about him, had coolly walked off with her under Ludovic's very nose. Worse—most unkindest cut of all—Theodora had gone with him willingly; nay, she had evidently enjoyed his company. Ludovic felt the stirring of a righteous anger in his easy-going soul.

When he reached the end of his lane, he paused at his gate, and looked at his house, set back from the lane in a crescent of birches. Even in the moonlight, its weather-worn aspect was plainly visible. He thought of the "palatial residence" rumour ascribed to Arnold Sherman in Boston, and stroked his chin nervously with his sunburnt fingers. Then he doubled up his fist and struck it smartly on the gate-post.

"Theodora needn't think she is going to jilt me in this fashion, after keeping company with me for fifteen years," he said. "*I'll* have something to say to it, Arnold Sherman or no Arnold Sherman. The impudence of the puppy!"

The next morning Ludovic drove to Carmody and engaged Joshua Pye to come and paint his house, and that evening, although he was not due till Saturday night, he went down to see Theodora.

Arnold Sherman was there before him, and was actually sitting in Ludovic's own prescriptive chair. Ludovic had to deposit himself in Theodora's new wicker rocker, where he looked and felt lamentably out of place.

If Theodora felt the situation to be awkward, she carried it off superbly. She had never looked handsomer, and Ludovic perceived that she wore her second best silk dress. He wondered miserably if she had donned it in expectation of his rival's call. She had never put on silk dresses for him. Ludovic had always been the meekest and mildest of mortals, but he felt quite murderous as he sat mutely there and listened to Arnold Sherman's polished conversation.

"You should just have been here to see him glowering," Theodora told the delighted Anne the next day. "It may be wicked of me, but I felt real glad. I was afraid he might stay away and sulk. So long as he comes here and sulks I don't worry. But he is feeling badly enough, poor soul, and I'm really eaten up by remorse. He tried to outstay Mr. Sherman last night, but he didn't manage it.

You never saw a more depressed-looking creature than he was as he hurried down the lane. Yes, he actually hurried."

The following Sunday evening Arnold Sherman walked to church with Theodora, and sat with her. When they came in, Ludovic Speed suddenly stood up in his pew under the gallery. He sat down again at once, but everybody in view had seen him, and that night folks in all the length and breadth of Grafton River discussed the dramatic occurrence with keen enjoyment.

"Yes, he jumped right up as if he was pulled to his feet, while the minister was reading the chapter," said his cousin, Lorella Speed, who had been in church, to her sister, who had not. "His face was as white as a sheet, and his eyes were just glaring out of his head. I never felt so thrilled, I declare! I almost expected him to fly at them then and there. But he just gave a sort of gasp and set down again. I don't know whether Theodora Dix saw him or not. She looked as cool and unconcerned as you please."

Theodora had not seen Ludovic, but if she looked cool and unconcerned, her appearance belied her, for she felt miserably flustered. She could not prevent Arnold Sherman coming to church with her, but it seemed to her like going too far. People did not go to church and sit together in Grafton unless they were the next thing to being engaged. What if this filled Ludovic with the narcotic of despair instead of wakening him up! She sat through the service in misery and heard not one word of the sermon.

But Ludovic's spectacular performances were not yet over. The Speeds might be hard to get started, but once they were started their momentum was irresistible. When Theodora and Mr. Sherman came out, Ludovic was waiting on the steps. He stood up straight and stern, with his head thrown back and his shoulders squared. There was open defiance in the look he cast on his rival, and masterfulness in the mere touch of the hand he laid on Theodora's arm.

"May I see you home, Miss Dix?" his words said. His tone said, "I am going to see you home whether or no."

Theodora, with a deprecating look at Arnold Sherman, took his arm, and Ludovic marched her across the green amid a silence which the very horses tied to the storm fence seemed to share. For Ludovic 'twas a crowded hour of glorious life.

Anne walked all the way over from Avonlea the next day to hear the news. Theodora smiled consciously.

"Yes, it is really settled at last, Anne. Coming home last night Ludovic asked me plump and plain to marry him—Sunday and all as it was. It's to be right away—for Ludovic won't be put off a week longer than necessary."

"So Ludovic Speed has been hurried up to some purpose at last," said Mr. Sherman, when Anne called in at Echo Lodge, brimful with her news. "And you are delighted, of course, and my poor pride must be the scapegoat. I shall always be remembered in Grafton as the man from Boston who wanted Theodora Dix and couldn't get her."

"But that won't be true, you know," said Anne comfortingly.

Arnold Sherman thought of Theodora's ripe beauty, and the mellow companionableness she had revealed in their brief intercourse.

"I'm not perfectly sure of that," he said, with a half-sigh.

2

Old Lady Lloyd

I. The May Chapter

SPENCERVALE gossip always said that "Old Lady Lloyd" was rich and mean and proud. Gossip, as usual, was one-third right and two-thirds wrong. Old Lady Lloyd was neither rich nor mean; in reality she was pitifully poor—so poor that "Crooked Jack" Spencer, who dug her garden and chopped her wood for her, was opulent by contrast; for he, at least, never lacked three meals a day, and the Old Lady could sometimes achieve no more than one. But she *was* very proud—so proud that she would have died rather than let the Spencervale people, among whom she had queened it in her youth, suspect how poor she was and to what straits was sometimes reduced. She much preferred to have them think her miserly and odd—a queer old recluse who never went anywhere, even to church, and who paid the smallest subscription to the minister's salary of anyone in the congregation.

"And her just rolling in wealth!" they said indignantly. "Well, she didn't get her miserly ways from her parents. *They* were real generous and neighbourly. There never was a finer gentleman than old Doctor Lloyd. He was always doing kindnesses to everybody; and he had a way of doing them that made you feel as if you was doing the favour, not him. Well, well, let Old Lady Lloyd keep herself and her money to herself if she wants to. If she doesn't want our company, she doesn't have to suffer it, that's all. Reckon she isn't none too happy for all her money and pride."

11

No, the Old Lady was none too happy, that was unfortunately true. It is not easy to be happy when your life is eaten up with loneliness and emptiness on the spiritual side, and when, on the material side, all you have between you and starvation is the little money your hens bring you in.

The Old Lady lived "away back at the old Lloyd place," as it was always called. It was a quaint, low-eaved house, with big chimneys and square windows and with spruces growing thickly all around it. The Old Lady lived there all alone and there were weeks at a time when she never saw a human being except Crooked Jack. What the Old Lady did with herself and how she put in her time was a puzzle the Spencervale people could not solve. The children believed she amused herself counting the gold in the big black box under her bed. Spencervale children held the Old Lady in mortal terror; some of them—the "Spencer Road" fry—believed she was a witch; all of them would run if, when wandering about the woods in search of berries or spruce gum, they saw at a distance the spare, upright form of the Old Lady, gathering sticks for her fire. Mary Moore was the only one who was quite sure she was not a witch.

"Witches are always ugly," she said decisively, "and Old Lady Lloyd isn't ugly. She's real pretty—she's got such soft white hair and big black eyes and a little white face. Those Road children don't know what they're talking of. Mother says they're a very ignorant crowd."

"Well, she doesn't ever go to church, and she mutters and talks to herself all the time she's picking up sticks," maintained Jimmy Kimball stoutly.

The Old Lady talked to herself because she was really very fond of company and conversation. To be sure, when you have talked to nobody but yourself for nearly twenty years, it is apt to grow somewhat monotonous; and there were times when the Old Lady would have sacrificed everything but her pride for a little human companionship. At such times she felt very bitter and resentful towards Fate for having taken everything from her. She had nothing to love, and that is about as unwholesome a condition as is possible to anyone.

It was always hardest in the spring. Once upon a time the Old Lady—when she had not been the Old Lady, but pretty, wilful, high-spirited Margaret Lloyd—had loved springs; now she hated them because they hurt her; and this particular spring of this particular May chapter hurt her more than any that had gone before. The Old Lady felt as if she could *not* endure the ache of it. Everything hurt her—the new green tips on the firs, the fairy mists down in the little beech hollow below the house, the fresh smell of the red earth Crooked Jack spaded up in her garden. The Old Lady lay awake all one moonlit night and cried for very heartache. She even forgot her body hunger in her soul hunger; and the Old Lady had been hungry, more or less, all that week. She was living on store biscuits and water, so that she might be able to pay Crooked Jack for digging her garden. When the pale, lovely dawn-colour came stealing up the sky behind the spruces, the Old Lady buried her face in her pillow and refused to look at it.

"I hate the new day," she said rebelliously. "It will be just like all the other hard, common days. I don't want to get up and live it. And, oh, to think that long ago I reached out my hands joyfully to every new day, as to a friend who was bringing me good tidings! I loved the mornings then— sunny or gray, they were as delightful as an unread book— and now I hate them—hate them—hate them!"

But the Old Lady got up nevertheless, for she knew Crooked Jack would be coming early to finish the garden. She arranged her beautiful thick, white hair very carefully, and put on her purple silk dress with the little gold spots in it. The Old Lady always wore silk from motives of economy. It was much cheaper to wear a silk dress that had belonged to her mother than to buy new print at the store. The Old Lady had plenty of silk dresses which had belonged to her mother. She wore them morning, noon, and night, and Spencervale people considered it an additional evidence of her pride. As for the fashion of them, it was, of course, just because she was too mean to have them made over. They did not dream that the Old Lady never put on one of the silk dresses without agonizing over its unfashionableness, and that even the eyes of

Crooked Jack cast on her antique flounces and overskirts was almost more than her feminine vanity could endure.

In spite of the fact that the Old Lady had not welcomed the new day, its beauty charmed her when she went out for a walk after her dinner—or, rather, after her mid-day biscuit. It was so fresh, so sweet, so virgin; and the spruce woods around the old Lloyd place were athrill with busy spring doings and all sprinkled through with young lights and shadows. Some of their delight found its way into the Old Lady's bitter heart as she wandered through them, and when she came out at the little plank bridge over the brook, down under the beeches, she felt almost gentle and tender once more. There was one big beech there, in particular, which the Old Lady loved for reasons best known to herself—a great, tall beech with a trunk like the shaft of a gray marble column and a leafy spread of branches over the still, golden-brown pool made beneath it by the brook. It had been a young sapling in the days that were haloed by the vanished glory of the Old Lady's life.

The Old Lady heard childish voices and laughter afar up the lane which led to William Spencer's place just above the woods. William Spencer's front lane ran out to the main road in a different direction, but this "back lane" furnished a short cut and his children always went to school that way.

The Old Lady shrank hastily back behind a clump of young spruces. She did not like the Spencer children because they always seemed so afraid of her. Through the spruce screen she could see them coming gaily down the lane—the two older ones in front, the twins behind, clinging to the hands of a tall, slim, young girl—the new music teacher, probably. The Old Lady had heard from the egg pedlar that she was going to board at William Spencer's, but she had not heard her name.

She looked at her with some curiosity as they drew near—and then, all at once, the Old Lady's heart gave a great bound and began to beat as it had not beaten for years, while her breath came quickly and she trembled violently. Who—*who* could this girl be?

Under the new music teacher's straw hat were masses

of fine chestnut hair of the very shade and wave that the Old Lady remembered on another head in vanished years; from under those waves looked large, violet-blue eyes with very black lashes and brows—and the Old Lady knew those eyes as well as she knew her own; and the new music teacher's face, with all its beauty of delicate outline and dainty colouring and glad, buoyant youth, was a face from the Old Lady's past—a perfect resemblance in every respect save one; the face which the Old Lady remembered had been weak, with all its charm; but this girl's face possessed a fine, dominant strength compact of sweetness and womanliness. As she passed by the Old Lady's hiding place she laughed at something one of the children said; and oh, but the Old Lady knew that laughter well. She had heard it before under that very beech tree.

She watched them until they disappeared over the wooded hill beyond the bridge; and then she went back home as if she walked in a dream. Crooked Jack was delving vigorously in the garden; ordinarily the Old Lady did not talk much with Crooked Jack, for she disliked his weakness for gossip; but now she went into the garden, a stately old figure in her purple, gold-spotted silk, with the sunshine gleaming on her white hair.

Crooked Jack had seen her go out and had remarked to himself that the Old Lady was losing ground; she was pale and peaked-looking. He now concluded that he had been mistaken. The Old Lady's cheeks were pink and her eyes shining. Somewhere in her walk she had shed ten years at least. Crooked Jack leaned on his spade and decided that there weren't many finer looking women anywhere than Old Lady Lloyd. Pity she was such an old miser!

"Mr. Spencer," said the Old Lady graciously—she always spoke very graciously to her inferiors when she talked to them at all—"can you tell me the name of the new music teacher who is boarding at Mr. William Spencer's?"

"Sylvia Gray," said Crooked Jack.

The Old Lady's heart gave another great bound. But she had known it—she had known that girl with Leslie

Gray's hair and eyes and laugh must be Leslie Gray's daughter.

Crooked Jack spat on his hand and resumed his work, but his tongue went faster than his spade, and the Old Lady listened greedily. For the first time she enjoyed and blessed Crooked Jack's garrulity and gossip. Every word he uttered was as an apple of gold in a picture of silver to her.

He had been working at William Spencer's the day the new music teacher had come, and what Crooked Jack couldn't find out about any person in one whole day—at least as far as outward life went—was hardly worth finding out. Next to discovering things did he love telling them, and it would be hard to say which enjoyed that ensuing half-hour more—Crooked Jack or the Old Lady.

Crooked Jack's account, boiled down, amounted to this; both Miss Gray's parents had died when she was a baby; she had been brought up by an aunt; she was very poor and very ambitious.

"Wants a moosical eddication," finished up Crooked Jack, "and, by jingo, she orter have it, for anything like the voice of her I never heerd. She sung for us that evening after supper and I thought 'twas an angel singing. It just went through me like a shaft o' light. The Spencer young ones are crazy over her already. She's got twenty pupils around here and in Grafton and Avonlea."

When the Old Lady had found out everything Crooked Jack could tell her, she went into the house and sat down by the window of her little sitting-room to think it all over. She was tingling from head to foot with excitement.

Leslie's daughter! This Old Lady had had her romance once. Long ago—forty years ago—she had been engaged to Leslie Gray, a young college student who taught in Spencervale for the summer term one year—the golden summer of Margaret Lloyd's life. Leslie had been a shy, dreamy, handsome fellow with literary ambitions, which, as he and Margaret both firmly believed, would one day bring him fame and fortune.

Then there had been a foolish, bitter quarrel at the end of that golden summer. Leslie had gone away in anger; afterwards he had written; but Margaret Lloyd, still

in the grasp of her pride and resentment, had sent a harsh
answer. No more letters came; Leslie Gray never returned; and one day Margaret wakened to the realization
that she had put love out of her life for ever. She knew it
would never be hers again; and from that moment her feet
were turned from youth to walk down the valley of shadow
to a lonely, eccentric age.

Many years later she heard of Leslie's marriage; then
came news of his death, after a life that had not fulfilled
his dreams for him. Nothing more she had heard or
known—nothing to this day, when she had seen his daughter pass her by unseeing in the beech hollow.

"His daughter! And she might have been *my* daughter," murmured the Old Lady. "Oh, if I could only know
her and love her—and perhaps win her love in return! But
I cannot. I could not have Leslie Gray's daughter know
how poor I am—how low I have been brought. I could not
bear that. And to think she is living so near me, the
darling—just up the lane and over the hill. I can see her
go by every day—I can have that dear pleasure, at least.
But oh, if I could only do something for her—give her
some little pleasure! It would be such a delight."

When the Old Lady happened to go into her spare
room that evening, she saw from it a light shining through
a gap in the trees on the hill. She knew that it shone from
the Spencers' spare room. So it was Sylvia's light. The Old
Lady stood in the darkness and watched it until it went
out—watched it with a great sweetness breathing in her
heart, such as rises from old rose-leaves when they are
stirred. She fancied Sylvia moving about her room, brushing and braiding her long, glistening hair—laying aside
her little trinkets and girlish adornments—making her
simple preparations for sleep. When the light went out,
the Old Lady pictured a slight white figure kneeling by
the window in the soft starshine; and the Old Lady knelt
down then and there and said her own prayers in fellow-
ship. She said the simple form of words she had always
used; but a new spirit seemed to inspire them; and she
finished with a new petition—"Let me think of something
I can do for her, dear Father—some little, little thing that
I can do for her."

The Old Lady had slept in the same room all her life—the one looking north into the spruces—and loved it; but the next day she moved into the spare room without a regret. It was to be her room after this; she must be where she could see Sylvia's light; she put the bed where she could lie in it and look at that earth star which had suddenly shone across the twilight shadows of her heart. She felt very happy; she had not felt happy for many years; but now a strange, new, dream-like interest, remote from the harsh realities of her existence, but none the less comforting and alluring, had entered into her life. Besides, she had thought of something she could do for Sylvia—"a little, little thing" that might give her pleasure.

Spencervale people were wont to say regretfully that there were no Mayflowers in Spencervale; the Spencervale young fry, when they wanted Mayflowers, thought they had to go over to the barrens at Avonlea, six miles away, for them. Old Lady Lloyd knew better. In her many long, solitary rambles, she had discovered a little clearing far back in the woods—a southward-sloping, sandy hill on a tract of woodland belonging to a man who lived in town—which in spring was starred over with the pink and white of arbutus.

To this clearing the Old Lady betook herself that afternoon, walking through wood lanes and under dim spruce arches like a woman with a glad purpose. All at once the spring was dear and beautiful to her once more; for love had entered again into her heart, and her starved soul was feasting on its divine nourishment.

Old Lady Lloyd found a wealth of Mayflowers on the sandy hill. She filled her basket with them, gloating over the loveliness which was to give pleasure to Sylvia. When she got home she wrote on a slip of paper, "For Sylvia." It was not likely anyone in Spencervale would know her handwriting, but, to make sure, she disguised it, writing in round, big letters like a child's. She carried her Mayflowers down to the hollow and heaped them in a recess between the big roots of the old beech, with the little note thrust through a stem on top.

Then the Old Lady deliberately hid behind the spruce

clump. She had put on her dark green silk on purpose for hiding. She had not long to wait. Soon Sylvia Gray came down the hill with Mattie Spencer. When she reached the bridge she saw the Mayflowers and gave an exclamation of delight. Then she saw her name and her expression changed to wonder. The Old Lady, peering through the boughs, could have laughed for very pleasure over the success of her little plot.

"For me!" said Sylvia, lifting the flowers. "*Can* they really be for me, Mattie? Who could have left them here?"

Mattie giggled.

"I believe it was Chris Stewart," she said. "I know he was over at Avonlea last night. And ma says he's taken a notion to you—she knows by the way he looked at you when you were singing night before last. It would be just like him to do something queer like this—he's such a shy fellow with the girls."

Sylvia frowned a little. She did not like Mattie's expressions; but she did like Mayflowers, and she did not dislike Chris Stewart, who had seemed to her merely a nice, modest, country boy. She lifted the flowers and buried her face in them.

"Anyway, I'm much obliged to the giver, whoever he or she is," she said merrily. "There's nothing I love like Mayflowers. Oh, how sweet they are!"

When they had passed the Old Lady emerged from her lurking place, flushed with triumph. It did not vex her that Sylvia should think Chris Stewart had given her the flowers; nay, it was all the better, since she would be the less likely to suspect the real donor. The main thing was that Sylvia should have the delight of them. That quite satisfied the Old Lady, who went back to her lonely house with the cockles of her heart all in a glow.

It soon was a matter of gossip in Spencervale that Chris Stewart was leaving Mayflowers at the beech hollow for the music teacher every other day. Chris himself denied it, but he was not believed. Firstly, there were no Mayflowers in Spencervale; secondly, Chris had to go to Carmody every other day to haul milk to the butter factory, and Mayflowers grew in Carmody; and, thirdly, the

Stewarts always had a romantic streak in them. Was not that enough circumstantial evidence for anybody?

As for Sylvia, she did not mind if Chris had a boyish admiration for her and expressed it thus delicately. She thought it very nice of him, indeed, when he did not vex her with any other advances, and she was quite content to enjoy his Mayflowers.

Old Lady Lloyd heard all the gossip about it from the egg pedlar, and listened to him with laughter glimmering far down in her eyes. The egg pedlar went away and vowed he'd never seen the Old Lady so spry as she was this spring; she seemed real interested in the young folk's doings.

The Old Lady kept her secret and grew young in it. She walked back to the Mayflower hill as long as the Mayflowers lasted; and she always hid in the spruces to see Sylvia Gray go by. Every day she loved her more, and yearned after her more deeply. All the long repressed tenderness of her nature overflowed to this girl who was unconscious of it. She was proud of Sylvia's grace and beauty, and sweetness of voice and laughter. She began to like the Spencer children because they worshipped Sylvia; she envied Mrs. Spencer because the latter could minister to Sylvia's needs. Even the egg pedlar seemed a delightful person because he brought news of Sylvia—her social popularity, her professional success, the love and admiration she had won already.

The Old Lady never dreamed of revealing herself to Sylvia. That, in her poverty, was not to be thought of for a moment. It would have been very sweet to know her— sweet to have her come to the old house—sweet to talk to her—to enter into her life. But it might not be. The Old Lady's pride was still far stronger than her love. It was the one thing she had never sacrificed and never—so she believed—could sacrifice.

II. The June Chapter

There were no Mayflowers in June; but now the Old

Lady's garden was full of blossoms and every morning Sylvia found a bouquet of them by the beech—the perfumed ivory of white narcissus, the flame of tulips, the fairy branches of bleeding-heart, the pink-and-snow of little, thorny, single, sweet-breathed early roses. The Old Lady had no fear of discovery, for the flowers that grew in her garden grew in every other Spencervale garden as well, including the Stewart garden. Chris Stewart, when he was teased about the music teacher, merely smiled and held his peace. Chris knew perfectly well who was the real giver of those flowers. He had made it his business to find out when the Mayflower gossip started. But since it was evident Old Lady Lloyd did not wish it to be known, Chris told no one. Chris had always liked Old Lady Lloyd ever since the day, ten years before, when she had found him crying in the woods with a cut foot and had taken him into her house, and bathed and bound the wound, and given him ten cents to buy candy at the store. The Old Lady went without her supper that night because of it, but Chris never knew that.

The Old Lady thought it a most beautiful June. She no longer hated the new days; on the contrary, she welcomed them.

"Every day is an uncommon day now," she said jubilantly to herself—for did not almost every day bring her a glimpse of Sylvia? Even on rainy days the Old Lady gallantly braved rheumatism to hide behind her clump of dripping spruces and watch Sylvia pass. The only days she could not see her were Sundays; and no Sundays had ever seemed so long to Old Lady Lloyd as those June Sundays did.

One day the egg pedlar had news for her.

"The music teacher is going to sing a solo for a collection piece to-morrow," he told her.

The Old Lady's black eyes flashed with interest.

"I didn't know Miss Gray was a member of the choir," she said.

"Jined two Sundays ago. I tell you, our music is something worth listening to now. The church'll be packed to-morrow, I reckon—her name's gone all over the country for singing. You ought to come and hear it, Miss Lloyd."

The pedlar said this out of bravado, merely to show he wasn't scared of the Old Lady, for all her grand airs. The Old Lady made no answer, and he thought he had offended her. He went away, wishing he hadn't said it. Had he but known it, the Old Lady had forgotten the existence of all and any egg pedlars. He had blotted himself and his insignificance out of her consciousness by his last sentence. All her thoughts, feelings, and wishes were submerged in a very whirlpool of desire to hear Sylvia sing that solo. She went into the house in a tumult and tried to conquer that desire. She could not do it, even though she summoned all her pride to her aid. Pride said:

"You will have to go to church to hear her. You haven't fit clothes to go to church in. Think what a figure you will make before them all."

But, for the first time, a more insistent voice than pride spoke to her soul—and, for the first time, the Old Lady listened to it. It was too true that she had never gone to church since the day on which she had to begin wearing her mother's silk dresses. The Old Lady herself thought that this was very wicked; and she tried to atone by keeping Sunday very strictly, and always having a little service of her own, morning and evening. She sang three hymns in her cracked voice, prayed aloud, and read a sermon. But she could not bring herself to go to church in her out-of-date clothes—she, who had once set the fashions in Spencervale; and the longer she stayed away, the more impossible it seemed that she should ever again go. Now the impossible had become, not only possible, but insistent. She must go to church and hear Sylvia sing, no matter how ridiculous she appeared, no matter how people talked and laughed at her.

Spencervale congregation had a mild sensation the next afternoon. Just before the opening of service Old Lady Lloyd walked up the aisle and sat down in the long-unoccupied Lloyd pew, in front of the pulpit.

The Old Lady's very soul was writhing within her. She recalled the reflection she had seen in her mirror before she left—the old black silk in the mode of thirty years agone and the queer little bonnet of shirred black satin. She thought how absurd she must look in the eyes of her world.

As a matter of fact, she did not look in the least absurd. Some women might have; but the Old Lady's stately distinction of carriage and figure was so subtly commanding that it did away with the consideration of garmenting altogether.

The Old Lady did not know this. But she did know that Mrs. Kimball, the storekeeper's wife, presently rustled into the next pew in the very latest fashion of fabric and mode; she and Mrs. Kimball were the same age, and there had been a time when the latter had been content to imitate Margaret Lloyd's costumes at a humble distance. But the storekeeper had proposed, and things were changed now; and there sat poor Old Lady Lloyd, feeling the change bitterly, and half-wishing she had not come to church at all.

Then all at once the Angel of Love touched these foolish thoughts, born of vanity and morbid pride, and they melted away as if they had never been. Sylvia Gray had come into the choir, and was sitting just where the afternoon sunshine fell over her beautiful hair like a halo. The Old Lady looked at her in a rapture of satisfied longing and thenceforth the service was blessed to her, as anything is blessed which comes through the medium of unselfish love, whether human or divine. Nay, are they not one and the same, differing in degree only, not in kind?

The Old Lady had never had such a good, satisfying look at Sylvia before. All her former glimpses had been stolen and fleeting. Now she sat and gazed upon her to her hungry heart's content, lingering delightedly over every little charm and loveliness—the way Sylvia's shining hair rippled back from her forehead, the sweet little trick she had of dropping quickly her long-lashed eyelids when she encountered too bold or curious a glance, and the slender, beautifully modelled hands—so like Leslie Gray's hands—that held her hymn book. She was dressed very plainly in a black skirt and a white shirtwaist; but none of the other girls in the choir, with all their fine feathers, could hold a candle to her—as the egg pedlar said to his wife, going home from church.

The Old Lady listened to the opening hymns with keen pleasure. Sylvia's voice thrilled through and dominated them all. But when the ushers got up to take the collection, an undercurrent of subdued excitement flowed over the congregation. Sylvia rose and came forward to Janet Moore's side at the organ. The next moment her beautiful voice soared through the building like the very soul of melody—true, clear, powerful, sweet. Nobody in Spencervale had ever listened to such a voice, except Old Lady Lloyd herself, who, in her youth, had heard enough good singing to enable her to be a tolerable judge of it. She realized instantly that this girl of her heart had a great gift—a gift that would some day bring her fame and fortune, if it could be duly trained and developed.

"Oh, I'm so glad I came to church," thought Old Lady Lloyd.

When the solo was ended, the Old Lady's conscience compelled her to drag her eyes and thoughts from Sylvia, and fasten them on the minister, who had been flattering himself all through the opening portion of the service that Old Lady Lloyd had come to church on his account. He was newly settled, having been in charge of the Spencervale congregation only a few months; he was a clever little fellow, and he honestly thought it was the fame of his preaching that had brought Old Lady Lloyd out to church.

When the service was over, all the Old Lady's neighbours came to speak to her, with kindly smile and handshake. They thought they ought to encourage her, now that she had made a start in the right direction; the Old Lady liked their cordiality, and liked it none the less because she detected in it the same unconscious respect and deference she had been wont to receive in the old days—a respect and deference which her personality compelled from all who approached her. The Old Lady was surprised to find that she could command it still, in defiance of unfashionable bonnet and ancient attire.

Janet Moore and Sylvia Gray walked home from church together.

"Did you see Old Lady Lloyd out to-day?" asked

Janet. "I was amazed when she walked in. She has never been to church in my recollection. What a quaint old figure she is! She's very rich, you know, but she wears her mother's old clothes and never gets a new thing. Some people think she is mean; but," concluded Janet charitably, "I believe it is simply eccentricity."

"I felt that was Miss Lloyd as soon as I saw her, although I had never seen her before," said Sylvia dreamily. "I have been wishing to see her—for a certain reason. She has a very striking face. I should like to meet her—to know her."

"I don't think it's likely you ever will," said Janet carelessly. "She doesn't like young people and she never goes anywhere. I don't think I'd like to know her. I'd be afraid of her—she has such stately ways and such strange, piercing eyes."

"*I* shouldn't be afraid of her," said Sylvia to herself, as she turned into the Spencer lane. "But I don't expect I'll ever become acquainted with her. If she knew who I am I suppose she would dislike me. I suppose she never suspects that I am Leslie Gray's daughter."

The minister, thinking it well to strike while the iron was hot, went up to call on Old Lady Lloyd the very next afternoon. He went in fear and trembling, for he had heard things about Old Lady Lloyd; but she made herself so agreeable in her high-bred fashion that he was delighted, and told his wife when he went home that Spencervale people didn't understand Miss Lloyd. This was perfectly true; but it is by no means certain that the minister understood her either.

He made only one mistake in tact, but, as the Old Lady did not snub him for it, he never knew he made it. When he was leaving he said, "I hope we shall see you at church next Sunday, Miss Lloyd."

"Indeed, you will," said the Old Lady emphatically.

III. The July Chapter

The first day of July Sylvia found a little birch bark

boat full of strawberries at the beech in the hollow. They were the earliest of the season; the Old Lady had found them in one of her secret haunts. They would have been a toothsome addition to the Old Lady's own slender bill of fare; but she never thought of eating them. She got far more pleasure out of the thought of Sylvia's enjoying them for her tea. Thereafter the strawberries alternated with the flowers as long as they lasted, and then came blueberries and raspberries. The blueberries grew far away and the Old Lady had many a tramp after them. Sometimes her bones ached at night because of it; but what cared the Old Lady for that? Bone ache is easier to endure than soul ache; and the Old Lady's soul had stopped aching for the first time in many a year. It was being nourished with heavenly manna.

One evening Crooked Jack came up to fix something that had gone wrong with the Old Lady's well. The Old Lady wandered affably out to him; for she knew he had been working at the Spencers' all day, and there might be crumbs of information about Sylvia to be picked up.

"I reckon the music teacher's feeling pretty blue this evening," Crooked Jack remarked, after straining the Old Lady's patience to the last verge of human endurance by expatiating on William Spencer's new pump, and Mrs. Spencer's new washing-machine, and Amelia Spencer's new young man.

"Why?" asked the Old Lady, turning very pale. Had anything happened to Sylvia?

"Well, she's been invited to a big party at Mrs. Moore's brother's in town, and she hasn't got a dress to go in," said Crooked Jack. "They're great swells and everybody will be got up regardless. Mrs. Spencer was telling me about it. She says Miss Gray can't afford a new dress because she's helping to pay her aunt's doctor's bills. She says she's sure Miss Gray feels awful disappointed over it, though she doesn't let on. But Mrs. Spencer says she knows she was crying after she went to bed last night."

The Old Lady turned and went into the house abruptly. This was dreadful. Sylvia must go to that party—she *must*. But how was it to be managed? Through the Old Lady's brain passed wild thoughts of her mother's silk dresses.

But none of them would be suitable, even if there were time to make one over. Never had the Old Lady so bitterly regretted her vanished wealth.

"I've only two dollars in the house," she said, "and I've got to live on that till the next day the egg pedlar comes round. Is there anything I can sell—*anything?* Yes, yes, the grape jug!"

Up to this time, the Old Lady would as soon have thought of trying to sell her head as the grape jug. The grape jug was two hundred years old and had been in the Lloyd family ever since it was a jug at all. It was a big, pot-bellied affair, festooned with pink-gilt grapes, and with a verse of poetry printed on one side, and it had been given as a wedding present to the Old Lady's great-grandmother. As long as the Old Lady could remember it had sat on the top shelf in the cupboard in the sitting-room wall, far too precious ever to be used.

Two years before, a woman who collected old china had explored Spencervale, and, getting word of the grape jug, had boldly invaded the old Lloyd place and offered to buy it. She never, to her dying day, forgot the reception the Old Lady gave her; but, being wise in her day and generation, she left her card, saying that if Miss Lloyd ever changed her mind about selling the jug, she would find that she, the aforesaid collector, had not changed hers about buying it. People who make a hobby of heirloom china must meekly overlook snubs, and this particular person had never seen anything she coveted so much as that grape jug.

The Old Lady had torn the card to pieces; but she remembered the name and address. She went to the cupboard and took down the beloved jug.

"I never thought to part with it," she said wistfully, "but Sylvia must have a dress, and there is no other way. And, after all, when I'm gone, who would there be to have it? Strangers would get it then—it might as well go to them now. I'll have to go to town to-morrow morning, for there's no time to lose if the party is Friday night. I haven't been to town for ten years. I dread the thought of going, more than parting with the jug. But for Sylvia's sake!"

It was all over Spencervale by the next morning that Old Lady Lloyd had gone to town, carrying a carefully guarded box. Everybody wondered why she went; most people supposed she had become too frightened to keep her money in a black box below her bed, when there had been two burglaries over at Carmody, and had taken it to the bank.

The Old Lady sought out the address of the china collector, trembling with fear that she might be dead or gone. But the collector was there, very much alive, and as keenly anxious to possess the grape jug as ever. The Old Lady, pallid with the pain of her trampled pride, sold the grape jug and went away, believing that her great-grandmother must have turned over in her grave at the moment of the transaction. Old Lady Lloyd felt like a traitor to her traditions.

But she went unflinchingly to a big store and, guided by that special Providence which looks after simple-minded old souls in their dangerous excursions into the world, found a sympathetic clerk who knew just what she wanted and got it for her. The Old Lady selected a very dainty muslin gown, with gloves and slippers in keeping; and she ordered it sent at once, expressage prepaid, to Miss Sylvia Gray, in care of William Spencer, Spencervale.

Then she paid down the money—the whole price of the jug, minus a dollar and a half for railroad fare—with a grand, careless air and departed. As she marched erectly down the aisle of the store, she encountered a sleek, portly, prosperous man coming in. As their eyes met, the man started and his bland face flushed crimson; he lifted his hat and bowed confusedly. But the Old Lady looked through him as if he wasn't there, and passed on with not a sign of recognition about her. He took one step after her, then stopped and turned away, with a rather disagreeable smile and a shrug of his shoulders.

Nobody would have guessed, as the Old Lady swept out, how her heart was seething with abhorrence and scorn. She would not have had the courage to come to town, even for Sylvia's sake, if she had thought she would meet Andrew Cameron. The mere sight of him opened up anew a sealed fountain of bitterness in her soul; but the thought of Sylvia somehow stemmed the torrent, and presently the Old Lady was smiling rather triumphantly, thinking rightly that she had come off best in that unwelcome encounter. *She,* at any rate, had not faltered and coloured, and lost her presence of mind.

"It is little wonder *he* did," thought the Old Lady vindictively. It pleased her that Andrew Cameron should lose, before her, the front of adamant he presented to the world. He was her cousin, and the only living creature Old Lady Lloyd hated; and she hated and despised him with all the intensity of her intense nature. She and hers had sustained grievous wrong at his hands, and the Old Lady was convinced that she would rather die than take any notice of his existence.

Presently, she resolutely put Andrew Cameron out of her mind. It was desecration to think of him and Sylvia together. When she laid her weary head on her pillow that night she was so happy that even the thought of the vacant shelf in the room below, where the grape jug had always been, gave her only a momentary pang.

"It's sweet to sacrifice for one we love—it's sweet to have someone to sacrifice for," thought the Old Lady.

Desire grows by what it feeds on. The Old Lady thought she was content; but Friday evening came and found her in a perfect fever to see Sylvia in her party dress. It was not enough to fancy her in it; nothing would do the Old Lady but seeing her.

"And I *shall* see her," said the Old Lady resolutely, looking out from her window at Sylvia's light gleaming through the firs. She wrapped herself in a dark shawl and crept out, slipping down to the hollow and up the wood lane. It was a misty, moonlight night, and a wind, fragrant with the aroma of clover fields, blew down the lane to meet her.

"I wish I could take your perfume—the soul of you— and pour it into her life," said the Old Lady aloud to that wind.

Sylvia Gray was standing in her room, ready for the party. Before her stood Mrs. Spencer and Amelia Spencer and all the little Spencer girls, in an admiring semi-circle. There was another spectator. Outside, under the lilac bush, Old Lady Lloyd was standing. She could see Sylvia plainly, in her dainty dress, with the pale pink roses Old Lady Lloyd had left at the beech that day for her in her hair. Pink as they were, they were not so pink as her cheeks, and her eyes shone like stars. Amelia Spencer put up her hand to push back a rose that had fallen a little out of place, and the Old Lady envied her fiercely.

"That dress couldn't have fitted better if it had been made for you," said Mrs. Spencer admiringly. "Ain't she lovely, Amelia? Who *could* have sent it?"

"Oh, I feel sure that Mrs. Moore was the fairy god-mother," said Sylvia. "There is nobody else who would. It was dear of her—she knew I wished so much to go to the party with Janet. I wish Aunty could see me now." Sylvia gave a little sigh in spite of her joy. "There's nobody else to care very much."

Ah, Sylvia, you were wrong! There was somebody else—somebody who cared very much—an Old Lady, with eager, devouring eyes, who was standing under the lilac bush and who presently stole away through the moonlit orchard to the woods like a shadow, going home with a vision of you in your girlish beauty to companion her through the watches of that summer night.

IV. The August Chapter

One day the minister's wife rushed in where Spencer-vale people had feared to tread, went boldly to Old Lady Lloyd, and asked her if she wouldn't come to their Sewing Circle, which met fortnightly on Saturday afternoons.

"We are filling a box to send to our Trinidad mission-ary," said the minister's wife, "and we should be so pleased to have you come, Miss Lloyd."

The Old Lady was on the point of refusing rather haughtily. Not that she was opposed to missions—or sewing circles either—quite the contrary; but she knew that each member of the Circle was expected to pay ten cents a week for the purpose of procuring sewing materials; and the poor Old Lady really did not see how she could afford it. But a sudden thought checked her refusal before it reached her lips.

"I suppose some of the young girls go to the Circle?" she said craftily.

"Oh, they all go," said the minister's wife. "Janet Moore and Miss Gray are our most enthusiastic members. It is very lovely of Miss Gray to give her Saturday afternoons—the only ones she has free from pupils—to our work. But she really has the sweetest disposition."

"I'll join your Circle," said the Old Lady promptly. She was determined she would do it, if she had to live on two meals a day to save the necessary fee.

She went to the Sewing Circle at James Martin's the next Saturday, and did the most beautiful hand sewing for them. She was so expert at it that she didn't need to think about it at all, which was rather fortunate, for all her thoughts were taken up with Sylvia, who sat in the opposite corner with Janet Moore, her graceful hands busy with a little boy's coarse gingham shirt. Nobody thought of introducing Sylvia to Old Lady Lloyd, and the Old Lady was glad of it. She sewed finely away, and listened with all her ears to the girlish chatter which went on in the opposite corner. One thing she found out—Sylvia's birthday was the twentieth of August. And the Old Lady was straightway fired with a consuming wish to give Sylvia a birthday present. She lay awake most of the night wondering if she could do it, and most sorrowfully concluded that it was utterly out of the question, no matter how she might pinch and contrive. Old Lady Lloyd worried quite absurdly over this, and it haunted her like a spectre until the next Sewing Circle day.

It met at Mrs. Moore's and Mrs. Moore was especially gracious to Old Lady Lloyd, and insisted on her taking the wicker rocker in the parlour. The Old Lady would rather have been in the sitting-room with the young girls, but she submitted for courtesy's sake—and she had her reward. Her chair was just behind the parlour door, and presently Janet Moore and Sylvia Gray came and sat on the stairs in the hall outside, where a cool breeze blew in through the maples before the front door.

They were talking of their favourite poets. Janet, it appeared, adored Byron and Scott. Sylvia leaned to Tennyson and Browning.

"Do you know," said Sylvia softly, "my father was a poet? He published a little volume of verse once; and, Janet, I've never seen a copy of it, and oh, how I would love to! It was published when he was at college—just a small, private edition to give his friends. He never published any more—poor father! I think life disappointed him. But I have such a longing to see that little book of his verse. I haven't a scrap of his writings. If I had it would seem as if I possessed something of him—of his heart, his soul, his inner life. He would be something more than a mere name to me."

"Didn't he have a copy of his own—didn't your mother have one?" asked Janet.

"Mother hadn't. She died when I was born, you know, but Aunty says there was no copy of father's poems among mother's books. Mother didn't care for poetry, Aunty says—Aunty doesn't either. Father went to Europe after mother died, and he died there the next year. Nothing that he had with him was ever sent home to us. He had sold most of his books before he went, but he gave a few of his favourite ones to Aunty to keep for me. *His* book wasn't among them. I don't suppose I shall ever find a copy; but I should be so delighted if I only could."

When the Old Lady got home she took from her top bureau drawer an inlaid box of sandalwood. It held a little, slim, limp volume, wrapped in tissue paper—the Old Lady's most treasured possession. On the fly-leaf was written, "To Margaret, with the author's love."

The Old Lady turned the yellowed leaves with trembling fingers and, through eyes brimming with tears, read the verses, although she had known them all by heart for years. She meant to give the book to Sylvia for a birthday present—one of the most precious gifts ever given, if the value of gifts is gauged by the measure of self-sacrifice involved. In that little book was immortal love— old laughter—old tears—old beauty which had bloomed like a rose years ago, holding still its sweetness like old rose leaves.

She removed the telltale fly-leaf; and late on the night before Sylvia's birthday, the Old Lady crept, under cover of the darkness, through byways and across fields, as if bent on some nefarious expedition, to the little Spencervale store where the post-office was kept. She slipped the thin parcel through the slit in the door, and then stole home again, feeling a strange sense of loss and loneliness. It was as if she had given away the last link between herself and her youth. But she did not regret it. It would give Sylvia pleasure, and that had come to be the overmastering passion of the Old Lady's heart.

The next night the light in Sylvia's room burned very late, and the Old Lady watched it triumphantly, knowing the meaning of it. Sylvia was reading her father's poems, and the Old Lady in her darkness read them too, murmuring the lines over and over to herself. After all, giving away the book had not mattered so very much. She had the soul of it still—and the fly-leaf with the name, in Leslie's writing, by which nobody ever called her now.

The Old Lady was sitting on the Marshall sofa the next Sewing Circle afternoon when Sylvia Gray came and sat down beside her. The Old Lady's hands trembled a little, and one side of a handkerchief, which was afterwards given as a Christmas present to a little olive-skinned coolie in Trinidad, was not quite so exquisitely done as the other three sides.

Sylvia at first talked of the Circle, and Mrs. Marshall's dahlias, and the Old Lady was in the seventh heaven of delight, though she took care not to show it, and was even a little more stately and finely mannered than usual. When she asked Sylvia how she liked living in Spencervale, Sylvia said,

"Very much. Everybody is so kind to me. Besides" —Sylvia lowered her voice so that nobody but the Old Lady could hear it—"I have a fairy godmother here who does the most beautiful and wonderful things for me."

Sylvia, being a girl of fine instincts, did not look at Old Lady Lloyd as she said this. But she would not have seen anything if she had looked. The Old Lady was not a Lloyd for nothing.

"How very interesting," she said, indifferently.

"Isn't it? I am so grateful to her and I have wished so much she might know how much pleasure she has given me. I have found lovely flowers and delicious berries on my path all summer; I feel sure she sent me my party dress. But the dearest gift came last week on my birthday—a little volume of my father's poems. I can't express what I felt on receiving them. But I longed to meet my fairy godmother and thank her."

"Quite a fascinating mystery, isn't it? Have you really no idea who she is?"

The Old Lady asked this dangerous question with marked success. She would not have been so successful if she had not been so sure that Sylvia had no idea of the old romance between her and Leslie Gray. As it was, she had a comfortable conviction that she herself was the very last person Sylvia would be likely to suspect.

Sylvia hesitated for an almost unnoticeable moment. Then she said, "I haven't tried to find out, because I don't think she wants me to know. At first, of course, in the matter of the flowers and dress, I did try to solve the mystery; but, since I received the book, I became convinced that it was my fairy godmother who was doing it all, and I have respected her wish for concealment and always shall. Perhaps some day she will reveal herself to me. I hope so, at least."

"I wouldn't hope it," said the Old Lady discouragingly. "Fairy godmothers—at least, in all the fairy tales I ever read—are somewhat apt to be queer, crochety people, much more agreeable when wrapped up in mystery than when met face to face."

"I'm convinced that mine is the very opposite, and that the better I became acquainted with her, the more charming a personage I should find her," said Sylvia gaily.

Mrs. Marshall came up at this juncture and entreated Miss Gray to sing for them. Miss Gray consenting sweetly, the Old Lady was left alone and was rather glad of it. She enjoyed her conversation with Sylvia much more in thinking it over after she got home than while it was taking place. When an Old Lady has a guilty conscience, it is apt to make her nervous and distract her thoughts from immediate pleasure. She wondered a little uneasily if Sylvia really did suspect her. Then she concluded that it was out of the question. Who would suspect a mean, unsociable Old Lady, who had no friends, and who gave only five cents to the Sewing Circle when everyone else gave ten or fifteen, to be a fairy godmother, the donor of beautiful party dresses, and the recipient of gifts from romantic, aspiring young poets?

V. The September Chapter

In September the Old Lady looked back on the summer and owned to herself that it had been a strangely happy one, with Sundays and Sewing Circle days standing out like golden punctuation marks in a poem of life. She felt like an utterly different woman; and other people thought her different also. The Sewing Circle women found her so pleasant, and even friendly, that they began to think they had misjudged her, and that perhaps it was eccentricity after all, and not meanness, which accounted for her peculiar mode of living. Sylvia Gray always came and talked to her on Circle afternoons now, and the Old Lady treasured every word she said in her heart and repeated them over and over to her lonely self in the watches of the night.

Sylvia never talked of herself or her plans, unless asked about them; and the Old Lady's self-consciousness prevented her from asking any personal questions: so their conversation kept to the surface of things, and it was not from Sylvia, but from the minister's wife that the Old Lady finally discovered what her darling's dearest ambition was.

The minister's wife had dropped in at the old Lloyd place one evening late in September, when a chilly wind was blowing up from the northeast and moaning about the eaves of the house, as if the burden of its lay were "harvest is ended and summer is gone." The Old Lady had been listening to it, as she plaited a little basket of sweet grass for Sylvia. She had walked all the way to Avonlea sand-hills for it the day before, and she was very tired. And her heart was sad. This summer, which had so enriched her life, was almost over; and she knew that Sylvia Gray talked of leaving Spencervale at the end of October. The Old Lady's heart felt like very lead within her at the thought, and she almost welcomed the advent of the minister's wife as a distraction, although she was desperately afraid that the minister's wife had called to ask for a subscription for the new vestry carpet, and the Old Lady simply could not afford to give one cent.

But the minister's wife had merely dropped in on her way home from the Spencers' and she did not make any embarrassing requests. Instead, she talked about Sylvia Gray, and her words fell on the Old Lady's ears like separate pearl notes of unutterably sweet music. The minister's wife had nothing but praise for Sylvia—she was so sweet and beautiful and winning.

"And with *such* a voice," said the minister's wife enthusiastically, adding with a sigh, "It's such a shame she can't have it properly trained. She would certainly become a great singer—competent critics have told her so. But she is so poor she doesn't think she can ever possibly manage it—unless she can get one of the Cameron scholarships, as they are called; and she has very little hope of that, although the professor of music who taught her has sent her name in."

"What are the Cameron scholarships?" asked the Old Lady.

"Well, I suppose you have heard of Andrew Cameron, the millionaire?" said the minister's wife, serenely unconscious that she was causing the very bones of the Old Lady's family skeleton to jangle in their closet.

Into the Old Lady's white face came a sudden faint stain of colour, as if a rough hand had struck her cheek.

"Yes, I've heard of him," she said.

"Well, it seems that he had a daughter, who was a very beautiful girl, and whom he idolized. She had a fine voice, and he was going to send her abroad to have it trained. And she died. It nearly broke his heart, I under-

stand. But ever since, he sends one young girl away to
Europe every year for a thorough musical education under
the best teachers—in memory of his daughter. He has
sent nine or ten already; but I fear there isn't much chance
for Sylvia Gray, and she doesn't think there is herself."

"Why not?" asked the Old Lady spiritedly. "I am sure
that there can be few voices equal to Miss Gray's."

"Very true. But you see, these so-called scholarships
are private affairs, dependent solely on the whim and
choice of Andrew Cameron himself. Of course, when a girl
has friends who use their influence with him, he will often
send her on their recommendation. They say he sent a girl
last year who hadn't much of a voice at all just because her
father had been an old business crony of his. But Sylvia
doesn't know anyone at all who would, to use a slang
term, have 'pull' with Andrew Cameron, and she is
not acquainted with him herself. Well, I must be going;
we'll see you at the Manse on Saturday, I hope, Miss
Lloyd. The Circle meets there, you know."

"Yes, I know," said the Old Lady absently. When the
minister's wife had gone, she dropped her sweet-grass
basket and sat for a long, long time with her hands lying
idly in her lap, and her big black eyes staring unseeingly
at the wall before her.

Old Lady Lloyd, so pitifully poor that she had to eat
six crackers the less a week to pay her fee to the Sewing
Circle, knew that it was in her power—*hers*—to send
Leslie Gray's daughter to Europe for her musical education! If she chose to use her "pull" with Andrew Cameron—
if she went to him and asked him to send Sylvia Gray
abroad the next year—she had no doubt whatever that it
would be done. It all lay with her—if—if— *if* she could so
far crush and conquer her pride as to stoop to ask a favour
of the man who had wronged her and hers so bitterly.

Years ago, her father, acting under the advice and
urgency of Andrew Cameron, had invested all his little
fortune in an enterprise that had turned out a failure.
Abraham Lloyd lost every dollar he possessed, and his
family were reduced to utter poverty. Andrew Cameron
might have been forgiven for a mistake; but there was a
strong suspicion, amounting to almost certainty, that he

had been guilty of something far worse than a mistake in regard to his uncle's investment. Nothing could be legally proved; but it was certain that Andrew Cameron, already noted for his "sharp practices," emerged with improved finances from an entanglement that had ruined many better men; and old Doctor Lloyd had died broken-hearted, believing that his nephew had deliberately victimized him.

Andrew Cameron had not quite done this; he had meant well enough by his uncle at first, and what he had finally done he tried to justify to himself by the doctrine that a man must look out for Number One.

Margaret Lloyd made no such excuses for him; she held him responsible, not only for her lost fortune, but for her father's death, and never forgave him for it. When Abraham Lloyd had died, Andrew Cameron, perhaps pricked by his conscience, had come to her, sleekly and smoothly, to offer her financial aid. He would see, he told her, that she never suffered want.

Margaret Lloyd flung his offer back in his face after a fashion that left nothing to be desired in the way of plain speaking. She would die, she told him passionately, before she would accept a penny or a favour from him. He had preserved an unbroken show of good temper, expressed his heartfelt regret that she should cherish such an unjust opinion of him, and had left her with an oily assurance that he would always be her friend, and would always be delighted to render her any assistance in his power whenever she should choose to ask for it.

The Old Lady had lived for twenty years in the firm conviction that she would die in the poorhouse—as, indeed, seemed not unlikely—before she would ask a favour of Andrew Cameron. And so, in truth, she would have, had it been for herself. But for Sylvia! Could she so far humble herself for Sylvia's sake?

The question was not easily or speedily settled, as had been the case in the matters of the grape jug and the book of poems. For a whole week the Old Lady fought her pride and bitterness. Sometimes, in the hours of sleepless night, when all human resentments and rancours seemed petty and contemptible, she thought she had conquered it. But in the daytime, with the picture of her father looking down at her from the wall, and the rustle of her unfashionable dresses, worn because of Andrew Cameron's double dealing, in her ears, it got the better of her again.

But the Old Lady's love for Sylvia had grown so strong and deep and tender that no other feeling could endure finally against it. Love is a great miracle worker; and never had its power been more strongly made manifest than on the cold, dull autumn morning when the Old Lady walked to Bright River railway station and took the train to Charlottetown, bent on an errand the very thought of which turned her soul sick within her. The station master who sold her her ticket thought Old Lady Lloyd looked uncommonly white and peaked—"as if she hadn't slept a wink or eaten a bite for a week," he told his wife at dinner time. "Guess there's something wrong in her business affairs. This is the second time she's gone to town this summer."

When the Old Lady reached the town, she ate her slender little lunch and then walked out to the suburb where the Cameron factories and warehouses were. It was a long walk for her, but she could not afford to drive. She felt very tired when she was shown into the shining, luxurious office where Andrew Cameron sat at his desk.

After the first startled glance of surprise, he came forward beamingly, with outstretched hand.

"Why, Cousin Margaret! This is a pleasant surprise. Sit down—allow me, this is a much more comfortable chair. Did you come in this morning? And how is everybody out in Spencervale?"

The Old Lady had flushed at his first words. To hear the name by which her father and mother and lover had called her on Andrew Cameron's lips seemed like profanation. But, she told herself, the time was past for squeamishness. If she could ask a favour of Andrew Cameron, she could bear lesser pangs. For Sylvia's sake she shook hands with him, for Sylvia's sake she sat down in the chair he offered. But for no living human being's sake could this determined Old Lady infuse any cordiality into her manner or her words. She went straight to the point with Lloyd simplicity.

"I have come to ask a favour of you," she said, looking

him in the eye, not at all humbly or meekly, as became a suppliant, but challengingly and defiantly, as if she dared him to refuse.

"*De*-lighted to hear it, Cousin Margaret." Never was anything so bland and gracious as his tone. "Anything I can do for you I shall be only too pleased to do. I am afraid you have looked upon me as an enemy, Margaret, and I assure you I have felt your injustice keenly. I realize that some appearances were against me, but—"

The Old Lady lifted her hand and stemmed his eloquence by that one gesture.

"I did not come here to discuss that matter," she said. "We will not refer to the past, if you please. I came to ask a favour, not for myself, but for a very dear young friend of mine—a Miss Gray, who has a remarkably fine voice which she wishes to have trained. She is poor, so I came to ask you if you would give her one of your musical scholarships. I understand her name has already been suggested to you, with a recommendation from her teacher. I do not know what he has said of her voice, but I do know he could hardly overrate it. If you send her abroad for training, you will not make any mistake."

The Old Lady stopped talking. She felt sure Andrew Cameron would grant her request; but she did hope he would grant it rather rudely or unwillingly. She could accept the favour so much more easily if it were flung to her like a bone to a dog. But not a bit of it, Andrew Cameron was suaver than ever. Nothing could give him greater pleasure than to grant his dear Cousin Margaret's request—he only wished it involved more trouble on his part. Her little protege should have her musical education assuredly—she should go abroad next year—and he was *de*-lighted—

"Thank you," said the Old Lady, cutting him short again. "I am much obliged to you—and I ask you not to let Miss Gray know anything of my interference. And I shall not take up any more of your valuable time. Good afternoon."

"Oh, you mustn't go so soon," he said, with some real kindness or clannishness permeating the hateful cordiality of his voice—for Andrew Cameron was not entirely without the homely virtues of the average man. He had been a good husband and father; he had once been very fond of his Cousin Margaret; and he was really very sorry that "circumstances" had "compelled" him to act as he had done in that old affair of her father's investment. "You must be my guest to-night."

"Thank you. I must return home to-night," said the Old Lady firmly, and there was that in her tone which told Andrew Cameron that it would be useless to urge her. But he insisted on telephoning for his carriage to drive her to the station. The Old Lady submitted to this, because she was secretly afraid her own legs would not suffice to carry her there; she even shook hands with him at parting, and thanked him a second time for granting her request.

"Not at all," he said. "Please try to think a little more kindly of me, Cousin Margaret."

When the Old Lady reached the station she found, to her dismay, that her train had just gone and that she would have to wait two hours for the evening one. She went into the waiting-room and sat down. She was very tired. All the excitement that had sustained her was gone, and she felt weak and old. She had nothing to eat, having expected to get home in time for tea; the waiting-room was chilly, and she shivered in her thin, old, silk mantilla. Her head ached and her heart likewise. She had won Sylvia's desire for her; but Sylvia would go out of her life, and the Old Lady did not see how she was to go on living after that. Yet she sat there unflinchingly for two hours, an upright, indomitable old figure, silently fighting her losing battle with the forces of physical and mental pain, while happy people came and went, and laughed and talked before her.

At eight o'clock the Old Lady got off the train at Bright River station, and slipped off unnoticed into the darkness of the wet night. She had two miles to walk, and a cold rain was falling. Soon the Old Lady was wet to the skin and chilled to the marrow. She felt as if she were walking in a bad dream. Blind instinct alone guided her over the last mile and up the lane to her own house. As she fumbled at her door, she realized that a burning heat had suddenly taken the place of her chilliness. She stumbled in over her threshold and closed the door.

VI. The October Chapter

On the second morning after Old Lady Lloyd's journey to town, Sylvia Gray was walking blithely down the wood lane. It was a beautiful autumn morning, clear and crisp and sunny; the frosted ferns, drenched and battered with the rain of yesterday, gave out a delicious fragrance; here and there in the woods a maple waved a gay crimson banner, or a branch of birch showed pale golden against the dark, unchanging spruces. The air was very pure and exhilarating. Sylvia walked with a joyous lightness of step and uplift of brow.

At the beech in the hollow she paused for an expectant moment, but there was nothing among the gray old roots for her. She was just turning away when little Teddy Kimball, who lived next door to the manse, came running down the slope from the direction of the old Lloyd place. Teddy's freckled face was very pale.

"Oh, Miss Gray!" he gasped. "I guess Old Lady Lloyd has gone clean crazy at last. The minister's wife asked me to run up to the Old Lady, with a message about the Sewing Circle—and I knocked—and knocked—and nobody came—so I thought I'd just step in and leave the letter on the table. But when I opened the door, I heard an awful queer laugh in the sitting-room, and next minute, the Old Lady came to the sitting-room door. Oh, Miss Gray, she looked awful. Her face was red and her eyes awful wild—and she was muttering and talking to herself and laughing like mad. I was so scared I just turned and run."

Sylvia, without stopping for reflection, caught Teddy's hand and ran up the slope. It did not occur to her to be frightened, although she thought with Teddy that the poor, lonely, eccentric Old Lady had really gone out of her mind at last.

The Old Lady was sitting on the kitchen sofa when

Sylvia entered. Teddy, too frightened to go in, lurked on the step outside. The Old Lady still wore the damp black silk dress in which she had walked from the station. Her face was flushed, her eyes wild, her voice hoarse. But she knew Sylvia and cowered down.

"Don't look at me," she moaned. "Please go away—I can't bear that *you* should know how poor I am. You're to go to Europe—Andrew Cameron is going to send you—I asked him—he couldn't refuse *me*. But please go away."

Sylvia did not go away. At a glance she had seen that this was sickness and delirium, not insanity. She sent Teddy off in hot haste for Mrs. Spencer, and when Mrs. Spencer came they induced the Old Lady to go to bed, and sent for the doctor. By night everybody in Spencervale knew that Old Lady Lloyd had pneumonia.

Mrs. Spencer announced that she meant to stay and nurse the Old Lady. Several other women offered assistance. Everybody was kind and thoughtful. But the Old Lady did not know it. She was in a high fever and delirium. She did not even know Sylvia Gray, who came and sat by her every minute she could spare. Sylvia Gray now knew all that she had suspected—the Old Lady was her fairy godmother. The Old Lady babbled of Sylvia incessantly, revealing all her love for her, betraying all the sacrifices she had made. Sylvia's heart ached with love and tenderness, and she prayed earnestly that the Old Lady might recover.

"I want her to know that I give her love for love," she murmured.

Everybody knew now how poor the Old Lady really was. She let slip all the jealously guarded secrets of her existence, except her old love for Leslie Gray. Even in delirium something sealed her lips as to that. But all else came out—her anguish over her unfashionable attire, her pitiful makeshifts and contrivances, her humiliation over wearing unfashionable dresses and paying only five cents where every other Sewing Circle member paid ten. The kindly women who waited on her listened to her with tear-filled eyes, and repented of their harsh judgments in the past.

"But who would have thought it?" said Mrs. Spencer to the minister's wife. "Nobody ever dreamed that her father had lost *all* his money, though folks supposed he had lost some in that old affair of the silver mine out west. It's shocking to think of the way she has lived all these years, often with not enough to eat— and going to bed in winter days to save fuel. Though I suppose if we had known we couldn't have done much for her, she's so desperate proud. But if she lives, and will let us help her, things will be different after this. Crooked Jack says he'll never forgive himself for taking pay for the few little jobs he did for her. He says, if she'll only let him, he'll do everything she wants done for her after this for nothing. Ain't it strange what a fancy she's took to Miss Gray? Think of her doing all those things for her all summer, and selling the grape jug and all. Well, the Old Lady certainly isn't mean, but nobody made a mistake in calling her queer. It all does seem desperate pitiful. Miss Gray's taking it awful hard. She seems to think about as much of the Old Lady as the Old Lady thinks of her. She's so worked up she don't even seem to care about going to Europe next year. She's really going—she's had word from Andrew Cameron. I'm awful glad, for there never was a sweeter girl in the world; but she says it will cost too much if the Old Lady's life is to pay for it."

Andrew Cameron heard of the Old Lady's illness and came out to Spencervale himself. He was not allowed to see the Old Lady, of course; but he told all concerned that no expense or trouble was to be spared, and the Spencervale doctor was instructed to send his bill to Andrew Cameron and hold his peace about it. Moreover, when Andrew Cameron went back home, he sent a trained nurse out to wait on the Old Lady, a capable, kindly woman who contrived to take charge of the case without offending Mrs. Spencer—than which no higher tribute could be paid to her tact!

The Old Lady did not die—the Lloyd constitution brought her through. One day, when Sylvia came in, the Old Lady smiled up at her, with a weak, faint, sensible smile, and murmured her name, and the nurse said that the crisis was past.

The Old Lady made a marvellously patient and tractable invalid. She did just as she was told, and accepted the presence of the nurse as a matter of course.

But one day, when she was strong enough to talk a little, she said to Sylvia,

"I suppose Andrew Cameron sent Miss Hayes here, did he?"

"Yes," said Sylvia, rather timidly.

The old lady noticed the timidity and smiled, with something of her old humour and spirit in her black eyes.

"Time has been when I'd have packed off unceremoniously any person Andrew Cameron sent here," she said. "But, Sylvia, I have gone through the Valley of the Shadow of Death, and I have left pride and resentment behind me for ever, I hope. I no longer feel as I felt towards Andrew. I can even accept a personal favour from him now. At last I can forgive him for the wrong he did me and mine. Sylvia, I find that I have been letting no ends of cats out of bags in my illness. Everybody knows now how poor I am—but I don't seem to mind it a bit. I'm only sorry that I ever shut my neighbours out of my life because of my foolish pride. Everyone has been so kind to me, Sylvia. In the future, if my life is spared, it is going to be a very different sort of life. I'm going to open it to all the kindness and companionship I can find in young and old. I'm going to help them all I can and let them help me. I *can* help people—I've learned that money isn't the only power for helping people. Anyone who has sympathy and understanding to give has a treasure that is without money and without price. And oh, Sylvia, you've found out what I never meant you to know. But I don't mind that now, either."

Sylvia took the Old Lady's thin white hand and kissed it.

"I can never thank you enough for what you have done for me, dearest Miss Lloyd," she said earnestly. "And I am so glad that all mystery is done away with between us, and I can love you as much and as openly as I have longed to do. I am so glad and so thankful that you love me, dear fairy godmother."

"Do you know *why* I love you so?" said the Old Lady wistfully. "Did I let *that* out in my raving, too?"

"No. But I think I know. It is because I am Leslie Gray's daughter, isn't it? I know that father loved you—his brother, Uncle Willis, told me all about it."

"I spoiled my own life because of my wicked pride," said the Old Lady sadly. "But you will love me in spite of it all, won't you, Sylvia? And you will come to see me sometimes? And write me after you go away?"

"I am coming to see you every day," said Sylvia. "I am going to stay in Spencervale for a whole year yet, just to be near you. And next year when I go to Europe— thanks to you, fairy godmother—I'll write you every day. We are going to be the best of chums, and we are going to have a most beautiful year of comradeship!"

The Old Lady smiled contentedly. Out in the kitchen, the minister's wife, who had brought up a dish of jelly, was talking to Mrs. Spencer about the Sewing Circle. Through the open window, where the red vines hung, came the pungent, sun-warm October air. The sunshine fell over Sylvia's chestnut hair like a crown of glory and youth.

"I do feel so perfectly happy," said the Old Lady, with a long, rapturous breath.

3

Each In His Own Tongue

THE honey-tinted autumn sunshine was falling thickly over the crimson and amber maples around old Abel Blair's door. There was only one outer door in old Abel's house, and it almost always stood wide open. A little black dog, with one ear missing and a lame forepaw, almost always slept on the worn red sandstone slab which served old Abel for a doorstep; and on the still more worn sill above it a large gray cat almost always slept. Just inside the door, on a bandy-legged chair of elder days, old Abel almost always sat.

He was sitting there this afternoon—a little old man, sadly twisted with rheumatism; his head was abnormally large, thatched with long, wiry black hair; his face was heavily lined and swarthily sunburned; his eyes were deep-set and black, with occasional peculiar golden flashes in them. A strange looking man was old Abel Blair; and as strange was he as he looked, Lower Carmody people would have told you.

Old Abel was almost always sober in these, his later years. He was sober to-day. He liked to bask in that ripe sunlight as well as his dog and cat did; and in such baskings he almost always looked out of his doorway at the far, fine blue sky over the tops of the crowding maples. But to-day he was not looking at the sky; instead, he was staring at the black, dusty rafters of his kitchen, where hung dried meats and strings of onions and bunches of herbs and fishing tackle and guns and skins.

But old Abel saw not these things; his face was the face of a man who beholds visions, compact of heavenly pleasure and hellish pain, for old Abel was seeing what he might have been—and what he was; as he always saw when Felix Moore played to him on the violin. And the awful joy of dreaming that he was young again, with unspoiled life before him, was so great and compelling that it counterbalanced the agony in the realization of a dishonoured old age, following years in which he had squandered the wealth of his soul in ways where Wisdom lifted not her voice.

Felix Moore was standing opposite to him, before an untidy stove, where the noon fire had died down into pallid, scattered ashes. Under his chin he held old Abel's brown, battered fiddle; his eyes, too, were fixed on the ceiling; and he, too, saw things not lawful to be uttered in any language save that of music; and of all music, only that given forth by the anguished, enraptured spirit of the violin. And yet this Felix was little more than twelve years old, and his face was still the face of a child who knows nothing of either sorrow or sin or failure or remorse. Only in his large, gray-black eyes was there something not of the child—something that spoke of an inheritance from many hearts, now ashes, which had aforetime grieved and joyed, and struggled and failed, and succeeded and grovelled. The inarticulate cries of their longings had passed into this child's soul, and transmuted themselves into the expression of his music.

Felix was a beautiful child. Carmody people, who stayed at home, thought so; and old Abel Blair, who had roamed afar in many lands, thought so; and even the Rev. Stephen Leonard, who taught, and tried to believe, that favour is deceitful and beauty is vain, thought so.

He was a slight lad, with sloping shoulders, a slim brown neck, and a head set on it with stag-like grace and uplift. His hair, cut straight across his brow and falling over his ears, after some caprice of Janet Andrews, the minister's housekeeper, was a glossy blue-black. The skin of his face and hands was like ivory; his eyes were large and beautifully tinted—gray, with dilating pupils; his features had the outlines of a cameo. Carmody mothers considered him delicate, and had long foretold that the minister would never bring him up; but old Abel pulled his grizzled moustache when he heard such forebodings and smiled.

"Felix Moore will live," he said positively. "You can't kill that kind until their work is done. He's got a work to do—if the minister'll let him do it. And if the minister don't let him do it, then I wouldn't be in that minister's shoes when he comes to the judgment—no, I'd rather be in my own. It's an awful thing to cross the purposes of the Almighty, either in your own life or anybody else's. Sometimes I think it's what's meant by the unpardonable sin—ay, that I do!"

Carmody people never asked what old Abel meant. They had long ago given up such vain questioning. When a man had lived as old Abel had lived for the greater part of his life, was it any wonder he said crazy things? And as for hinting that Mr. Leonard, a man who was really almost too good to live, was guilty of any sin, much less an unpardonable one—well, there now! what use was it to be taking any account of old Abel's queer speeches? Though, to be sure, there was no great harm in a fiddle, and maybe Mr. Leonard was a mite too strict that way with the child. But then, could you wonder at it? There was his father, you see.

Felix finally lowered the violin, and came back to old Abel's kitchen with a long sigh. Old Abel smiled drearily at him—the smile of a man who has been in the hands of the tormentors.

"It's awful the way you play—it's awful," he said with a shudder. "I never heard anything like it—and you that never had any teaching since you were nine years old, and not much practice, except what you could get here now and then on my old, battered fiddle. And to think you make it up yourself as you go along! I suppose your grandfather would never hear to your studying music—would he now?"

Felix shook his head.

"I know he wouldn't, Abel. He wants me to be a minister. Ministers are good things to be, but I'm afraid I can't be a minister."

"Not a pulpit minister. There's different kinds of ministers, and each must talk to men in his own tongue if he's going to do 'em any real good," said old Abel meditatively.

"*Your* tongue is music. Strange that your grandfather can't see that for himself, and him such a broad-minded man! He's the only minister I ever had much use for. He's God's own if ever a man was. And he loves you—yes, sir, he loves you like the apple of his eye."

"And I love him," said Felix warmly. "I love him so much that I'll even try to be a minister for his sake, though I don't want to be."

"What do you want to be?"

"A great violinist," answered the child, his ivory-hued face suddenly warming into living rose. "I want to play to thousands—and see their eyes look as yours do when I play. Sometimes your eyes frighten me, but oh, it's a splendid fright! If I had father's violin I could do better. I remember that he once said it had a soul that was doing purgatory for its sins when it had lived on earth. I don't know what he meant, but it did seem to me that *his* violin was alive. He taught me to play on it as soon as I was big enough to hold it."

"Did you love your father?" asked old Abel, with a keen look.

Again Felix crimsoned; but he looked straightly and steadily into his old friend's face.

"No," he said, "I didn't; but," he added, gravely and deliberately, "I don't think you should have asked me such a question."

It was old Abel's turn to blush. Carmody people would not have believed he could blush; and perhaps no living being could have called that deepening hue into his weather-beaten cheek save only this gray-eyed child of the rebuking face.

"No, I guess I shouldn't," he said. "But I'm always making mistakes. I've never made anything else. That's why I'm nothing more than 'Old Abel' to the Carmody people. Nobody but you and your grandfather ever calls me 'Mr. Blair.' Yet William Blair at the store up there, rich and respected as he is, wasn't half as clever a man as I was when we started in life: you mayn't believe that, but it's true. And the worst of it is, young Felix, that most of the time I don't care whether I'm Mr. Blair or old Abel. Only when you play I care. It makes me feel just as a look

I saw in a little girl's eyes some years ago made me feel. Her name was Anne Shirley and she lived with the Cuthberts down at Avonlea. We got into a conversation at Blair's store. She could talk a blue streak to anyone, that girl could. I happened to say about something that it didn't matter to a battered old hulk of sixty odd like me. She looked at me with her big, innocent eyes, a little reproachful like, as if I'd said something awful heretical. 'Don't you think, Mr. Blair,' she says, 'that the older we get the more things ought to matter to us?'—as grave as if she'd been a hundred instead of eleven. 'Things matter *so* much to me now,' she says, clasping her hands thisaway, 'and I'm sure that when I'm sixty they'll matter just five times as much to me.' Well, the way she looked and the way she spoke made me feel downright ashamed of myself because things had stopped mattering with me. But never mind all that. My miserable old feelings don't count for much. What come of your father's fiddle?"

"Grandfather took it away when I came here. I think he burned it. And I long for it so often."

"Well, you've always got my old brown fiddle to come to when you must."

"Yes, I know. And I'm glad for that. But I'm hungry for a violin all the time. And I only come here when the hunger gets too much to bear. I feel as if I outghtn't to come even then—I'm always saying I won't do it again, because I know grandfather wouldn't like it, if he knew."

"He has never forbidden it, has he?"

"No, but that is because he doesn't know I come here for that. He never thinks of such a thing. I feel sure he *would* forbid it, if he knew. And that makes me very wretched. And yet I *have* to come. Mr. Blair, do you know why grandfather can't bear to have me play on the violin? He loves music, and he doesn't mind my playing on the organ, if I don't neglect other things. I can't understand it, can you?"

"I have a pretty good idea, but I can't tell you. It isn't my secret. Maybe he'll tell you himself some day. But, mark you, young Felix, he has got good reasons for it all. Knowing what I know, I can't blame him over much, though I think he's mistaken. Come now, play something more for me before you go—something that's bright and happy this time, so as to leave me with a good taste in my mouth. That last thing you played took me straight to heaven—but heaven's awful near to hell, and at the last you tipped me in."

"I don't understand you," said Felix, drawing his fine, narrow black brows together in a perplexed frown.

"No—and I wouldn't want you to. You couldn't understand unless you was an old man who had it in him once to do something and be a *man*, and just went and made himself a devilish fool. But there must be something in you that understands things—all kinds of things—or you couldn't put it all into music the way you do. How do you do it? How in—how *do* you do it, young Felix?"

"I don't know. But I play differently to different people. I don't know how that is. When I'm alone with you I have to play one way; and when Janet comes over here to listen I feel quite another way—not so thrilling, but happier and lonelier. And that day when Jessie Blair was here listening, I felt as if I wanted to laugh and sing—as if the violin wanted to laugh and sing all the time."

The strange, golden gleam flashed through old Abel's sunken eyes.

"God," he muttered under his breath, "I believe the boy can get into other folk's souls somehow, and play out what *his* soul sees there."

"What's that you say?" inquired Felix, petting his fiddle.

"Nothing—never mind—go on. Something lively now, young Felix. Stop probing into my soul, where you haven't no business to be, you infant, and play me something out of your own—something sweet and happy and pure."

"I'll play the way I feel on sunshiny mornings, when the birds are singing and I forget I have to be a minister," said Felix simply.

A witching, gurgling, mirthful strain, like mingled bird and brook song, floated out on the still air, along the path where the red and golden maple leaves were falling very softly, one by one. The Reverend Stephen Leonard heard it, as he came along the way, and the Reverend Stephen Leonard smiled. Now, when Stephen Leonard smiled, children ran to him, and grown people felt as if they looked from Pisgah over to some fair land of promise beyond the fret and worry of their care-dimmed earthly lives.

Mr. Leonard loved music, as he loved all things beautiful, whether in the material or the spiritual world, though he did not realize how much he loved them for their beauty alone, or he would have been shocked and remorseful. He himself was beautiful. His figure was erect and youthful, despite seventy years. His face was as mobile and charming as a woman's, yet with all a man's tried strength and firmness in it, and his dark blue eyes flashed with the brilliance of one and twenty; even his silken silvery hair could not make an old man of him. He was worshipped by everyone who knew him, and he was, in so far as mortal man may be, worthy of that worship.

"Old Abel is amusing himself with his violin again," he thought. "What a delicious thing he is playing! He has quite a gift for the violin. But how can he play such a thing as that—a battered old hulk of a man who has, at one time or another, wallowed in almost every sin to which human nature can sink? He was on one of his sprees three days ago—the first one for over a year—lying dead-drunk in the market square in Charlottetown among the dogs; and now he is playing something that only a young archangel on the hills of heaven ought to be able to play. Well, it will make my task all the easier. Abel is always repentant by the time he is able to play on his fiddle."

Mr. Leonard was on the door-stone. The little black dog had frisked down to meet him, and the gray cat rubbed her head against his leg. Old Abel did not notice him; he was beating time with uplifted hand and smiling face to Felix's music, and his eyes were young again, glowing with laughter and sheer happiness.

"Felix! what does this mean?"

The violin bow clattered from Felix's hand upon the floor; he swung around and faced his grandfather. As he met the passion of grief and hurt in the old man's eyes, his own clouded with an agony of repentance.

"Grandfather—I'm sorry," he cried brokenly.

"Now, now!" Old Abel had risen deprecatingly. "It's all my fault, Mr. Leonard. Don't you blame the boy. I coaxed him to play a bit for me. I didn't feel fit to touch the fiddle yet myself—too soon after Friday, you see. So I coaxed him on—wouldn't give him no peace till he played. It's all my fault."

"No," said Felix, throwing back his head. His face was as white as marble, yet it seemed ablaze with desperate truth and scorn of old Abel's shielding lie. "No, grandfather, it isn't Abel's fault. I came over here on purpose to play, because I thought you had gone to the harbour. I have come here often, ever since I have lived with you."

"Ever since you have lived with me you have been deceiving me like this, Felix?"

There was no anger in Mr. Leonard's tone—only measureless sorrow. The boy's sensitive lips quivered.

"Forgive me, grandfather," he whispered beseechingly.

"You never forbid him to come," old Abel broke in angrily. "Be just, Mr. Leonard—be just."

"I *am* just. Felix knows that he has disobeyed me, in the spirit if not in the letter. Do you not know it, Felix?"

"Yes, grandfather, I have done wrong—I've known that I was doing wrong every time I came. Forgive me, grandfather."

"Felix, I forgive you, but I ask you to promise me, here and now, that you will never again, as long as you live, touch a violin."

Dusky crimson rushed madly over the boy's face. He gave a cry as if he had been lashed with a whip. Old Abel sprang to his feet.

"Don't you ask such a promise of him, Mr. Leonard," he cried furiously. "It's a sin, that's what it is. Man, man, what blinds you? You *are* blind. Can't you see what is in the boy? His soul is full of music. It'll torture him to death—or to worse—if you don't let it have way."

"There is a devil in such music," said Mr. Leonard hotly.

"Ay, there may be, but don't forget that there's a Christ in it, too," retorted old Abel in a low, tense tone.

Mr. Leonard looked shocked; he considered that old

Abel had uttered blasphemy. He turned away from him rebukingly.

"Felix, promise me."

There was no relenting in his face or tone. He was merciless in the use of the power he possessed over that young, loving spirit. Felix understood that there was no escape; but his lips were very white as he said,

"I promise, grandfather."

Mr. Leonard drew a long breath of relief. He knew that promise would be kept. So did old Abel. The latter crossed the floor and sullenly took the violin from Felix's relaxed hand. Without a word or look he went into the little bedroom off the kitchen and shut the door with a slam of righteous indignation. But from its window he stealthily watched his visitors go away. Just as they entered on the maple path, Mr. Leonard laid his hand on Felix's head and looked down at him. Instantly, the boy flung his arm up over the old man's shoulder and smiled at him. In the look they exchanged there was boundless love and trust—ay, and good-fellowship. Old Abel's scornful eyes again held the golden flash.

"How those two love each other!" he muttered enviously. "And how they torture each other!"

Mr. Leonard went to his study to pray when he got home. He knew that Felix had run for comforting to Janet Andrews, the little, thin, sweet-faced, rigid-lipped woman who kept house for them. Mr. Leonard knew that Janet would disapprove of his action as deeply as old Abel had done. She would say nothing, she would only look at him with reproachful eyes over the teacups at suppertime. But Mr. Leonard believed he had done what was best and his conscience did not trouble him, though his heart did.

Thirteen years before this, his daughter Margaret had almost broken that heart by marrying a man of whom he could not approve. Martin Moore was a professional violinist. He was a popular performer, though not in any sense a great one. He met the slim, golden haired daughter of the manse at the house of a college friend she was visiting in Toronto, and fell straightway in love with her. Margaret had loved him with all her virginal heart in return, and married him, despite her father's disapproval. It was not to Martin Moore's profession that Mr. Leonard objected, but to the man himself. He knew that the violinist's past life had not been such as became a suitor for Margaret Leonard; and his insight into character warned him that Martin Moore could never make any woman lastingly happy.

Margaret Leonard did not believe this. She married Martin Moore and lived one year in paradise. Perhaps that atoned for the three bitter years which followed—that, and her child. At all events, she died as she had lived, loyal and uncomplaining. She died alone, for her husband was away on a concert tour, and her illness was so brief that her father had not time to reach her before the end. Her body was taken home to be buried beside her mother in the little Carmody churchyard. Mr. Leonard wished to take the child, but Martin Moore refused to give him up.

Six years later Moore, too, died, and at last Mr. Leonard had his heart's desire—the possession of Margaret's son. The grandfather awaited the child's coming with mingled feelings. His heart yearned for him, yet he dreaded to meet a second edition of Martin Moore. Suppose Margaret's son resembled his handsome vagabond of a father! Or, worse still, suppose he were cursed with his father's lack of principle, his instability, his Bohemian instincts. Thus Mr. Leonard tortured himself wretchedly before the coming of Felix.

The child did not look like either father or mother. Instead, Mr. Leonard found himself looking into a face which he had put away under the grasses thirty years before—the face of his girl bride, who had died at Margaret's birth. Here again were her lustrous gray-black eyes, her ivory outlines, her fine-traced arch of brow; and here, looking out of those eyes, seemed her very spirit again. From that moment the soul of the old man was knit to the soul of the child, and they loved each other with a love surpassing that of women.

Felix's only inheritance from his father was his love of music. But the child had genius, where his father had possessed only talent. To Martin Moore's outward mastery of the violin was added the mystery and intensity of his mother's nature, with some more subtle quality still, which had perhaps come to him from the grandmother he so strongly resembled. Moore had understood what a career was naturally before the child, and he had trained him in the technique of his art from the time the slight fingers could first grasp the bow. When nine-year-old Felix came to the Carmody manse, he had mastered as much of the science of the violin as nine out of ten musicians acquire in a lifetime; and he brought with him his father's violin; it was all Martin Moore had to leave his son—but it was an Amati, the commercial value of which nobody in Carmody suspected. Mr. Leonard had taken possession of it and Felix had never seen it since. He cried himself to sleep many a night for the loss of it. Mr. Leonard did not know this, and if Janet Andrews suspected it, she held her tongue—an art in which she excelled. She "saw no harm in a fiddle," herself, and thought Mr. Leonard absurdly strict in the matter, though it would not have been well for the luckless outsider who might have ventured to say as much to her. She had connived at Felix's visits to old Abel Blair, squaring the matter with her Presbyterian conscience by some peculiar process known only to herself.

When Janet heard of the promise which Mr. Leonard had exacted from Felix she seethed with indignation; and, though she "knew her place" better than to say anything to Mr. Leonard about it, she made her disapproval so plainly manifest in her bearing that the stern, gentle old man found the atmosphere of his hitherto peaceful manse unpleasantly chill and hostile for a time.

It was the wish of his heart that Felix should be a minister, as he would have wished his own son to be, had one been born to him. Mr. Leonard thought rightly that the highest work to which any man could be called was a life of service to his fellows; but he made the mistake of supposing the field of service much narrower than it is—of failing to see that a man may minister to the needs of humanity in many different but equally effective ways.

Janet hoped that Mr. Leonard might not exact the fulfilment of Felix's promise; but Felix himself, with the instinctive understanding of perfect love, knew that it was vain to hope for any change of viewpoint in his grandfather. He addressed himself to the keeping of his promise in letter and in spirit. He never went again to old Abel's; he did not even play on the organ, though this was not forbidden, because any music wakened in him a passion of longing and ecstasy which demanded expression with an intensity not to be borne. He flung himself grimly into his studies and conned Latin and Greek verbs with a persistency which soon placed him at the head of all competitors.

Only once in the long winter did he come near to breaking his promise. One evening, when March was melting into April, and the pulses of spring were stirring under the lingering snow, he was walking home from school alone. As he descended into the little hollow below the manse, a lively lilt of music drifted up to meet him. It was only the product of a mouth-organ, manipulated by a little black-eyed, French-Canadian hired boy, sitting on the fence by the brook; but there was music in the ragged urchin and it came out through his simple toy. It tingled over Felix from head to foot; and, when Leon held out the mouth-organ with a fraternal grin of invitation, he snatched at it as a famished creature might snatch at food.

Then, with it half-way to his lips, he paused. True, it was only the violin he had promised never to touch; but he felt that if he gave way ever so little to the desire that was in him, it would sweep everything before it. If he played on Leon Buote's mouth-organ, there in that misty spring dale, he would go to old Abel's that evening; he *knew* he would go. To Leon's amazement, Felix threw the mouth-organ back at him and ran up the hill as if he were pursued. There was something in his boyish face that frightened Leon; and it frightened Janet Andrews as Felix rushed past her in the hall of the manse.

"Child, what's the matter with you?" she cried. "Are you sick? Have you been scared?"

"No, no. Leave me alone, Janet," said Felix chokingly, dashing up the stairs to his own room.

He was quite composed when he came down to tea, an hour later, though he was unusually pale and had purple shadows under his large eyes.

Mr. Leonard scrutinized him somewhat anxiously; it

suddenly occurred to the old minister that Felix was looking more delicate than his wont this spring. Well, he had studied hard all winter, and he was certainly growing very fast. When vacation came, he must be sent away for a visit.

"They tell me Naomi Clark is real sick," said Janet. "She has been ailing all winter, and now she's fast to her bed. Mrs. Murphy says she believes the woman is dying, but nobody dares tell her so. She won't give in she's sick, nor take medicine. And there's nobody to wait on her except that simple creature, Maggie Peterson."

"I wonder if I ought to go and see her," said Mr. Leonard uneasily.

"What use would it be to bother yourself? You know she wouldn't see you—she'd shut the door in your face like she did before. She's an awful wicked woman—but it's kind of terrible to think of her lying there sick, with no responsible person to tend her."

"Naomi Clark is a bad woman and she lived a life of shame, but I like her, for all that," remarked Felix, in the grave, meditative tone in which he occasionally said rather startling things.

Mr. Leonard looked somewhat reproachfully at Janet Andrews, as if to ask her why Felix should have attained to this dubious knowledge of good and evil under her care; and Janet shot a dour look back which, being interpreted, meant that if Felix went to the district school, she could not and would not be held responsible if he learned more there than arithmetic and Latin.

"What do you know of Naomi Clark to like or dislike?" she asked curiously. "Did you ever see her?"

"Oh, yes," Felix replied, addressing himself to his cherry preserve with considerable gusto. "I was down at Spruce Cove one night last summer when a big thunderstorm came up. I went to Naomi's house for shelter. The door was open, so I walked right in, because nobody answered my knock. Naomi Clark was at the window, watching the cloud coming up over the sea. She just looked at me once, but didn't say anything, and then went on watching the cloud. I didn't like to sit down because she hadn't asked me to, so I went to the window by her and watched it, too. It was a dreadful sight—the cloud was so black and the water so green, and there was such a strange light between the cloud and the water; yet there was something splendid in it, too. Part of the time I watched the storm, and the other part I watched Naomi's face. It was dreadful to see, like the storm, and yet I liked to see it.

"After the thunder was over it rained a while longer, and Naomi sat down and talked to me. She asked me who I was, and when I told her she asked me to play something for her on her violin,"—Felix shot a deprecating glance at Mr. Leonard—"because, she said, she'd heard I was a great hand at it. She wanted something lively, and I tried just as hard as I could to play something like that. But I couldn't. I played something that was terrible—it just played itself—it seemed as if something was lost that could never be found again. And before I got through, Naomi came at me, and tore the violin from me, and—*swore*. And she said, 'You big-eyed brat, how did you know *that?*' Then she took me by the arm—and she hurt me, too, I can tell you—and she put me right out in the rain and slammed the door."

"The rude, unmannerly creature!" said Janet indignantly.

"Oh, no, she was quite in the right," said Felix composedly. "It served me right for what I played. You see, she didn't know I couldn't help playing it. I suppose she thought I did it on purpose."

"What on earth did you play, child?"

"I don't know." Felix shivered. "It was awful—it was dreadful. It was fit to break your heart. But it *had* to be played, if I played anything at all."

"I don't understand what you mean—I declare I don't," said Janet in bewilderment.

"I think we'll change the subject of conversation," said Mr. Leonard.

It was a month later when "the simple creature, Maggie" appeared at the manse door one evening and asked for the preacher.

"Naomi wants ter see yer," she mumbled. "Naomi sent Maggie ter tell yer ter come at onct."

"I shall go, certainly," said Mr. Leonard gently. "Is she very ill?"

"Her's dying," said Maggie with a broad grin. "And her's awful skeered of hell. Her just knew ter-day her was dying. Maggie told her—her wouldn't believe the harbour women, but her believed Maggie. Her yelled awful."

Maggie chuckled to herself over the gruesome remembrance. Mr. Leonard, his heart filled with pity, called Janet and told her to give the poor creature some refreshment. But Maggie shook her head.

"No, no, preacher, Maggie must get right back to Naomi. Maggie'll tell her the preacher's coming ter save her from hell."

She uttered an eerie cry, and ran at full speed shoreward through the spruce woods.

"The Lord save us!" said Janet in an awed tone. "I knew the poor girl was simple, but I didn't know she was like *that*. And are you going, sir?"

"Yes, of course. I pray God I may be able to help the poor soul," said Mr. Leonard sincerely. He was a man who never shirked what he believed to be his duty; but duty had sometimes presented itself to him in pleasanter guise than this summons to Naomi Clark's death-bed.

The woman had been the plague spot of Lower Carmody and Carmody Harbour for a generation. In the earlier days of his ministry to the congregation he had tried to reclaim her, and Naomi had mocked and flouted him to his face. Then, for the sake of those to whom she was a snare or a heart-break, he had endeavoured to set the law in motion against her, and Naomi had laughed the law to scorn. Finally, he had been compelled to let her alone.

Yet Naomi had not always been an outcast. Her girl-hood had been innocent; but she was the possessor of a dangerous beauty, and her mother was dead. Her father was a man notorious for his harshness and violence of temper. When Naomi made the fatal mistake of trusting to a false love that betrayed and deserted, he drove her from his door with taunts and curses.

Naomi took up her quarters in a little deserted house

at Spruce Cove. Had her child lived, it might have saved her. But it died at birth, and with its little life went her last chance of worldly redemption. From that time forth, her feet were set in the way that takes hold on hell.

For the past five years, however, Naomi had lived a tolerably respectable life. When Janet Peterson had died, her idiot daughter, Maggie, had been left with no kith or kin in the world. Nobody knew what was to be done with her, for nobody wanted to be bothered with her. Naomi Clark went to the girl and offered her a home. People said she was no fit person to have charge of Maggie, but everybody shirked the unpleasant task of interfering in the matter, except Mr. Leonard, who went to expostulate with Naomi, and, as Janet said, for his pains got her door shut in his face.

But from the day when Maggie Peterson went to live with her, Naomi ceased to be the harbour Magdalen.

The sun had set when Mr. Leonard reached Spruce Cove, and the harbour was veiling itself in a wondrous twilight splendour. Afar out, the sea lay throbbing and purple, and the moan of the bar came through the sweet, chill spring air with its burden of hopeless, endless longing and seeking. The sky was blossoming into stars above the afterglow; out to the east the moon was rising, and the sea beneath it was a thing of radiance and silver and glamour; and a little harbour boat that went sailing across it was transmuted into an elfin shallop from the coast of fairyland.

Mr. Leonard sighed as he turned from the sinless beauty of the sea and sky to the threshold of Naomi Clark's house. It was very small—one room below, and a sleeping-loft above; but a bed had been made up for the sick woman by the down-stairs window looking out on the harbour; and Naomi lay on it, with a lamp burning at her head and another at her side, although it was not yet dark. A great dread of darkness had always been one of Naomi's peculiarities.

She was tossing restlessly on her poor couch, while Maggie crouched on a box at the foot. Mr. Leonard had not seen her for five years, and he was shocked at the change in her. She was much wasted; her clear-cut, aquiline features had been of the type which becomes indescribably witch-like in old age, and, though Naomi Clark was barely sixty, she looked as if she might be a hundred. Her hair streamed over the pillow in white, uncared-for tresses, and the hands that plucked at the bed-clothes were like wrinkled claws. Only her eyes were unchanged; they were as blue and brilliant as ever, but now filled with such agonized terror and appeal that Mr. Leonard's gentle heart almost stood still with the horror of them. They were the eyes of a creature driven wild with torture, hounded by furies, clutched by unutterable fear.

Naomi sat up and dragged at his arm.

"Can you help me? Can you help me?" she gasped imploringly. "Oh, I thought you'd never come! I was skeered I'd die before you got here—die and go to hell. I didn't know before today that I was dying. None of those cowards would tell me. Can you help me?"

"If I cannot, God can," said Mr. Leonard gently. He felt himself very helpless and inefficient before this awful terror and frenzy. He had seen sad death-beds—troubled death-beds—ay, and despairing death-beds, but never anything like this.

"God!" Naomi's voice shrilled terribly as she uttered the name. "I can't go to God for help. Oh, I'm skeered of hell, but I'm skeereder still of God. I'd rather go to hell a thousand times over than face God after the life I've lived. I tell you, I'm sorry for living wicked—I was always sorry for it all the time. There ain't never been a moment I wasn't sorry, though nobody would believe it. I was driven on by fiends of hell. Oh, you don't understand—you *can't* understand—but I was always sorry!"

"If you repent, that is all that is necessary. God will forgive you if you ask Him."

"No, He can't! Sins like mine can't be forgiven. He can't—and He won't."

"He can and He will. He is a God of love, Naomi."

"No," said Naomi with stubborn conviction. "He isn't a God of love at all. That's why I'm skeered of him. No, no. He's a God of wrath and justice and punishment.

Love! There ain't no such thing as love! I've never found it on earth, and I don't believe it's to be found in God."

"Naomi, God loves us like a father."

"Like *my* father?" Naomi's shrill laughter, pealing through the still room, was hideous to hear.

The old minister shuddered.

"No—no! As a kind, tender, all-wise father, Naomi—as you would have loved your little child if it had lived."

Naomi cowered and moaned.

"Oh, I wish I could believe *that*. I wouldn't be frightened if I could believe that. *Make* me believe it. Surely you can make me believe that there's love and forgiveness in God if you believe it yourself."

"Jesus Christ forgave and loved the Magdalen, Naomi."

"Jesus Christ? Oh, I ain't afraid of *Him*. Yes, *He* could understand and forgive. He was half-human. I tell you, it's God I'm skeered of."

"They are one and the same," said Mr. Leonard helplessly. He knew he could not make Naomi realize it. This anguished death-bed was no place for a theological exposition on the mysteries of the Trinity.

"Christ died for you, Naomi. He bore your sins in His own body on the cross."

"We bear our own sins," said Naomi fiercely. "I've borne mine all my life—and I'll bear them for all eternity. I can't believe anything else. I *can't* believe God can forgive me. I've ruined people body and soul—I've broken hearts and poisoned homes—I'm worse than a murderess. No—no—no, there's no hope for me." Her voice rose again into that shrill, intolerable shriek. "I've got to go to hell. It ain't so much the fire I'm skeered of as the outer darkness. I've always been so skeered of darkness—it's so full of awful things and thoughts. Oh, there ain't nobody to help me! Man ain't no good and I'm too skeered of God."

She wrung her hands. Mr. Leonard walked up and down the room in the keenest anguish of spirit he had ever known. What could he do? What could he say? There was healing and peace in his religion for this woman as for all others, but he could express it in no language which this tortured soul could understand. He looked at her writing face; he looked at the idiot girl chuckling to herself at the foot of the bed; he looked through the open door to the remote, starlit night—and a horrible sense of utter helplessness overcame him. He could do nothing—nothing! In all his life he had never known such bitterness of soul as the realization brought home to him.

"What is the good of you if you can't help me?" moaned the dying woman. "Pray—pray—pray!" she shrilled suddenly.

Mr. Leonard dropped on his knees by the bed. He did not know what to say. No prayer that he had ever prayed was of use here. The old, beautiful formulas, which had soothed and helped the passing of many a soul, were naught save idle, empty words to Naomi Clark. In his anguish of mind, Stephen Leonard gasped out the briefest and sincerest prayer his lips had ever uttered.

"O God, our Father! Help this woman. Speak to her in a tongue which she can understand."

A beautiful, white face appeared for a moment in the light that streamed out of the doorway into the darkness of the night. No one noticed it, and it quickly drew back into the shadow. Suddenly, Naomi fell back on her pillow, her lips blue, her face horribly pinched, her eyes rolled up in her head. Maggie started up, pushed Mr. Leonard aside, and proceeded to administer some remedy with surprising skill and deftness. Mr. Leonard, believing Naomi to be dying, went to the door, feeling sick and bruised in soul.

Presently a figure stole out into the light.

"Felix, is that you?" said Mr. Leonard in a startled tone.

"Yes, sir." Felix came up to the stone step. "Janet got frightened that you might fall on that rough road after dark, so she made me come after you with a lantern. I've been waiting behind the point, but at last I thought I'd better come and see if you would be staying much longer, If you will be, I'll go back to Janet and leave the lantern here with you."

"Yes, that will be the best thing to do. I may not be ready to go home for some time yet," said Mr. Leonard,

thinking that the death-bed of sin behind him was no sight
for Felix's young eyes.

"Is that your grandson you're talking to?" Naomi spoke
clearly and strongly. The spasm had passed. "If it is, bring
him in. I want to see him."

Reluctantly, Mr. Leonard signed Felix to enter. The
boy stood by Naomi's bed and looked down at her with
sympathetic eyes. But at first she did not look at him—she
looked past him at the minister.

"I might have died in that spell," she said, with sullen
reproach in her voice, "and if I had, I'd been in hell now.
You can't help me—I'm done with you. There ain't any
hope for me, and I know it now."

She turned to Felix.

"Take down that fiddle on the wall and play something for me," she said imperiously "I'm dying—and I'm
going to hell—and I don't want to think of it. Play me
something to take my thoughts off it—I don't care what
you play. I was always fond of music—there was always
something in it for me I never found anywhere else."

Felix looked at his grandfather. The old man nodded;
he felt too ashamed to speak; he sat with his fine silver
head in his hands, while Felix took down and tuned the
old violin, on which so many godless lilts had been played
in many a wild revel. Mr. Leonard felt that he had failed
his religion. He could not give Naomi the help that was in
it for her.

Felix drew the bow softly, perplexedly over the strings.
He had no idea what he should play. Then his eyes were
caught and held by Naomi's burning, mesmeric, blue gaze
as she lay on her crumpled pillow. A strange, inspired
look came over the boy's face. He began to play as if it
were not he who played, but some mightier power, of
which he was but the passive instrument.

Sweet and soft and wonderful was the music that stole
through the room. Mr. Leonard forgot his heart-break and
listened to it in puzzled amazement. He had never heard
anything like it before. How could the child play like that?
He looked at Naomi and marvelled at the change in her
face. The fear and frenzy were going out of it; she listened

breathlessly, never taking her eyes from Felix. At the foot of the bed the idiot girl sat with tears on her cheeks.

In that strange music was the joy of innocent, mirthful childhood, blent with the laughter of waves and the call of glad winds. Then it held the wild, wayward dreams of youth, sweet and pure in all their wildness and waywardness. They were followed by a rapture of young love—allsurrendering, all-sacrificing love.

The music changed. It held the torture of unshed tears, the anguish of a heart deceived and desolate. Mr. Leonard almost put his hands over his ears to shut out its intolerable poignancy. But on the dying woman's face was only a strange relief, as if some dumb, long-hidden pain had at last won to the healing of utterance.

The sullen indifference of despair came next, the bitterness of smouldering revolt and misery, the reckless casting away of all good. There was something indescribably evil in the music now—so evil that Mr. Leonard's white soul shuddered away in loathing, and Maggie cowered and whined like a frightened animal.

Again the music changed. And in it now there was agony and fear—and repentance and a cry for pardon. To Mr. Leonard there was something strangely familiar in it. He struggled to recall where he had heard it before; then he suddenly knew—he had heard it before Felix came, in Naomi's terrible words! He looked at his grandson with something like awe. Here was a power of which he knew nothing—a strange and dreadful power. Was it of God? Or of Satan?

For the last time the music changed. And now it was not music at all—it was a great, infinite forgiveness, an all-comprehending love. It was healing for a sick soul; it was light and hope and peace. A Bible text, seemingly incongruous, came into Mr. Leonard's mind—"This is the house of God; this is the gate of heaven."

Felix lowered the violin and dropped wearily on a chair by the bed. The inspired light faded from his face; once more he was only a tired boy. But Stephen Leonard was on his knees, sobbing like a child; and Naomi Clark was lying still, with her hands clasped over her breast.

"I understand now," she said very softly. "I couldn't

see it before—and now it's so plain. I just *feel* it. God *is* a God of love. He can forgive anybody—even me—even me. He knows all about it. I ain't skeered any more. He just loves me and forgives me as I'd have loved and forgiven my baby if she'd lived, no matter how bad she was, or what she did. The minister told me that but I couldn't believe it. I *know* it now. And He sent you here to-night, boy, to tell it to me in a way that I could feel it."

Naomi Clark died just as the dawn came up over the sea. Mr. Leonard rose from his watch at her bedside and went to the door. Before him spread the harbour, gray and austere in the faint light, but afar out the sun was rending asunder the milk-white mists in which the sea was scarfed, and under it was a virgin glow of sparkling water.

The fir trees on the point moved softly and whispered together. The whole world sang of spring and resurrection and life; and behind him Naomi Clark's dead face took on the peace that passes understanding.

The old minister and his grandson walked home together in a silence that neither wished to break. Janet Andrews gave them a good scolding and an excellent breakfast. Then she ordered them both to bed; but Mr. Leonard, smiling at her, said:

"Presently, Janet, presently. But now, take this key, go up to the black chest in the garret, and bring me what you will find there."

When Janet had gone, he turned to Felix.

"Felix, would you like to study music as your life-work?"

Felix looked up, with a transfiguring flush on his wan face.

"Oh, grandfather! Oh, grandfather!"

"You may do so, my child. After this night I dare not hinder you. Go with my blessing, and may God guide and keep you, and make you strong to do His work and tell His message to humanity in your own appointed way. It is not the way I desired for you—but I see that I was mistaken. Old Abel spoke truly when he said there was a Christ in your violin as well as a devil. I understand what he meant now."

He turned to meet Janet, who came into the study with a violin. Felix's heart throbbed; he recognized it. Mr. Leonard took it from Janet and held it out to the boy.

"This is your father's violin, Felix. See to it that you never make your music the servant of the power of evil—never debase it to unworthy ends. For your responsibility is as your gift, and God will exact the accounting of it from you. Speak to the world in your own tongue through it, with truth and sincerity; and all I have hoped for you will be abundantly fulfilled."

4

Little Joscelyn

"IT simply isn't to be thought of, Aunty Nan," said Mrs. William Morrison decisively. Mrs. William Morrison was one of those people who always speak decisively. If they merely announce that they are going to peel the potatoes for dinner, their hearers realize that there is no possible escape for the potatoes. Moreover, these people are always given their full title by everybody. William Morrison was called Billy oftener than not; but, if you had asked for Mrs. Billy Morrison, nobody in Avonlea would have known what you meant at first guess.

"You must see that for yourself, Aunty," went on Mrs. William, hulling strawberries nimbly with her large, firm, white fingers as she talked. Mrs. William always improved every shining moment. "It is ten miles to Kensington, and just think how late you would be getting back. You are not able for such a drive. You wouldn't get over it for a month. You know you are anything but strong this summer."

Aunty Nan sighed, and patted the tiny, furry, gray morsel of a kitten in her lap with trembling fingers. She knew, better than anyone else could know it, that she was not strong that summer. In her secret soul, Aunty Nan, sweet and frail and timid under the burden of her seventy years, felt with mysterious unmistakable prescience that it was to be her last summer at the Gull Point Farm. But that was only the more reason why she should go to hear little Joscelyn sing; she would never have another chance. And oh, to hear little Joscelyn sing just once—Joscelyn, whose voice was delighting thousands out in the big world,

70

just as in the years gone by it had delighted Aunty Nan and the dwellers at the Gull Point Farm for a whole golden summer with carols at dawn and dusk about the old place!

"Oh, I know I'm not very strong, Maria," said Aunty Nan pleadingly, "but I am strong enough for that. Indeed I am. I could stay at Kensington over night with George's folks, you know, and so it wouldn't tire me much. I do so want to hear Joscelyn sing. Oh, how I love little Joscelyn."

"It passes my understanding, the way you hanker after that child," cried Mrs. William impatiently. "Why, she was a perfect stranger to you when she came here, and she was here only one summer!"

"But oh, such a summer!" said Aunty Nan softly. "We all loved little Joscelyn. She just seemed like one of our own. She was one of God's children, carrying love with them everywhere. In some ways that little Anne Shirley the Cuthberts have got up there at Green Gables reminds me of her, though in other ways they're not a bit alike. Joscelyn was a beauty."

"Well, that Shirley snippet certainly isn't that," said Mrs. William sarcastically. "And if Joscelyn's tongue was one third as long as Anne Shirley's, the wonder to me is that she didn't talk you all to death out of hand."

"Little Joscelyn wasn't much of a talker," said Aunty Nan dreamily. "She was kind of a quiet child. But you remembered what she did say. And I've never forgotten little Joscelyn."

Mrs. William shrugged her plump, shapely shoulders.

"Well, it was fifteen years ago, Aunty Nan, and Joscelyn can't be very 'little' now. She is a famous woman, and she has forgotten all about you, you can be sure of that."

"Joscelyn wasn't the kind that forgets," said Aunty Nan loyally. "And, anyway, the point is, *I* haven't forgotten *her*. Oh, Maria, I've longed for years and years just to hear her sing once more. It seems as if I *must* hear my little Joscelyn sing once again before I die. I've never had the chance before and I never will have it again. Do please ask William to take me to Kensington."

"Dear me, Aunty Nan, this is really childish," said Mrs. William, whisking her bowlful of berries into the pantry. "You must let other folks be the judge of what is best for you now. You aren't strong enough to drive to Kensington, and, even if you were, you know well enough that William couldn't go to Kensington to-morrow night. He has got to attend that political meeting at Newbridge. They can't do without him."

"Jordan could take me to Kensington," pleaded Aunty Nan, with very unusual persistence.

"Nonsense! You couldn't go to Kensington with the hired man. Now, Aunty Nan, do be reasonable. Aren't William and I kind to you? Don't we do everything for your comfort?"

"Yes, oh, yes," admitted Aunty Nan deprecatingly.

"Well, then, you ought to be guided by our opinion. And you must just give up thinking about the Kensington concert, Aunty, and not worry yourself and me about it any more. I am going down to the shore field now to call William to tea. Just keep an eye on the baby in chance he wakes up, and see that the teapot doesn't boil over."

Mrs. William whisked out of the kitchen, pretending not to see the tears that were falling over Aunty Nan's withered pink cheeks. Aunty Nan was really getting very childish, Mrs. William reflected as she marched down to the shore field. Why, she cried now about every little thing! And such a notion—to want to go to the Old Timers' concert at Kensington and be so set on it! Really, it was hard to put up with her whims. Mrs. William sighed virtuously.

As for Aunty Nan, she sat alone in the kitchen, and cried bitterly, as only lonely old age can cry. It seemed to her that she could not bear it, that she *must* go to Kensington. But she knew that it was not to be, since Mrs. William had decided otherwise. Mrs. William's word was law at Gull Point Farm.

"What's the matter with my old Aunty Nan?" cried a hearty young voice from the doorway. Jordan Sloane stood there, his round, freckled face looking as anxious and sympathetic as it was possible for such a very round, very freckled face to look. Jordan was the Morrisons' hired boy that summer, and he worshipped Aunty Nan.

"Oh, Jordan," sobbed Aunty Nan, who was not above telling her troubles to the hired help, although Mrs. William thought she ought to be, "I can't go to Kensington to-morrow night to hear little Joscelyn sing at the Old Timers' concert. Maria says I can't."

"That's too bad," said Jordan. "Old cat," he muttered after the retreating and serenely unconscious Mrs. William. Then he shambled in and sat down on the sofa beside Aunty Nan.

"There, there, don't cry," he said, patting her thin little shoulder with his big, sunburned paw. "You'll make yourself sick if you go on crying, and we can't get along without you at Gull Point Farm."

Aunty Nan smiled wanly.

"I'm afraid you'll soon have to get on without me, Jordan. I'm not going to be here very long now. No, I'm not, Jordan, I know it. Something tells me so very plainly. But I would be willing to go—glad to go, for I'm very tired, Jordan—if I could only have heard little Joscelyn sing once more."

"Why are you so set on hearing her?" asked Jordan. "She ain't no kin to you, is she?"

"No, but dearer to me—dearer to me than many of my own. Maria thinks that is silly, but you wouldn't if you'd known her, Jordan. Even Maria herself wouldn't, if she had known her. It is fifteen years since she came here one summer to board. She was a child of thirteen then, and hadn't any relations except an old uncle who sent her to school in winter and boarded her out in summer, and didn't care a rap about her. The child was just starving for love, Jordan, and she got it here. William and his brothers were just children then, and they hadn't any sister. We all just worshipped her. She was so sweet, Jordan. And pretty, oh my! like a little girl in a picture, with great long curls, all black and purply and fine as spun silk, and big dark eyes, and such pink cheeks—real wild rose cheeks. And sing! My land! But couldn't she sing! Always singing, every hour of the day that voice was ringing round the old place. I used to hold my breath to hear it. She always said that she meant to be a famous singer some day, and I

never doubted it a mite. It was born in her. Sunday
evening she used to sing hymns for us. Oh, Jordan, it
makes my old heart young again to remember it. A sweet
child she was, my little Joscelyn! She used to write me for
three or four years after she went away, but I haven't
heard a word from her for long and long. I daresay she has
forgotten me, as Maria says. 'Twouldn't be any wonder.
But I haven't forgotten her, and oh, I want to see and hear
her terrible much. She is to sing at the Old Timers'
concert to-morrow night at Kensington. The folks who are
getting the concert up are friends of hers, or, of course,
she'd never have come to a little country village. Only
sixteen miles away—and I can't go."

Jordan couldn't think of anything to say. He reflected
savagely that if he had a horse of his own he would take
Aunty Nan to Kensington, Mrs. William or no Mrs. William. Though, to be sure, it *was* a long drive for her; and
she was looking very frail this summer.

"Ain't going to last long," muttered Jordan, making
his escape by the porch door as Mrs. William puffed in by
the other. "The sweetest old creetur that ever was created'll
go when she goes. Yah, ye old madam, I'd like to give you
a piece of my mind, that I would!"

This last was for Mrs. William, but was delivered in a
prudent undertone. Jordan detested Mrs. William, but
she was a power to be reckoned with, all the same. Meek,
easy-going Billy Morrison did just what his wife told him
to.

So Aunty Nan did not get to Kensington to hear little
Joscelyn sing. She said nothing more about it but after
that night she seemed to fail very rapidly. Mrs. William
said it was the hot weather, and that Aunty Nan gave way
too easily. But Aunty Nan could not help giving way now;
she was very, very tired. Even her knitting wearied her.
She would sit for hours in her rocking chair with the gray
kitten in her lap, looking out of the window with dreamy,
unseeing eyes. She talked to herself a good deal, generally
about little Joscelyn. Mrs. William told Avonlea folk that
Aunty Nan had got terribly childish and always accompa-
nied the remark with a sigh that intimated how much she,
Mrs. William, had to contend with.

Justice must be done to Mrs. William, however. She was not unkind to Aunty Nan; on the contrary, she was very kind to her in the letter. Her comfort was scrupulously attended to, and Mrs. William had the grace to utter none of her complaints in the old woman's hearing. If Aunty Nan felt the absence of the spirit, she never murmured at it.

One day, when the Avonlea slopes were golden-hued with the ripened harvest, Aunty Nan did not get up. She complained of nothing but great weariness. Mrs. William remarked to her husband that if *she* lay in bed every day she felt tired, there wouldn't be much done at Gull Point Farm. But she prepared an excellent breakfast and carried it patiently up to Aunty Nan, who ate little of it.

After dinner, Jordan crept up by way of the back stairs to see her. Aunty Nan was lying with her eyes fixed on the pale pink climbing roses that nodded about the window. When she saw Jordan she smiled.

"Them roses put me so much in mind of little Joscelyn," she said softly. "She loved them so. If I could only see her! Oh, Jordan, if I could only see her! Maria says it's terrible childish to be always harping on that string, and mebbe it is. But—oh, Jordan, there's such a hunger in my heart for her, such a hunger!"

Jordan felt a queer sensation in his throat, and twisted his ragged straw hat about in his big hands. Just then a vague idea which had hovered in his brain all day crystallized into decision. But all he said was:

"I hope you'll feel better soon, Aunty Nan."

"Oh, yes, Jordan dear, I'll be better soon," said Aunty Nan with her own sweet smile. "'The inhabitant shall not say I am sick,' you know. But if I could only see little Joscelyn first!"

Jordan went out and hurried down-stairs. Billy Morrison was in the stable, when Jordan stuck his head over the half-door.

"Say, can I have the rest of the day off, sir? I want to go to Kensington."

"Well, I don't mind," said Billy Morrison amiably. "May's well get your jaunting done 'fore harvest comes on.

And here, Jord; take this quarter and get some oranges for Aunty Nan. Needn't mention it to headquarters."

Billy Morrison's face was solemn, but Jordan winked as he pocketed the money.

"If I've any luck, I'll bring her something that'll do her more good than the oranges," he muttered, as he hurried off to the pasture. Jordan had a horse of his own now, a rather bony nag, answering to the name of Dan. Billy Morrison had agreed to pasture the animal if Jordan used him in the farm work, an arrangement scoffed at by Mrs. William in no measured terms.

Jordan hitched Dan into the second best buggy, dressed himself in his Sunday clothes, and drove off. On the road he re-read a paragraph he had clipped from the *Charlottown Daily Enterprise* of the previous day.

"Joscelyn Burnett, the famous contralto, is spending a few days in Kensington on her return from her Maritime concert tour. She is the guest of Mr. and Mrs. Bromley, of The Beeches."

"Now if I can get there in time," said Jordan emphatically.

Jordan got to Kensington, put Dan up in a livery stable, and inquired the way to The Beeches. He felt rather nervous when he found it, it was such a stately, imposing place, set back from the street in an emerald green seclusion of beautiful grounds.

"Fancy me stalking up to that front door and asking for Miss Joscelyn Burnett," grinned Jordan sheepishly. "Mebbe they'll tell me to go around to the back and inquire for the cook. But you're going just the same, Jordan Sloane, and no skulking. March right up now. Think of Aunty Nan and don't let style down you."

A pert-looking maid answered Jordan's ring, and stared at him when he asked for Miss Burnett.

"I don't think you can see her," she said shortly, scanning his country cut of hair and clothes rather superciliously. "What is your business with her?"

The maid's scorn roused Jordan's "dander," as he would have expressed it.

"I'll tell her that when I see her," he retorted coolly.

"Just you tell her that I've a message for her from Aunty Nan Morrison of Gull Point Farm, Avonlea. If she hain't forgot, that'll fetch her. You might as well hurry up, if you please, I've not overly too much time."

The pert maid decided to be civil at least, and invited Jordan to enter. But she left him standing in the hall while she went in search of Miss Burnett. Jordan gazed about him in amazement. He had never been in any place like this before. The hall was wonderful enough, and through the open doors on either hand stretched vistas of lovely rooms that, to Jordan's eyes, looked like those of a palace.

"Gee whiz! How do they ever move around without knocking things over?"

Then Joscelyn Burnett came, and Jordan forgot everything else. This tall, beautiful woman, in her silken draperies, with a face like nothing Jordan had ever seen, or even dreamed about—could this be Aunty Nan's little Joscelyn? Jordan's round, freckled countenance grew crimson. He felt horribly tongue-tied and embarrassed. What could he say to her? How could he say it?

Joscelyn Burnett looked at him with her large, dark eyes—the eyes of a woman who had suffered much, and learned much, and won through struggle to victory.

"You have come from Aunty Nan?" she said. "Oh, I am so glad to hear from her. Is she well? Come in here and tell me all about her."

She turned towards one of those fairy-like rooms, but Jordan interrupted her desperately.

"Oh, not in there, ma'am. I'd never get it out. Just let me blunder through it out here someways. Yes'm, Aunty Nan, she ain't very well. She's—she's dying, I guess. And she's longing for you night and day. Seems as if she couldn't die in peace without seeing you. She wanted to get to Kensington to hear you sing, but that old cat of a Mrs. William—begging your pardon, ma'am—wouldn't let her come. She's always talking of you. If you can come out to Gull Point Farm and see her, I'll be most awful obliged to you, ma'am."

Joscelyn Burnett looked troubled. She had not forgotten Gull Point Farm, nor Aunty Nan; but for years the memory had been dim, crowded into the background of consciousness by the more exciting events of her busy life. Now it came back with a rush. She recalled it all tenderly— the peace and beauty and love of that olden summer, and sweet Aunty Nan, so very wise in the lore of all things simple and good and true. For the moment, Joscelyn Burnett was a lonely, hungry-hearted little girl again, seeking for love and finding it not, until Aunty Nan had taken her into her great mother-heart and taught her its meaning.

"Oh, I don't know," she said perplexedly. "If you had come sooner—I leave on the 11:30 train to-night. I *must* leave by then or I shall not reach Montreal in time to fill a very important engagement. And yet I must see Aunty Nan, too. I have been careless and neglectful. I might have gone to see her before. How can we manage it?"

"I'll bring you back to Kensington in time to catch that train," said Jordan eagerly. "There's nothing I wouldn't do for Aunty Nan—me and Dan. Yes, sir, you'll get back in time. Just think of Aunty Nan's face when she sees you!"

"I will come," said the great singer, gently.

It was sunset when they reached Gull Point Farm. An arc of warm gold was over the spruces behind the house. Mrs. William was out in the barn-yard, milking, and the house was deserted, save for the sleeping baby in the kitchen and the little old woman with the watchful eyes in the up-stairs room.

"This way, ma'am," said Jordan, inwardly congratulat-. ing himself that the coast was clear. "I'll take you right up to her room."

Up-stairs, Joscelyn tapped at the half-open door and went in. Before it closed behind her, Jordan heard Aunty Nan say, "Joscelyn! Little Joscelyn!" in a tone that made him choke again. He stumbled thankfully down-stairs, to be pounced upon by Mrs. William in the kitchen.

"Jordan Sloane, who was that stylish woman you drove into the yard with? And what have you done with her?"

"That was Miss Joscelyn Burnett," said Jordan, expanding himself. This was his hour of triumph over Mrs. William. "I went to Kensington and brung her out to see Aunty Nan. She's up with her now."

"Dear me," said Mrs. William helplessly. "And me in

my milking rig! Jordan, for pity's sake, hold the baby while I go and put on my black silk. You might have given a body some warning. I declare I don't know which is the greatest idiot, you or Aunty Nan!"

As Mrs. William flounced out of the kitchen, Jordan took his satisfaction in a quiet laugh.

Up-stairs in the little room was a great glory of sunset and gladness of human hearts. Joscelyn was kneeling by the bed, with her arms about Aunty Nan; and Aunty Nan, with her face all irradiated, was stroking Joscelyn's dark hair fondly.

"O little Joscelyn," she murmured, "it seems too good to be true. It seems like a beautiful dream. I knew you the minute you opened the door, my dearie. You haven't changed a bit. And you're a famous singer now, little Joscelyn! I always knew you would be. Oh, I want you to sing a piece for me—just one, won't you, dearie? Sing that piece people like to hear you sing best. I forget the name, but I've read about it in the papers. Sing it for me, little Joscelyn."

And Joscelyn, standing by Aunty Nan's bed, in the sunset light, sang the song she had sung to many a brilliant audience on many a noted concert-platform—sang it as even she had never sung before, while Aunty Nan lay and listened beatifically, and down-stairs even Mrs. William held her breath, entranced by the exquisite melody that floated through the old farmhouse.

"O little Joscelyn!" breathed Aunty Nan in rapture, when the song ended.

Joscelyn knelt by her again and they had a long talk of old days. One by one they recalled the memories of that vanished summer. The past gave up its tears and its laughter. Heart and fancy alike went roaming through the ways of the long ago. Aunty Nan was perfectly happy. And then Joscelyn told her all the story of her struggles and triumphs since they had parted.

When the moonlight began to creep in through the low window, Aunty Nan put out her hand and touched Joscelyn's bowed head.

"Little Joscelyn," she whispered, "if it ain't asking too

much, I want you to sing just one other piece. Do you
remember when you were here how we sung hymns in
the parlour every Sunday night, and my favourite always
was 'The Sands of Time are Sinking'? I ain't never forgot
how you used to sing that, and I want to hear it just once
again, dearie. Sing it for me, little Joscelyn."

Joscelyn rose and went to the window. Lifting back
the curtain, she stood in the splendour of the moonlight,
and sang the grand old hymn. At first Aunty Nan beat
time to it feebly on the counterpane; but when Joscelyn
came to the verse, "With mercy and with judgment," she
folded her hands over her breast and smiled.

When the hymn ended, Joscelyn came over to the
bed.

"I am afraid I must say good-bye now, Aunty Nan,"
she said.

Then she saw that Aunty Nan had fallen asleep. She
would not waken her, but she took from her breast the
cluster of crimson roses she wore and slipped them gently
between the toil-worn fingers.

"Good-bye, dear, sweet mother-heart," she murmured.

Down-stairs she met Mrs. William, splendid in rus-
tling black silk, her broad, rubicund face smiling, overflowing with apologies and welcomes, which Joscelyn cut
short coldly.

"Thank you, Mrs. Morrison, but I cannot possibly
stay longer. No, thank you, I don't care for any refresh-
ments. Jordan is going to take me back to Kensington at
once. I came out to see Aunty Nan."

"I'm certain she'd be delighted," said Mrs. William
effusively. "She's been talking about you for weeks."

"Yes, it has made her very happy," said Joscelyn
gravely. "And it has made me happy, too. I love Aunty
Nan, Mrs. Morrison, and I owe her much. In all my life I
have never met a woman so purely, unselfishly good and
noble and true."

"Fancy now," said Mrs. William, rather overcome at
hearing this great singer pronounce such an encomium on
quiet, timid old Aunty Nan.

Jordan drove Joscelyn back to Kensington; and up-
stairs in her room Aunty Nan slept, with that rapt smile on

her face and Joscelyn's red roses in her hands. Thus it was that Mrs. William found her, going in the next morning with her breakfast. The sunlight crept over the pillow, lighting up the sweet old face and silver hair, and stealing downward to the faded red roses on her breast. Smiling and peaceful and happy lay Aunty Nan, for she had fallen on the sleep that knows no earthly waking, while little Joscelyn sang.

5

The Winning of Lucinda

THE marriage of a Penhallow was always the signal for
a gathering of the Penhallows. From the uttermost parts of
the earth they would come—Penhallows by birth, and
Penhallows by marriage and Penhallows by ancestry. East
Grafton was the ancient habitat of the race, and Penhallow
Grange, where "old" John Penhallow lived, was a Mecca
to them.

As for the family itself, the exact kinship of all its
various branches and ramifications was a hard thing to
define. Old Uncle Julius Penhallow was looked upon as a
veritable wonder because he carried it all in his head and
could tell on sight just what relation any one Penhallow
was to any other Penhallow. The rest made a blind guess
at it, for the most part, and the younger Penhallows let it
go at loose cousinship.

In this instance it was Alice Penhallow, daughter of
"young" John Penhallow, who was to be married. Alice
was a nice girl, but she and her wedding only pertain to
this story in so far as they furnish a background for Lucinda; hence nothing more need be said of her.

On the afternoon of her wedding day—the Penhallows
held to the good, old-fashioned custom of evening wed-
dings, with a rousing dance afterwards—Penhallow Grange
was filled to overflowing with guests who had come there
to have tea and rest themselves before going down to
"young" John's. Many of them had driven fifty miles. In
the big autumnal orchard the younger fry foregathered
and chatted and coquetted. Up-stairs, in "old" Mrs. John's
bedroom, she and her married daughters held high con-

clave. "Old" John had established himself with his sons and sons-in-law in the parlour, and the three daughters-in-law were making themselves at home in the blue sitting-room, ear-deep in harmless family gossip. Lucinda and Romney Penhallow were also there.

Thin Mrs. Nathaniel Penhallow sat in a rocking chair and toasted her toes at the grate, for the brilliant autumn afternoon was slightly chilly, and Lucinda, as usual, had the window open. She and plump Mrs. Frederick Penhallow did most of the talking, Mrs. George Penhallow being rather out of it by reason of her newness. She was George Penhallow's second wife, married only a year. Hence, her contributions to the conversation were rather spasmodic, hurled in, as it were, by dead reckoning, being sometimes appropriate and sometimes savouring of a point of view not strictly Penhallowesque.

Romney Penhallow was sitting in a corner, listening to the chatter of the women, with the inscrutable smile that always vexed Mrs. Frederick. Mrs. George wondered within herself what he did there among the women. She also wondered just where he belonged on the family tree. He was not one of the uncles, yet he could not be much younger than George.

"Forty, if he is a day," was Mrs. George's mental dictum, "but a very handsome and fascinating man. I never saw such a splendid chin and dimple."

Lucinda, with bronze-colored hair and the whitest of skins, defiant of merciless sunlight and revelling in the crisp air, sat on the sill of the open window behind the crimson vine leaves, looking out into the garden, where dahlias flamed and asters broke into waves of purple and snow. The ruddy light of the autumn afternoon gave a sheen to the waves of her hair and brought out the exceeding purity of her Greek outlines.

Mrs. George knew who Lucinda was—a cousin of the second generation, and, in spite of her thirty-five years, the acknowledged beauty of the whole Penhallow connection.

She was one of those rare women who keep their loveliness unmarred by the passage of years. She had ripened and matured, but she had not grown old. The older Penhallows were still inclined, from sheer force of habit, to look upon her as a girl, and the younger Penhallows hailed her as one of themselves. Yet Lucinda never aped girlishness; good taste and a strong sense of humour preserved her amid many temptations thereto. She was simply a beautiful, fully developed woman, with whom Time had declared a truce, young with a mellow youth which had nothing to do with years.

Mrs. George liked and admired Lucinda. Now, when Mrs. George liked and admired any person, it was a matter of necessity with her to impart her opinions to the most convenient confidant. In this case it was Romney Penhallow to whom Mrs. George remarked sweetly:

"Really, don't you think our Lucinda is looking remarkably well this fall?"

It seemed a very harmless, inane, well-meant question. Poor Mrs. George might well be excused for feeling bewildered over the effect. Romney gathered his long legs together, stood up, and swept the unfortunate speaker a crushing Penhallow bow of state.

"Far be it from me to disagree with the opinion of a lady—especially when it concerns another lady," he said, as he left the blue room.

Overcome by the mordant satire in his tone, Mrs. George glanced speechlessly at Lucinda. Behold, Lucinda had squarely turned her back on the party and was gazing out into the garden, with a very decided flush on the snowy curves of her neck and cheek. Then Mrs. George looked at her sisters-in-law. They were regarding her with the tolerant amusement they might bestow on a blundering child. Mrs. George experienced that subtle prescience whereby it is given us to know that we have put our foot in it. She felt herself turning an uncomfortable brick-red. What Penhallow skeleton had she unwittingly jangled? Why, oh, why, was it such an evident breach of the proprieties to praise Lucinda?

Mrs. George was devoutly thankful that a summons to the tea-table rescued her from her mire of embarrassment. The meal was spoiled for her, however; the mortifying recollection of her mysterious blunder conspired with her curiosity to banish appetite. As soon as possible after tea she decoyed Mrs. Frederick out into the garden, and in the dahlia walk solemnly demanded the reason of it all.

Mrs. Frederick indulged in a laugh which put the mettle of her festal brown silk seams to the test.

"My dear Cecilia, it was *so* amusing," she said, a little patronizingly.

"But *why!*" cried Mrs. George, resenting the patronage and the mystery. "What was so dreadful in what I said? Or so funny? And *who* is this Romney Penhallow who mustn't be spoken to?"

"Oh, Romney is one of the Charlottetown Penhallows," explained Mrs. Frederick. "He is a lawyer there. He is a first cousin of Lucinda's and a second of George's—or is he? Oh, bother! You must go to Uncle Julius if you want the genealogy. I'm in a chronic muddle concerning Penhallow relationship. And, as for Romney, of course you can speak to him about anything you like except Lucinda. Oh, you innocent! To ask him if he didn't think Lucinda was looking well! And right before her, too! Of course he thought you did it on purpose to tease him. That was what made him so savage and sarcastic."

"But *why?*" persisted Mrs. George, sticking tenaciously to her point.

"Hasn't George told you?"

"No," said George's wife in mild exasperation. "George has spent most of his time since we were married telling me odd things about the Penhallows, but he hasn't got to that yet, evidently."

"Why, my dear, it is our family romance. Lucinda and Romney are in love with each other. They have been in love with each other for fifteen years, and in all that time they have never spoken to each other once!"

"Dear me!" murmured Mrs. George, feeling the inadequacy of mere language. Was this a Penhallow method of courtship? "But *why?*"

"They had a quarrel fifteen years ago," said Mrs. Frederick patiently. "Nobody knows how it originated or anything about it, except that Lucinda was in the wrong. We know that, because Lucinda herself admitted it to us afterwards. But, in the first flush of her rage, she told Romney that she would never speak to him again as long as she lived. And *he* said he would never speak to her until she spoke first—because, you see, as she was in the wrong she ought to make the first advance. And they never have spoken. Everybody in the connection, I suppose, has taken turns trying to reconcile them, but nobody has succeeded. I don't believe that Romney has ever so much as *thought* of any other woman in his whole life, and certainly Lucinda has never thought of any other man. You will notice she still wears Romney's ring. They're practically engaged still, of course. And Romney said once that if Lucinda would just say one word, no matter what it was, even if it were something insulting, he would speak, too, and beg her pardon for his share in the quarrel— because then, you see, he would not be breaking his word. He hasn't referred to the matter for years, but I presume that he is of the same mind still. And they are just as much in love with each other as they ever were. He's always hanging about where she is—when other people are there, too, that is. He avoids her like a plague when she is alone. That was why he was stuck out in the blue room with us to-day. There doesn't seem to be a particle of resentment between them. If Lucinda would only speak! But that Lucinda will not do."

"Don't you think she will yet?" said Mrs. George.

Mrs. Frederick shook her crimped head sagely.

"Not now. The whole thing has hardened too long. Her pride will never let her speak. We used to hope she would be tricked into it by forgetfulness or accident—we used to lay traps for her—but all to no effect. It is such a shame, too. They were made for each other. Do you know, I get cross when I begin to thrash the whole silly affair over like this. Doesn't it sound as if we were talking of the quarrel of two school-children? Of late years we have learned that it does not do to speak of Lucinda to Romney, even in the most commonplace way. He seems to resent it."

"*He* ought to speak," cried Mrs. George warmly. "Even if she were in the wrong ten times over, he ought to overlook it and speak first."

"But he won't. And she won't. You never saw two such determined mortals. They get it from their grandfa-

ther on the mother's side—old Absalom Gordon. There is
no such stubbornness on the Penhallow side. His obsti-
nacy was a proverb, my dear—actually a proverb. Whatever he said, he would stick to if the skies fell. He was a
terrible old man to swear, too," added Mrs. Frederick,
dropping into irrelevant reminiscence. "He spent a long
while in a mining camp in his younger days and he never
got over it—the habit of swearing, I mean. It would have
made your blood run cold, my dear, to have heard him go
on at times. And yet he was a real good old man every
other way. He couldn't help it someway. He tried to, but
he used to say that profanity came as natural to him as
breathing. It used to mortify his family terribly. Fortunately, none of them took after him in that respect. But
he's dead—and one shouldn't speak ill of the dead. I must
go and get Mattie Penhallow to do my hair. I would burst
these sleeves clean out if I tried to do it myself, and I don't
want to dress over again. You won't be likely to talk to
Romney about Lucinda again, my dear Cecilia?"

"Fifteen years!" murmured Mrs. George helplessly to
the dahlias. "Engaged for fifteen years and never speaking
to each other! Dear heart and soul, think of it! Oh, these
Penhallows!"

Meanwhile, Lucinda, serenely unconscious that her
love story was being mouthed over by Mrs. Frederick in
the dahlia garden, was dressing for the wedding. Lucinda
still enjoyed dressing for a festivity, since the mirror still
dealt gently with her. Moreover, she had a new dress.
Now, a new dress—and especially one as nice as this—was
a rarity with Lucinda, who belonged to a branch of the
Penhallows noted for being chronically hard up. Indeed,
Lucinda and her widowed mother were positively poor,
and hence a new dress was an event in Lucinda's existence. An uncle had given her this one—a beautiful, per-
ishable thing, such as Lucinda would never have dared to
choose for herself, but in which she revelled with feminine delight.

It was of pale green voile—a colour which brought out
admirably the ruddy gloss of her hair and the clear brilliance of her skin. When she had finished dressing, she
looked at herself in the mirror with frank delight. Lucinda

was not vain, but she was quite well aware of the fact of her beauty and took an impersonal pleasure in it, as if she were looking at some finely painted picture by a master hand.

The form and face reflected in the glass satisfied her. The puffs and draperies of the green voile displayed to perfection the full, but not over-full, curves of her fine figure. Lucinda lifted her arm and touched a red rose to her lips with the hand upon which shone the frosty glitter of Romney's diamond, looking at the graceful slope of her shoulder and the splendid line of chin and throat with critical approval.

She noted, too, how well the gown became her eyes, bringing out all·the deeper colour in them. Lucinda had magnificent eyes. Once Romney had written a sonnet to them in which he compared their colour to ripe blueberries. This may not sound poetical to you unless you know or remember just what the tints of ripe blueberries are— dusky purple in some lights, clear slate in others, and yet again in others the misty hue of early meadow violets.

"You really look very well," remarked the real Lucinda to the mirrored Lucinda. "Nobody would think you were an old maid. But you are. Alice Penhallow, who is to be married to-night, was a child of five when you thought of being married fifteen years ago. That makes you an old maid, my dear. Well, it is your own fault, and it will continue to be your own fault, you stubborn offshoot of a stubborn breed!"

She flung her train out straight and pulled on her gloves.

"I do hope I won't get any spots on this dress to-night," she reflected. "It will have to do me for a gala dress for a year at least—and I have a creepy conviction that it is fearfully spottable. Bless Uncle Mark's good, uncalculating heart! How I would have detested it if he had given me something sensible and useful and ugly—as Aunt Emilia would have done."

They all went to "young" John Penhallow's at early moonrise. Lucinda drove over the two miles of hill and dale with a youthful second cousin, by name, Carey Penhallow. The wedding was quite a brilliant affair. Lucinda seemed to pervade the social atmosphere, and everywhere she went a little ripple of admiration trailed after her like a wave. She was undeniably a belle, yet she found herself feeling faintly bored and was rather glad than otherwise when the guests began to fray off.

"I'm afraid I'm losing my capacity for enjoyment," she thought, a little drearily. "Yes, I must be growing old. That is what it means when social functions begin to bore you."

It was that unlucky Mrs. George who blundered again. She was standing on the veranda when Carey Penhallow dashed up.

"Tell Lucinda that I can't take her back to the Grange. I have to drive Mark and Cissy Penhallow to Bright River to catch the two o'clock express. There will be plenty of chances for her with the others."

At this moment George Penhallow, holding his rearing horse with difficulty, shouted for his wife. Mrs. George, all in a flurry, dashed back into the still-crowded hall. Exactly to whom she gave her message was never known to any of the Penhallows. But a tall, ruddy-haired girl, dressed in pale green organdy—Anne Shirley from Avonlea—told Marilla Cuthbert and Rachel Lynde as a joke the next morning how a chubby little woman in a bright pink fascinator had clutched her by the arm, and gasped out:

"Carey Penhallow can't take you—he says you're to look out for someone else," and was gone before she could answer or turn around.

Thus it was that Lucinda, when she came out to the veranda step, found herself unaccountably deserted. All the Grange Penhallows were gone; Lucinda realized this after a few moments of bewildered seeking, and she understood that if she were to get to the Grange that night she must walk. Plainly there was nobody to take her.

Lucinda was angry. It is not pleasant to find yourself forgotten and neglected. It is still less pleasant to walk home alone along a country road, at one o'clock in the morning, wearing a pale green voile. Lucinda was not prepared for such a walk. She had nothing on her feet save thin-soled shoes, and her only wraps were a flimsy fascinator and a short coat.

"What a guy I shall look, stalking home alone in this rig," she thought crossly.

There was no help for it, unless she confessed her plight to some of the stranger guests and begged a drive home. Lucinda's pride scorned such a request and the admission of neglect it involved. No, she would walk, since that was all there was to it; but she would not go by the main road to be stared at by all and sundry who might pass her. There was a short cut by way of a lane across the fields; she knew every inch of it, although she had not traversed it for years.

She gathered up the green voile as trimly as possible, slipped around the house in the kindly shadows, picked her way across the side lawn, and found a gate which opened into a birch-bordered lane where the frosted trees shone with silvery-golden radiance in the moonlight. Lucinda flitted down the lane, growing angrier at every step as the realization of how shamefully she seemed to have been treated came home to her. She believed that nobody had thought about her at all, which was tenfold worse than premeditated neglect.

As she came to the gate at the lower end of the lane, a man who was leaning over it started, with a quick intake of his breath, which, in any other man than Romney Penhallow, or for any other woman than Lucinda Penhallow, would have been an exclamation of surprise.

Lucinda recognized him with a great deal of annoyance and a little relief. She would not have to walk home alone. But with Romney Penhallow! Would he think she had contrived it so purposely?

Romney silently opened the gate for her, silently latched it behind her, and silently fell into step beside her. Down across a velvety sweep of field they went; the air was frosty, calm, and still; over the world lay a haze of moonshine and mist that converted East Grafton's prosaic hills and fields into a shimmering fairyland.

At first Lucinda felt angrier than ever. What a ridiculous situation! How the Penhallows would laugh over it!

As for Romney, he, too, was angry with the trick impish chance had played him. He liked being the butt of an awkward situation as little as most men; and certainly to be obliged to walk home over moonlit fields at one o'clock in the morning with the woman he had loved and never spoken to for fifteen years was the irony of fate with a vengeance. Would she think he had schemed for it? And how the deuce did she come to be walking home from the wedding at all?

By the time they had crossed the field and reached the wild cherry lane beyond it, Lucinda's anger was mastered by her saving sense of humour. She was even smiling a little maliciously under her fascinator.

The lane was a place of enchantment—a long, moonlit colonnade adown which beguiling wood nymphs might have footed it featly. The moonshine fell through the arching boughs and made a mosaic of silver light and clear-cut shadow for the unfriendly lovers to walk in. On either side was the hovering gloom of the woods, and around them a great silence unstirred by wind or murmur.

Midway in the lane, Lucinda was attacked by a sentimental recollection. She thought of the last time Romney and she had walked home together through this very lane, from a party at "young" John's. It had been moonlight then, too, and—Lucinda checked a sigh—they had walked hand in hand. Just here, by the big gray beech, he had stopped her and kissed her. Lucinda wondered if he were thinking of it, too, and stole a look at him from under the lace border of her fascinator.

But he was striding moodily along with his hands in his pockets, and his hat pulled down over his eyes, passing the old beech without a glance at it. Lucinda checked another sigh, gathered up an escaped flutter of voile, and marched on.

Past the lane a range of three silvery harvest fields sloped down to Peter Penhallow's brook—a wide, shallow stream bridged over in the olden days by the mossy trunk of an ancient fallen tree. When Lucinda and Romney arrived at the brook, they gazed at the brawling water blankly. Lucinda remembered that she must not speak to Romney just in time to prevent an exclamation of dismay. There was no tree! There was no bridge of any kind over the brook!

Here was a predicament! But before Lucinda could do more than despairingly ask herself what was to be done now, Romney answered—not in words, but in deeds. He coolly picked Lucinda up in his arms, as if she had been a child instead of a full grown woman of no mean avoirdupois, and began to wade with her through the water.

Lucinda gasped helplessly. She could not forbid him, and she was so choked with rage over his presumption that she could not have spoken in any case. Then came the catastrophe. Romney's foot slipped on a treacherous round stone—there was a tremendous splash—and Romney and Lucinda Penhallow were sitting down in the middle of Peter Penhallow's brook.

Lucinda was the first to regain her feet. About her clung, in heart-breaking limpness, the ruined voile. The remembrance of all her wrongs that night rushed over her soul, and her eyes blazed in the moonlight. Lucinda Penhallow had never been so angry in her life.

"*You d—d idiot!*" she said, in a voice that literally shook with rage.

Romney meekly scrambled up the bank after her.

"I'm awfully sorry, Lucinda," he said, striving with uncertain success to keep a suspicious quiver of laughter out of his tone. "It was wretchedly clumsy of me, but that pebble turned right under my foot. Please forgive me—for that—and for other things."

Lucinda deigned no answer. She stood on a flat stone and wrung the water from the poor green voile. Romney surveyed her apprehensively.

"Hurry, Lucinda," he entreated. "You will catch your death of cold."

"I never take cold," answered Lucinda, with chattering teeth. "And it is my dress I am thinking of—was thinking of. You have more need to hurry. You are sopping wet yourself and you know you are subject to colds. There—come."

Lucinda picked up the stringy train, which had been so brave and buoyant five minutes before, and started up the field at a brisk rate. Romney came up to her and slipped his arm through hers in the old way. For a time they walked along in silence. Then Lucinda began to shake with inward laughter. She laughed silently for the whole length of the field; and at the line fence between Peter Penhallow's land and the Grange acres she paused, threw back the fascinator from her face, and looked at Romney defiantly.

"You are thinking of—*that*," she cried, "and I am thinking of it. And we will go on, thinking of it at intervals for the rest of our lives. But if you ever mention it to me I'll never forgive you, Romney Penhallow!"

"I never will," Romney promised. There was more than a suspicion of laughter in his voice this time, but Lucinda did not choose to resent it. She did not speak again until they reached the Grange gate. Then she faced him solemnly.

"It was a case of atavism," she said. "Old Grandfather Gordon was to blame for it."

At the Grange, almost everybody was in bed. What with the guests straggling home at intervals and hurrying sleepily off to their rooms, nobody had missed Lucinda, each set supposing she was with some other set. Mrs. Frederick, Mrs. Nathaniel and Mrs. George alone were up. The perennially chilly Mrs. Nathaniel had kindled a fire of chips in the blue room grate to warm her feet before retiring, and the three women were discussing the wedding in subdued tones when the door opened and the stately form of Lucinda, stately even in the draggled voile, appeared, with the damp Romney behind her.

"Lucinda Penhallow!" gasped they, one and all.

"I was left to walk home," said Lucinda coolly. "So Romney and I came across the fields. There was no bridge over the brook, and when he was carrying me over, he slipped and we fell in. That is all. No, Cecilia, I never take cold, so don't worry. Yes, my dress is ruined, but that is of no consequence. No, thank you, Cecilia, I do not care for a hot drink. Romney, do go and take off those wet clothes of yours immediately. No, Cecilia, I will *not* take a hot footbath. I am going straight to bed. Good night."

When the door closed on the pair, the three sisters-in-laws stared at each other. Mrs. Frederick, feeling herself incapable of expressing her sensations originally, took refuge in a quotation:

" 'Do I sleep, do I dream, do I wonder and doubt?
Is things what they seem, or is visions about?' "

"There will be another Penhallow wedding soon," said Mrs. Nathaniel, with a long breath. "Lucinda has spoken to Romney *at last.*"

"Oh, *what* do you suppose she said to him?" cried Mrs. George.

"My dear Cecilia," said Mrs. Frederick, "we shall never know."

They never did know.

6

Old Man Shaw's Girl

"DAY after to-morrow—day after to-morrow," said Old Man Shaw, rubbing his long slender hands together gleefully. "I have to keep saying it over and over, so as to really believe it. It seems far too good to be true that I'm to have Blossom again. And everything is ready. Yes, I think everything is ready, except a bit of cooking. And won't this orchard be a surprise to her! I'm just going to bring her out here as soon as I can, never saying a word. I'll fetch her through the spruce lane, and when we come to the end of the path I'll step back casual-like, and let her go out from under the trees alone, never suspecting. It'll be worth ten times the trouble to see her big, brown eyes open wide and hear her say, 'Oh, daddy! Why, daddy!'"

He rubbed his hands again and laughed softly to himself. He was a tall, bent old man, whose hair was snow white, but whose face was fresh and rosy. His eyes were a boy's eyes, large, blue, and merry, and his mouth had never got over a youthful trick of smiling at any provocation—and, oft-times, at no provocation at all.

To be sure, White Sands people would not have given you the most favourable opinion in the world of Old Man Shaw. First and foremost, they would have told you that he was "shiftless," and had let his bit of a farm run out while he pottered with flowers and bugs, or rambled aimlessly about in the woods, or read books along the shore. Perhaps it was true; but the old farm yielded him a living, and further than that Old Man Shaw had no ambition. He was as blithe as a pilgrim on a pathway climbing to the west. He had learned the rare secret that you must take happiness when you find it—that there is no use in marking the place and coming back to it at a more convenient season, because it will not be there then. And it is very easy to be happy if you know, as Old Man Shaw most thoroughly knew, how to find pleasure in little things. He enjoyed life, he had always enjoyed life and helped others to enjoy it; consequently, his life was a success, whatever White Sands people might think of it. What if he had not "improved" his farm? There are some people to whom life will never be anything more than a kitchen garden; and there are others to whom it will always be a royal palace with domes and minarets of rainbow fancy.

The orchard of which he was so proud was as yet little more than the substance of things hoped for—a flourishing plantation of young trees which would amount to something later on. Old Man Shaw's house was on the crest of a bare, sunny hill, with a few staunch old firs and spruces behind it—the only trees that could resist the full sweep of the winds that blew bitterly up from the sea at times. Fruit trees would never grow near it, and this had been a great grief to Sara.

"Oh, daddy, if we could just have an orchard!" she had been wont to say wistfully, when other farmhouses in White Sands were smothered whitely in apple bloom. And when she had gone away, and her father had nothing to look forward to save her return, he was determined she should find an orchard when she came back.

Over the southward hill, warmly sheltered by spruce woods and sloping to the sunshine, was a little field, so fertile that all the slack management of a life-time had not availed to exhaust it. Here Old Man Shaw set out his orchard and saw it flourish, watching and tending it until he came to know each tree as a child and loved it. His neighbours laughed at him, and said that the fruit of an orchard so far away from the house would all be stolen. But as yet there was no fruit, and when the time came for bearing, there would be enough and to spare.

"Blossom and me'll get all we want, and the boys can have the rest, if they want 'em worse'n they want a good conscience," said that unworldly, unbusiness-like Old Man Shaw.

On his way back home from his darling orchard, he found a rare fern in the woods and dug it up for Sara—she had loved ferns. He planted it at the shady, sheltered side of the house and then sat down on the old bench by the garden gate to read her last letter—the letter that was only a note, because she was coming home soon. He knew every word of it by heart, but that did not spoil the pleasure of re-reading it every half-hour.

Old Man Shaw had not married until late in life, and had, so White Sands people said, selected a wife with his usual judgment—which, being interpreted, meant no judgment at all; otherwise, he would never have married Sara Glover, a mere slip of a girl, with big brown eyes like a frightened wood creature's, and the delicate, fleeting bloom of a spring Mayflower.

"The last woman in the world for a farmer's wife—no strength or get-up about her."

Neither could White Sands folk understand what on earth Sara Glover had married him for.

"Well, the fool crop was the only one that never failed."

Old Man Shaw—he was Old Man Shaw even then, although he was only forty—and his girl bride had troubled themselves not at all about White Sands opinions. They had one year of perfect happiness, which is always worth living for, even if the rest of life be a dreary pilgrimage, and then Old Man Shaw found himself alone again, except for little Blossom. She was christened Sara, after her dead mother, but she was always Blossom to her father—the precious little blossom whose plucking had cost the mother her life.

Sara Glover's people, especially a wealthy aunt in Montreal, had wanted to take the child, but Old Man Shaw grew almost fierce over the suggestion. He would give his baby to no one. A woman was hired to look after the house, but it was the father who cared for the baby in the main. He was as tender and faithful and deft as a woman. Sara never missed a mother's care, and she grew up into a creature of life and light and beauty, a constant delight to all who knew her. She had a way of embroidering life with stars. She was dowered with all the charming characteristics of both parents, with a resilient vitality and activity which had pertained to neither of them. When she was ten years old, she had packed all hirelings off, and kept house for her father for six delightful years—years in which they were father and daughter, brother and sister, and "chums." Sara never went to school, but her father saw to her education after a fashion of his own. When their work was done, they lived in the woods and fields, in the little garden they had made on the sheltered side of the house, or on the shore, where sunshine and storm were to them equally lovely and beloved. Never was comradeship more perfect or more wholly satisfactory.

"Just wrapped up in each other," said White Sands folk, half-enviously, half-disapprovingly.

When Sara was sixteen, Mrs. Adair, the wealthy aunt aforesaid, pounced down on White Sands in a glamour of fashion and culture and outer worldliness. She bombarded Old Man Shaw with such arguments that he had to succumb. It was a shame that a girl like Sara should grow up in a place like White Sands, "with no advantages and no education," said Mrs. Adair scornfully, not understanding that wisdom and knowledge are two entirely different things.

"At least let me give my dear sister's child what I would have given my own daughter if I had had one," she pleaded tearfully. "Let me take her with me and send her to a good school for a few years. Then, if she wishes, she may come back to you, of course."

Privately, Mrs. Adair did not for a moment believe that Sara would want to come back to White Sands and her queer old father, after three years of the life she would give her.

Old Man Shaw yielded, influenced thereto not at all by Mrs. Adair's readily flowing tears, but greatly by his conviction that justice to Sara demanded it. Sara herself did not want to go; she protested and pleaded; but her father, having become convinced that it was best for her to go, was inexorable. Everything, even her own feelings, must give way to that. But she was to come back to him without let or hindrance when her "schooling" was done. It was only on having this most clearly understood that

Sara would consent to go at all. Her last words, called back to her father through her tears as she and her aunt drove down the lane, were,

"I'll be back, daddy. In three years I'll be back. Don't cry, but just look forward to that."

He had looked forward to it through the three long, lonely years that followed, in all of which he never saw his darling. Half a continent was between them, and Mrs. Adair had vetoed vacation visits, under some specious pretence. But every week brought its letter from Sara. Old Man Shaw had every one of them, tied up with one of her old blue hair ribbons, and kept in her mother's little rosewood work-box in the parlour. He spent every Sunday afternoon re-reading them, with her photograph before him. He lived alone, refusing to be pestered with kind help, but he kept the house in beautiful order.

"A better housekeeper than farmer," said White Sands people. He would have nothing altered. When Sara came back she was not to be hurt by changes. It never occurred to him that she might be changed herself.

And now those three interminable years were gone, and Sara was coming home. She wrote him nothing of her aunt's pleadings and reproaches and ready, futile tears; she wrote only that she would graduate in June and start for home a week later. Thenceforth Old Man Shaw went about in a state of beatitude, making ready for her homecoming. As he sat on the bench in the sunshine, with the blue sea sparkling and crinkling down at the foot of the green slope, he reflected with satisfaction that all was in perfect order. There was nothing left to do save count the hours until that beautiful, longed-for day after to-morrow. He gave himself over to a reverie, as sweet as a day-dream in a haunted valley.

The red roses were out in bloom. Sara had always loved those red roses—they were as vivid as herself, with all her own fullness of life and joy of living. And, besides these, a miracle had happened in Old Man Shaw's garden. In one corner was a rose-bush which had never bloomed, despite all the coaxing they had given it—"the sulky rose-bush," Sara had been wont to call it. Lo! this summer had flung the hoarded sweetness of years into plentiful white blossoms, like shallow ivory cups with a haunting, spicy fragrance. It was in honour of Sara's home-coming—so Old Man Shaw liked to fancy. All things, even the sulky rose-bush, knew she was coming back, and were making glad because of it.

He was gloating over Sara's letter when Mrs. Peter Blewett came. She told him she had run up to see how he was getting on, and if he wanted anything seen to before Sara came.

Old Man Shaw shook his head.

"No'm, thank you, ma'am. Everything is attended to. I couldn't let anyone else prepare for Blossom. Only to think, ma'am, she'll be home the day after to-morrow. I'm just filled clear through, body, soul, and spirit, with joy to think of having my little Blossom at home again."

Mrs. Blewett smiled sourly. When Mrs. Blewett smiled, it foretokened trouble, and wise people had learned to have sudden business elsewhere before the smile could be translated into words. But Old Man Shaw had never learned to be wise where Mrs. Blewett was concerned; although she had been his nearest neighbour for years, and had pestered his life out with advice and "neighbourly turns."

Mrs. Blewett was one with whom life had gone awry. The effect on her was to render happiness in other people a personal insult. She resented Old Man Shaw's beaming delight in his daughter's return, and she "considered it her duty" to rub the bloom off straightway.

"Do you think Sary'll be contented in White Sands now?" she asked.

Old Man Shaw looked slightly bewildered.

"Of course she'll be contented," he said slowly. "Isn't it her home? And ain't I here?"

Mrs. Blewett smiled again, with double distilled contempt for such simplicity.

"Well, it's a good thing you're so sure of it, I suppose. If 'twas my daughter that was coming back to White Sands, after three years of fashionable life among rich, stylish folks, and at a swell school, I wouldn't have a minute's peace of mind. I'd know perfectly well that she'd look down on everything here, and be discontented and miserable."

"*Your* daughter might," said Old Man Shaw, with more sarcasm than he had supposed he had possessed, "but Blossom won't."

Mrs. Blewett shrugged her sharp shoulders.

"Maybe not. It's to be hoped not, for both your sakes, I'm sure. But I'd be worried if 'twas me. Sary's been living among fine folks, and having a gay, exciting time, and it stands to reason she'll think White Sands fearful lonesome and dull. Look at Lauretta Bradley. She was up in Boston for just a month last winter and she's never been able to endure White Sands since."

"Lauretta Bradley and Sara Shaw are two different people," said Sara's father, trying to smile.

"And your house, too," pursued Mrs. Blewett ruthlessly. "It's such a queer, little, old place. What'll she think of it after her aunt's? I've heard tell Mrs. Adair lives in a perfect palace. I'll just warn you kindly that Sary'll probably look down on you, and you might as well be prepared for it. Of course, I suppose she kind of thinks she has to come back, seeing she promised you so solemn she would. But I'm certain she doesn't want to, and I don't blame her either."

Even Mrs. Blewett had to stop for breath, and Old Man Shaw found his opportunity. He had listened, dazed and shrinking, as if she were dealing him physical blows, but now a swift change swept over him. His blue eyes flashed ominously, straight into Mrs. Blewett's straggling, ferrety gray orbs.

"If you've said your say, Martha Blewett, you can go," he said passionately. "I'm not going to listen to another such word. Take yourself out of my sight, and your malicious tongue out of my hearing!"

Mrs. Blewett went, too dumfounded by such an unheard-of outburst in mild Old Man Shaw to say a word of defence or attack. When she had gone, Old Man Shaw, the fire all faded from his eyes, sank back on his bench. His delight was dead; his heart was full of pain and bitterness. Martha Blewett was a warped and ill-natured woman, but he feared there was altogether too much truth in what she said. Why had he never thought of it before? Of course White Sands would seem dull and lonely to Blossom; of course the little gray house where she was born would seem a poor abode after the splendours of her aunt's home. Old Man Shaw walked through his garden and looked at everything with new eyes. How poor and simple everything was! How sagging and weather-beaten the old house! He went in, and up-stairs to Sara's room. It was neat and clean, just as she had left it three years ago. But it was small and dark; the ceiling was discoloured, the furniture old-fashioned and shabby; she would think it a poor, mean place. Even the orchard over the hill brought him no comfort now. Blossom would not care for orchards. She would be ashamed of her stupid old father and the barren farm. She would hate White Sands, and chafe at the dull existence, and look down on everything that went to make up his uneventful life.

Old Man Shaw was unhappy enough that night to have satisfied even Mrs. Blewett, had she known. He saw himself as he thought White Sands folk must see him—a poor, shiftless, foolish old man, who had only one thing in the world worthwhile, his little girl, and had not been of enough account to keep her.

"Oh, Blossom, Blossom!" he said, and when he spoke her name it sounded as if he spoke the name of one dead.

After a little the worst sting passed away. He refused to believe long that Blossom would be ashamed of him; he knew she would not. Three years could not so alter her loyal nature—no, nor ten times three years. But she would be changed—she would have grown away from him in those three busy, brilliant years. His companionship could no longer satisfy her. How simple and childish he had been to expect it! She would be sweet and kind— Blossom could never be anything else. She would not show open discontent or dissatisfaction; she would not be like Lauretta Bradley; but it would be there, and he would divine it, and it would break his heart. Mrs. Blewett was right. When he had given Blossom up he should not have made a half-hearted thing of his sacrifice—he should not have bound her to come back to him.

He walked about in his little garden until late at night, under the stars, with the sea crooning and calling to him down the slope. When he finally went to bed he did not sleep, but lay until morning with tear-wet eyes and despair in his heart. All the forenoon he went about his usual daily work absently. Frequently he fell into long reveries, standing motionless wherever he happened to be, and looking dully before him. Only once did he show any animation. When he saw Mrs. Blewett coming up the lane, he darted into the house, locked the door, and listened to her knocking in grim silence. After she had gone he went out and found a plate of fresh doughnuts, covered with a napkin, placed on the bench at the door. Mrs. Blewett meant to indicate thus that she bore him no malice for her curt dismissal the day before; possibly her conscience gave her some twinges also. But her doughnuts could not minister to the mind she had diseased. Old Man Shaw took them up, carried them to the pig-pen, and fed them to the pigs. It was the first spiteful thing he had done in his life, and he felt a most immoral satisfaction in it.

In mid-afternoon he went out to the garden, finding the new loneliness of the little house unbearable. The old bench was warm in the sunshine. Old Man Shaw sat down with a long sigh, and dropped his white head wearily on his breast. He had decided what he must do. He would tell Blossom that she might go back to her aunt and never mind about him—he would do very well by himself and he did not blame her in the least.

He was still sitting broodingly there when a girl came up the lane. She was tall and straight, and walked with a kind of uplift in her motion, as if it would be rather easier to fly than not. She was dark, with a rich dusky sort of darkness, suggestive of the bloom on purple plums, or the glow of deep red apples among bronze leaves. Her big brown eyes lingered on everything in sight, and little gurgles of sound now and again came through her parted lips, as if inarticulate joy were thus expressing itself.

At the garden gate she saw the bent figure on the old bench, and the next minute she was flying along the rose walk.

"Daddy!" she called, "daddy!"

Old Man Shaw stood up in hasty bewilderment; then a pair of girlish arms were about his neck, and a pair of warm red lips were on his; girlish eyes, full of love, were looking up into his, and a never-forgotten voice, tingling with laughter and tears blended into one delicious chord, was crying,

"Oh, daddy, is it really you? Oh, I can't tell you how good it is to see you again!"

Old Man Shaw held her tightly in a silence of amazement and joy too deep for wonder. Why, this was his Blossom—the very Blossom who had gone away three years ago! A little taller, a little more womanly, but his own dear Blossom, and no stranger. There was a new heaven and a new earth for him in the realization.

"Oh, Baby Blossom!" he murmured, "little Baby Blossom!"

Sara rubbed her cheek against the faded coat sleeve.

"Daddy darling, this moment makes up for everything, doesn't it?"

"But—but—where did you come from?" he asked, his senses beginning to struggle out of their bewilderment of surprise. "I didn't expect you till to-morrow. You didn't have to walk from the station, did you? And your old daddy not there to welcome you!"

Sara laughed, swung herself back by the tips of her fingers and danced around him in the childish fashion of long ago.

"I found I could make an earlier connection with the C.P.A. yesterday and get to the Island last night. I was in such a fever to get home that I jumped at the chance. Of course I walked from the station—it's only two miles and every step was a benediction. My trunks are over there. We'll go after them to-morrow, daddy, but just now I want to go straight to every one of the dear old nooks and spots at once."

"You must get something to eat first," he urged fondly. "And there ain't much in the house, I'm afraid. I was going to bake to-morrow morning. But I guess I can forage you out something, darling."

He was sorely repenting having given Mrs. Blewett's doughnuts to the pigs, but Sara brushed all such considerations aside with a wave of her hand.

"I don't want anything to eat just now. By and by

we'll have a snack; just as we used to get up for ourselves whenever we felt hungry. Don't you remember how scandalized White Sands folks used to be at our irregular hours? I'm hungry; but it's soul hunger, for a glimpse of all the dear old rooms and places. Come—there are four hours yet before sunset, and I want to cram into them all I've missed out of these three years. Let us begin right here with the garden. Oh, daddy, by what witchcraft have you coaxed that sulky rose-bush into bloom?"

"No witchcraft at all—it just bloomed because you were coming home, baby," said her father.

They had a glorious afternoon of it, those two children. They explored the garden and then the house. Sara danced through every room, and then up to her own, holding fast to her father's hand.

"Oh, it's lovely to see my little room again, daddy. I'm sure all my old hopes and dreams are waiting here for me."

She ran to the window and threw it open, leaning out.

"Daddy, there's no view in the world so beautiful as that curve of sea between the headlands. I've looked at magnificent scenery—and then I'd shut my eyes and conjure up that picture. Oh, listen to the wind keening in the trees! How I've longed for that music!"

He took her to the orchard and followed out his crafty plan of surprise perfectly. She rewarded him by doing exactly what he had dreamed of her doing, clapping her hands and crying out:

"Oh, daddy! Why, daddy!"

They finished up with the shore, and then at sunset they came back and sat down on the old garden bench. Before them a sea of splendour, burning like a great jewel, stretched to the gateways of the west. The long headlands on either side were darkly purple, and the sun left behind him a vast, cloudless arc of fiery daffodil and elusive rose. Back over the orchard in a cool, green sky glimmered a crystal planet, and the night poured over them a clear wine of dew from her airy chalice. The spruces were rejoicing in the wind, and even the battered firs were singing of the sea. Old memories trooped into their hearts like shining spirits.

"Baby Blossom," said Old Man Shaw falteringly, "are you quite sure you'll be contented here? Out there"—with a vague sweep of his hand towards horizons that shut out a world far removed from White Sands—"there's pleasure and excitement and all that. Won't you miss it? Won't you get tired of your old father and White Sands?"

Sara patted his hand gently.

"The world out there is a good place," she said thoughtfully. "I've had three splendid years and I hope they'll enrich my whole life. There are wonderful things out there to see and learn, fine, noble people to meet, beautiful deeds to admire; but," she wound her arm about his neck and laid her cheek against his—"there was no daddy!"

And Old Man Shaw looked silently at the sunset—or, rather, through the sunset to still grander and more radiant splendours beyond, of which the things seen were only the pale reflections, not worthy of attention from those who had the gift of further sight.

7

Aunt Olivia's Beau

AUNT OLIVIA told Peggy and me about him on the afternoon we went over to help her gather her late roses for pot-pourri. We found her strangely quiet and preoccupied. As a rule she was fond of mild fun, alert to hear East Grafton gossip, and given to sudden little trills of almost girlish laughter, which for the time being dispelled the atmosphere of gentle old-maidishness which seemed to hang about her as a garment. At such moments we did not find it hard to believe—as we did at other times—that Aunt Olivia had once been a girl herself.

This day she picked the roses absently, and shook the fairy petals into her little sweet-grass basket with the air of a woman whose thoughts were far away. We said nothing, knowing that Aunt Olivia's secrets always came our way in time. When the rose-leaves were picked, we carried them in and upstairs in single file, Aunt Olivia bringing up the rear to pick up any stray rose-leaf we might drop. In the south-west room, where there was no carpet to fade, we spread them on newspapers on the floor. Then we put our sweet-grass baskets back in the proper place in the proper closet in the proper room. What would have happened to us, or to the sweet-grass baskets, if this had not been done I do not know. Nothing was ever permitted to remain an instant out of place in Aunt Olivia's house.

When we went downstairs, Aunt Olivia asked us to go into the parlour. She had something to tell us, she said, and as she opened the door a delicate pink flush spread over her face. I noted it, with surprise, but no inkling of the truth came to me—for nobody ever connected the

107

idea of possible lovers or marriage with this prim little old maid, Olivia Sterling.

Aunt Olivia's parlour was much like herself—painfully neat. Every article of furniture stood in exactly the same place it had always stood. Nothing was ever suffered to be disturbed. The tassels of the crazy cushion lay just so over the arm of the sofa, and the crochet antimacassar was always spread at precisely the same angle over the horse-hair rocking chair. No speck of dust was ever visible; no fly ever invaded that sacred apartment.

Aunt Olivia pulled up a blind, to let in what light could sift finely through the vine leaves, and sat down in a high-backed old chair that had appertained to her great-grandmother. She folded her hands in her lap, and looked at us with shy appeal in her blue-gray eyes. Plainly, she found it hard to tell us her secret, yet all the time there was an air of pride and exultation about her; somewhat, also, of a new dignity. Aunt Olivia could never be self-assertive, but if it had been possible, that would have been her time for it.

"Have you ever heard me speak of Mr. Malcolm MacPherson?" asked Aunt Olivia.

We had never heard her, or anybody else, speak of Mr. Malcolm MacPherson; but volumes of explanation could not have told us more about him than did Aunt Olivia's voice when she pronounced his name. We knew, as if it had been proclaimed to us in trumpet tones, that Mr. Malcolm MacPherson must be Aunt Olivia's beau, and the knowledge took away our breath. We even forgot to be curious, so astonished were we.

And there sat Aunt Olivia, proud and shy and exulting and shamefaced, all at once!

"He is a brother of Mrs. John Seaman's across the bridge," explained Aunt Olivia with a little simper. "Of course you don't remember him. He went out to British Columbia twenty years ago. But he is coming home now—and—and—tell your father, won't you—I—I—don't like to tell him—Mr. Malcolm MacPherson and I are going to be married."

"Married!" gasped Peggy. And "Married!" I echoed stupidly.

Aunt Olivia bridled a little.

"There is nothing unsuitable in that, is there?" she asked, rather crisply.

"Oh, no, no," I hastened to assure her, giving Peggy a surreptitious kick to divert her thoughts from laughter. "Only you must realize, Aunt Olivia, that this is a very great surprise to us."

"I thought it would be so," said Aunt Olivia complacently. "But your father will know—he will remember. I do hope he won't think me foolish. He did not think Mr. Malcolm MacPherson was a fit person for me to marry once. But that was long ago, when Mr. Malcolm MacPherson was very poor. He is in very comfortable circumstances now."

"Tell us all about it, Aunt Olivia," said Peggy. She did not look at me, which was my salvation. Had I caught Peggy's eye when Aunt Olivia said "Mr. Malcolm MacPherson" in that tone I must have laughed, willy-nilly.

"When I was a girl, the MacPhersons used to live across the road from here. Mr. Malcolm MacPherson was my beau then. But my family—and your father especially—dear me, I do hope he won't be very cross—were opposed to his attentions and were very cool to him. I think that was why he never said anything to me about getting married then. And after a time he went away, as I have said, and I never heard anything from him directly for many a year. Of course, his sister sometimes gave me news of him. But last June I had a letter from him. He said he was coming home to settle down for good on the old Island, and he asked me if I would marry him. I wrote back and said I would. Perhaps I ought to have consulted your father, but I was afraid he would think I ought to refuse Mr. Malcolm MacPherson."

"Oh, I don't think father will mind," said Peggy reassuringly.

"I hope not, because, of course, I would consider it my duty in any case to fulfil the promise I have given to Mr. Malcolm MacPherson. He will be in Grafton next week, the guest of his sister, Mrs. John Seaman, across the bridge."

Aunt Olivia said that exactly as if she were reading it from the personal column of the *Daily Enterprise*.

"When is the wedding to be?" I asked.

"Oh!" Aunt Olivia blushed distressfully. "I do not know the exact date. Nothing can be definitely settled until Mr. Malcolm MacPherson comes. But it will not be before September, at the earliest. There will be so much to do. You will tell your father, won't you?"

We promised that we would, and Aunt Olivia arose with an air of relief. Peggy and I hurried over home, stopping, when we were safely out of earshot, to laugh. The romances of the middle-aged may be to them as tender and sweet as those of youth, but they are apt to possess a good deal of humour for onlookers. Only youth can be sentimental without being mirth-provoking. We loved Aunt Olivia and were glad for her late, new-blossoming happiness; but we felt amused over it also. The recollection of her "Mr. Malcolm MacPherson" was too much for us every time we thought of it.

Father pooh-poohed incredulously at first, and, when we had convinced him, guffawed with laughter. Aunt Olivia need not have dreaded any more opposition from her cruel family.

"MacPherson was a good fellow enough, but horribly poor," said father. "I hear he has done very well out west, and if he and Olivia have a notion of each other, they are welcome to marry as far as I am concerned. Tell Olivia she mustn't take a spasm if he tracks some mud into her house once in a while."

Thus it was all arranged, and, before we realized it at all, Aunt Olivia was mid-deep in marriage preparations, in all of which Peggy and I were quite indispensable. She consulted us in regard to everything, and we almost lived at her place in those days preceding the arrival of Mr. Malcolm MacPherson.

Aunt Olivia plainly felt very happy and important. She had always wished to be married; she was not in the least strong-minded and her old-maidenhood had always been a sore point with her. I think she looked upon it as somewhat of a disgrace. And yet she was a born old maid; looking at her, and taking all her primness and little set ways into consideration, it was quite impossible to picture her as the wife of Mr. Malcolm MacPherson, or anybody else.

We soon discovered that, to Aunt Olivia, Mr. Malcolm MacPherson represented a merely abstract proposition—the man who was to confer on her the long-withheld dignity of matronhood. Her romance began and ended there, although she was quite unconscious of this herself, and believed that she was deeply in love with him.

"What will be the result, Mary, when he arrives in the flesh and she is compelled to deal with 'Mr. Malcolm MacPherson' as a real, live man, instead of a nebulous 'party of the second part' in the marriage ceremony?" queried Peggy, as she hemmed table-napkins for Aunt Olivia, sitting on her well-scoured sandstone steps, and carefully putting all thread-clippings and ravellings into the little basket which Aunt Olivia had placed there for that purpose.

"It may transform her from a self-centered old maid into a woman for whom marriage does not seem such an incongruous thing," I said.

The day on which Mr. Malcolm MacPherson was expected, Peggy and I went over. We had planned to remain away, thinking that the lovers would prefer their first meeting to be unwitnessed, but Aunt Olivia insisted on our being present. She was plainly nervous; the abstract was becoming concrete. Her little house was in spotless, speckless order from top to bottom. Aunt Olivia had herself scrubbed the garret floor and swept the cellar steps that very morning with as much painstaking care as if she expected that Mr. Malcolm MacPherson would hasten to inspect each at once and she must stand or fall by his opinion of them.

Peggy and I helped her to dress. She insisted on wearing her best black silk, in which she looked unnaturally fine. Her soft muslin became her much better, but we could not induce her to wear it. Anything more prim and bandboxy than Aunt Olivia when her toilet was finished it has never been my lot to see. Peggy and I watched her as she went downstairs, her skirt held stiffly up all around her that it might not brush the floor.

" 'Mr. Malcolm MacPherson' will be inspired with such awe that he will only be able to sit back and gaze at her," whispered Peggy. "I wish he would come and have it over. This is getting on my nerves."

Aunt Olivia went into the parlour, settled herself in the old carved chair, and folded her hands. Peggy and I sat down on the stairs to await his coming in a crisping suspense. Aunt Olivia's kitten, a fat, bewhiskered creature, looking as if it were cut out of black velvet, shared our vigil and purred in maddening peace of mind.

We could see the garden path and gate through the hall window, and therefore supposed we should have full warning of the approach of Mr. Malcolm MacPherson. It was no wonder, therefore, that we positively jumped when a thunderous knock crashed against the front door and re-echoed through the house. Had Mr. Malcolm Mac-Pherson dropped from the skies?

We afterwards discovered that he had come across lots and around the house from the back, but just then his sudden advent was almost uncanny. I ran downstairs and opened the door. On the step stood a man about six feet two in height, and proportionately broad and sinewy. He had splendid shoulders, a great crop of curly black hair, big, twinkling blue eyes, and a tremendous crinkly black beard that fell over his breast in shining waves. In brief, Mr. Malcolm MacPherson was what one would call instinctively, if somewhat tritely, "a magnificent specimen of manhood."

In one hand he carried a bunch of early goldenrod and smoke-blue asters.

"Good afternoon," he said in a resonant voice which seemed to take possession of the drowsy summer afternoon. "Is Miss Olivia Sterling in? And will you please tell her that Malcolm MacPherson is here?"

I showed him into the parlour. Then Peggy and I peeped through the crack of the door. Anyone would have done it. We would have scorned to excuse ourselves. And, indeed, what we saw would have been worth several conscience spasms, if we had felt any.

Aunt Olivia arose and advanced primly, with outstretched hand.

"Mr. MacPherson, I am very glad to see you," she said formally.

"It's yourself, Nillie!" Mr. Malcolm MacPherson gave two strides.

He dropped his flowers on the floor, knocked over a small table, and sent the ottoman spinning against the wall. Then he caught Aunt Olivia in his arms and—smack, smack, smack! Peggy sank back upon the stair-step with her handkerchief stuffed in her mouth. Aunt Olivia was being kissed!

Presently, Mr. Malcolm MacPherson held her back at arm's length in his big paws and looked her over. I saw Aunt Olivia's eyes roam over his arm to the inverted table and the litter of asters and goldenrod. Her sleek crimps were all ruffled up, and her lace fichu twisted half around her neck. She looked distressed.

"It's not a bit changed you are, Nillie," said Mr. Malcolm MacPherson admiringly. "And it's good I'm feeling to see you again. Are you glad to see me, Nillie?"

"Oh, of course," said Aunt Olivia.

She twisted herself free and went to set up the table. Then she turned to the flowers, but Mr. Malcolm MacPherson had already gathered them up, leaving a goodly sprinkling of leaves and stalks on the carpet.

"I picked these for you in the river field, Nillie," he said. "Where will I be getting something to stick them in? Here, this will do."

He grasped a frail, painted vase on the mantel, stuffed the flowers in it, and set it on the table. The look on Aunt Olivia's face was too much for me at last. I turned, caught Peggy by the shoulder, and dragged her out of the house.

"He will horrify the very soul out of Aunt Olivia's body if he goes on like this," I gasped. "But he's splendid— and he thinks the world of her—and, oh, Peggy, did you *ever* hear such kisses? Fancy Aunt Olivia!"

It did not take us long to get well acquainted with Mr. Malcolm MacPherson. He almost haunted Aunt Olivia's house, and Aunt Olivia insisted on our staying with her most of the time. She seemed to be very shy of finding herself alone with him. He horrified her a dozen times in an hour; nevertheless, she was very proud of him, and liked to be teased about him, too. She was delighted that we admired him.

"Though, to be sure, he is very different in his looks from what he used to be," she said. "He is so dreadfully big! And I do not like a beard, but I have not the courage to ask him to shave it off. He might be offended. He has bought the old Lynde place in Avonlea and wants to be married in a month. But, dear me, that is too soon. It—it would be hardly proper."

Peggy and I liked Mr. Malcolm MacPherson very much. So did father. We were glad that he seemed to think Aunt Olivia perfection. He was as happy as the day was long; but poor Aunt Olivia, under all her surface pride and importance, was not. Amid all the humour of the circumstances, Peggy and I snuffed tragedy compounded with the humour.

Mr. Malcolm MacPherson could never be trained to old-maidishness, and even Aunt Olivia seemed to realize this. He never stopped to clean his boots when he came in, although she had an ostentatiously new scraper put at each door for his benefit. He seldom moved in the house without knocking some of Aunt Olivia's treasures over. He smoked cigars in her parlour and scattered the ashes over the floor. He brought her flowers every day and stuck them into whatever receptacle came handiest. He sat on her cushions and rolled her antimacassars up into balls. He put his feet on her chair rungs—and all with the most distracting unconsciousness of doing anything out of the way. He never noticed Aunt Olivia's fluttering nervousness at all. Peggy and I laughed more than was good for us those days. It was so funny to see Aunt Olivia hovering anxiously around, picking up flower stems, and smoothing out tidies, and generally following him about to straighten out things. Once she even got a wing and a dustpan and swept the cigar ashes under his very eyes.

"Now don't be worrying yourself over that, Nillie," he protested. "Why, I don't mind a litter, bless you!"

How good and jolly he was, that Mr. Malcolm Mac-Pherson! Such songs as he sang, such stories as he told, such a breezy, unconventional atmosphere as he brought into that prim little house, where stagnant dulness had reigned for years! He worshipped Aunt Olivia, and his worship took the concrete form of presents galore. He brought her a present almost every visit— generally some article of jewelry. Bracelets, rings, chains, ear-drops, lockets, bangles, were showered upon our precise little aunt; she accepted them deprecatingly, but never wore them. This hurt him a little, but she assured him she would wear them all sometime.

"I am not used to jewelry, Mr. MacPherson," she would tell him.

Her engagement ring she did wear—it was a rather "loud" combination of engraved gold and opals. Sometimes we caught her turning it on her finger with a very troubled face.

"I would be sorry for Mr. Malcolm MacPherson if he were not so much in love with her," said Peggy. "But as he thinks that she is perfection, he doesn't need sympathy."

"I am sorry for Aunt Olivia," I said. "Yes, Peggy, I am. Mr. MacPherson is a splendid man, but Aunt Olivia is a born old maid, and it is outraging her very nature to be anything else. Don't you see how it's hurting her? His big, splendid man-ways are harrowing her very soul up—she can't get out of her little, narrow groove, and it is killing her to be pulled out."

"Nonsense!" said Peggy. Then she added with a laugh, "Mary, did you ever see anything so funny as Aunt Olivia sitting on 'Mr. Malcolm MacPherson's' knee?"

It *was* funny. Aunt Olivia thought it very unbecoming to sit there before us, but he made her do it. He would say, with his big, jolly laugh, "Don't be minding the little girls," and pull her down on his knee and hold her there. To my dying day I shall never forget the expression on the poor little woman's face.

But, as the days went by and Mr. Malcolm MacPherson began to insist on a date being set for the wedding, Aunt Olivia grew to have a strangely disturbed look. She became very quiet, and never laughed except under protest. Also, she showed signs of petulance when any of us, but especially father, teased her about her beau. I pitied her, for I think I understood better than the others what her feelings really were. But even I was not prepared for what did happen. I would not have believed that Aunt Olivia could do it. I thought that her desire for marriage in the abstract would outweigh the disadvantages of the concrete. But one can never reckon with real, bred-in-the-bone old-maidism.

One morning Mr. Malcolm MacPherson told us all that he was coming up that evening to make Aunt Olivia set the day. Peggy and I laughingly approved, telling him that it was high time for him to assert his authority, and he went off in great good humour across the river field, whistling a Highland strathspey. But Aunt Olivia looked like a martyr. She had a fierce attack of housecleaning that day, and put everything in flawless order, even to the corners.

"As if there was going to be a funeral in the house," sniffed Peggy.

Peggy and I were up in the south-west room at dusk that evening, piecing a quilt, when we heard Mr. Malcolm MacPherson shouting out in the hall below to know if anyone was home. I ran out to the landing, but as I did so Aunt Olivia came out of her room, brushed past me, and flitted downstairs.

"Mr. MacPherson," I heard her say with double-distilled primness, "will you please come into the parlour? I have something to say to you."

They went in, and I returned to the southwest room.

"Peg, there's trouble brewing," I said. "I'm sure of it by Aunt Olivia's face—it was *gray*. And she has gone down *alone*—and shut the door."

"I am going to hear what she says to him," said Peggy resolutely. "It is her own fault—she has spoiled us by always insisting that we should be present at their interviews. That poor man has had to do his courting under our very eyes. Come on, Mary."

The south-west room was directly over the parlour, and there was an open stovepipe-hole leading up therefrom. Peggy removed the hat box that was on it, and we both deliberately and shamelessly crouched down and listened with all our might.

It was easy enough to hear what Mr. Malcolm Mac-Pherson was saying.

"I've come up to get the date settled, Nillie, as I told you. Come now, little woman, name the day."

Smack!

"Don't, Mr. MacPherson," said Aunt Olivia. She spoke

as a woman who has keyed herself up to the doing of some very distasteful task and is anxious to have it over and done with as soon as possible. "There is something I must say to you. I cannot marry you, Mr. MacPherson."

There was a pause. I would have given much to have seen the pair of them. When Mr. Malcolm MacPherson spoke, his voice was that of blank, uncomprehending amazement.

"Nillie, what is it you are meaning?" he said.

"I cannot marry you, Mr. MacPherson," repeated Aunt Olivia.

"Why not?" Surprise was giving way to dismay.

"I don't think you will understand, Mr. MacPherson," said Aunt Olivia, faintly. "You don't realize what it means for a woman to give up everything—her own home and friends and all her past life, so to speak, and go far away with a stranger."

"Why, I suppose it will be rather hard. But, Nillie, Avonlea isn't very far away—not more than twelve miles, if it will be that."

"Twelve miles! It might as well be at the other side of the world to all intents and purposes," said Aunt Olivia obstinately. "I don't know a living soul there, except Rachel Lynde."

"Why didn't you say so before I bought the place, then? But it's not too late. I can be selling it and buying right here in East Grafton if that will please you—though there isn't half as nice a place to be had. But I'll fix it up somehow!"

"No, Mr. MacPherson," said Aunt Olivia firmly, "that doesn't cover the difficulty. I knew you would not understand. My ways are not your ways and I cannot make them over. For—you track mud in—and—and—you don't care whether things are tidy or not."

Poor Aunt Olivia had to be Aunt Olivia; if she were being burned at the stake, I verily believe she would have dragged some grotesqueness into the tragedy of the moment.

"The devil!" said Mr. Malcolm MacPherson—not profanely or angrily, but as in sheer bewilderment. Then he added, "Nillie, you must be joking. It's careless enough I am—the west isn't a good place to learn finicky ways—but you can teach me. You're not going to throw me over because I track mud in!"

"I cannot marry you, Mr. MacPherson," said Aunt Olivia again.

"You can't be meaning it!" he exclaimed, because he was beginning to understand that she did mean it, although it was impossible for his man mind to understand anything else about the puzzle. "Nillie, it's breaking my heart you are! I'll do anything—go anywhere—be anything you want—only don't be going back on me like this."

"I cannot marry you, Mr. MacPherson," said Aunt Olivia for the fourth time.

"Nillie!" exclaimed Mr. Malcolm MacPherson. There was such real agony in his tone that Peggy and I were suddenly stricken with contrition. What were we doing? We had no right to be listening to this pitiful interview. The pain and protest in his voice had suddenly banished all the humour from it, and left naught but the bare, stark tragedy. We rose and tiptoed out of the room, wholesomely ashamed of ourselves.

When Mr. Malcolm MacPherson had gone, after an hour of useless pleading, Aunt Olivia came up to us, pale and prim and determined, and told us that there was to be no wedding. We could not pretend surprise, but Peggy ventured a faint protest.

"Oh, Aunt Olivia, do you think you have done right?"

"It was the only thing I could do," said Aunt Olivia stonily. "I could not marry Mr. Malcolm MacPherson and I told him so. Please tell your father—and kindly say nothing more to me about the matter."

Then Aunt Olivia went downstairs, got a broom, and swept up the mud Mr. Malcolm MacPherson had tracked over the steps.

Peggy and I went home and told father. We felt very flat, but there was nothing to be done or said. Father laughed at the whole thing, but I could not laugh. I was sorry for Mr. Malcolm MacPherson and, though I was angry with her, I was sorry for Aunt Olivia, too. Plainly, she felt badly enough over her vanished hopes and plans, but she had developed a strange and baffling reserve which nothing could pierce.

"It's nothing but a chronic case of old-maidism," said father impatiently.

Things were very dull for a week. We saw no more of Mr. Malcolm MacPherson, and we missed him dreadfully. Aunt Olivia was inscrutable, and worked with fierceness at superfluous tasks.

One evening father came home with some news.

"Malcolm Macpherson is leaving on the 7:30 train for the west," he said. "He has rented the Avonlea place and he's off. They say he is mad as a hatter at the trick Olivia played on him."

After tea, Peggy and I went over to see Aunt Olivia, who had asked our advice about a wrapper. She was sewing as for dear life, and her face was primmer and colder than ever. I wondered if she knew of Mr. Malcolm MacPherson's departure. Delicacy forbade me to mention it, but Peggy had no such scruples.

"Well, Aunt Olivia, your beau is off," she announced cheerfully. "You won't be bothered with him again. He is leaving on the mail train for the west."

Aunt Olivia dropped her sewing and stood up. I have never seen anything like the transformation that came over her. It was so thorough and sudden as to be almost uncanny. The old maid vanished completely, and in her place was a woman, full to the lips with primitive emotion and pain.

"What shall I do?" she cried in a terrible voice. "Mary—Peggy—what shall I do?"

It was almost a shriek. Peggy turned pale.

"Do you care?" she said stupidly.

"Care! Girls, I shall *die* if Malcolm MacPherson goes away! I have been mad—I must have been mad. I have almost died of loneliness since I sent him away. But I thought he would come back! I must see him—there is time to reach the station before the train goes if I go by the fields."

She took a wild step towards the door, but I caught her back with a sudden mind-vision of Aunt Olivia flying bareheaded and distraught across the fields.

"Wait a moment, Aunt Olivia. Peggy, run home and get father to harness Dick in the buggy as quickly as he can. We'll drive Aunt Olivia to the station. We'll get you there in time, Aunty."

Peggy flew, and Aunt Olivia dashed upstairs. I lingered behind to pick up her sewing, and when I got to her room she had her hat and cape on. Spread out on the bed were all the boxes of gifts which Mr. Malcolm MacPherson had brought her, and Aunt Olivia was stringing their contents feverishly about her person. Rings, three brooches, a locket, three chains and a watch all went on—anyway and anyhow. A wonderful sight it was to see Aunt Olivia bedizened like that!

"I would never wear them before—but I'll put them all on now to show him I'm sorry," she gasped, with trembling lips.

When the three of us crowded into the buggy, Aunt Olivia grasped the whip before we could prevent her and, leaning out, gave poor Dick such a lash as he had never felt in his life before. He went tearing down the steep, stony, fast-darkening road in a fashion which made Peggy and me cry out in alarm. Aunt Olivia was usually the most timid of women, but now she didn't seem to know what fear was. She kept whipping and urging poor Dick the whole way to the station, quite oblivious to our assurances that there was plenty of time. The people who met us that night must have thought we were quite mad. I held on the reins, Peggy gripped the swaying side of the buggy, and Aunt Olivia bent forward, hat and hair blowing back from her set face with its strangely crimson cheeks, and plied the whip. In such a guise did we whirl through the village and over the two-mile station road.

When we drove up to the station, where the train was shunting amid the shadows, Aunt Olivia made a flying leap from the buggy and ran along the platform, with her cape streaming behind her and all her brooches and chains glittering in the lights. I tossed the reins to a boy standing near and we followed. Just under the glare of the station lamp we saw Mr. Malcolm MacPherson, grip in hand. Fortunately, no one else was very near, but it would have been all the same had they been the centre of a crowd. Aunt Olivia fairly flung herself against him.

"Malcolm," she cried, "don't go—don't go—I'll marry you—I'll go anywhere—and I don't care how much mud you bring in!"

That truly Aunt Olivian touch relieved the tension of the situation a little. Mr. MacPherson put his arm about her and drew her back into the shadows.

"There, there," he soothed. "Of course I won't be going. Don't cry, Nillie-girl."

"And you'll come right back with me now?" implored Aunt Olivia, clinging to him as if she feared he would be whisked away from her yet if she let go for a moment.

"Of course, of course," he said.

Peggy got a chance home with a friend, and Aunt Olivia and Mr. Malcolm MacPherson and I drove back in the buggy. Mr. MacPherson held Aunt Olivia on his knee because there was no room, but she would have sat there, I think, had there been a dozen vacant seats. She clung to him in the most barefaced fashion, and all her former primness and reserve were swept away completely. She kissed him a dozen times or more and told him she loved him—and I did not even smile, nor did I want to. Somehow, it did not seem in the least funny to me then, nor does it now, although it doubtless will to others. There was too much real intensity of feeling in it all to leave any room for the ridiculous. So wrapped up in each other were they that I did not even feel superfluous.

I set them safely down in Aunt Olivia's yard and turned homeward, completely forgotten by the pair. But in the moonlight, which flooded the front of the house, I saw something that testified eloquently to the transformation in Aunt Olivia. It had rained that afternoon and the yard was muddy. Nevertheless, she went in at her front door and took Mr. Malcolm MacPherson in with her without even a glance at the scraper!

8

The Quarantine at Alexander Abraham's

I REFUSED to take that class in Sunday School the first time I was asked. It was not that I objected to teaching in the Sunday School. On the contrary, I rather liked the idea; but it was the Rev. Mr. Allan who asked me, and it had always been a matter of principle with me never to do anything a man asked me to do if I could help it. I was noted for that. It saves a great deal of trouble and it simplifies everything beautifully. I had always disliked men. It must have been born in me, because, as far back as I can remember, an antipathy to men and dogs was one of my strongest characteristics. I was noted for that. My experiences through life only served to deepen it. The more I saw of men, the more I liked cats.

So, of course, when the Rev. Allan asked me if I would consent to take a class in Sunday School, I said no in a fashion calculated to chasten him wholesomely. If he had sent his wife the first time, as he did the second, it would have been wiser. People generally do what Mrs. Allan asks them to do because they know it saves time.

Mrs. Allan talked smoothly for half an hour before she mentioned the Sunday School, and paid me several compliments. Mrs. Allan is famous for her tact. Tact is a faculty for meandering around to a given point instead of making a bee-line. I have no tact. I am noted for that. As soon as Mrs. Allan's conversation came in sight of the Sunday School, I, who knew all along whither it was tending, said, straight out,

"What class do you want me to teach?"

122

Mrs. Allan was so surprised that she forgot to be tactful, and answered plainly for once in her life,

"There are two classes—one of boys and one of girls—needing a teacher. I have been teaching the girls' class, but I shall have to give it up for a little time on account of the baby's health. You may have your choice, Miss MacPherson."

"Then I shall take the boys," I said decidedly. I am noted for my decision. "Since they have to grow up to be men, it's well to train them properly betimes. Nuisances they are bound to become under any circumstances; but if they are taken in hand young enough, they may not grow up to be such nuisances as they otherwise would and that will be some unfortunate woman's gain."

Mrs. Allan looked dubious. I knew she had expected me to choose the girls.

"They are a very wild set of boys," she said.

"I never knew boys who weren't," I retorted.

"I—I—think perhaps you would like the girls best," said Mrs. Allan hesitatingly. If it had not been for one thing—which I would never in this world have admitted to Mrs. Allan—I might have liked the girls' class best myself. But the truth was, Anne Shirley was in that class; and Anne Shirley was the one living human being that I was afraid of. Not that I disliked her. But she had such a habit of asking weird, unexpected questions, which a Philadelphia lawyer couldn't answer. Miss Rogerson had that class once and Anne routed her, horse, foot, and artillery. *I* wasn't going to undertake a class with a walking interrogation point in it like that. Besides, I thought Mrs. Allan required a slight snub. Ministers' wives are rather apt to think they can run everything and everybody, if they are not wholesomely corrected now and again.

"It is not what *I* like best that must be considered, Mrs. Allan," I said rebukingly. "It is what is best for those boys. I feel that *I* shall be best for *them*."

"Oh, I've no doubt of that, Miss MacPherson," said Mrs. Allan amiably. It was a fib for her, minister's wife though she was. She *had* doubt. She thought I would be a dismal failure as teacher of a boys' class.

But I was not. I am not often a dismal failure when I make up my mind to do a thing. I am noted for that.

"It is wonderful what a reformation you have worked in that class, Miss MacPherson—wonderful," said the Rev. Mr. Allan some weeks later. He didn't mean to show how amazing a thing he thought it that an old maid noted for being a man-hater should have managed it, but his face betrayed him.

"Where does Jimmy Spencer live?" I asked him crisply. "He came one Sunday three weeks ago and hasn't been back since. I mean to find out why."

Mr. Allan coughed.

"I believe he is hired as handy boy with Alexander Abraham Bennett, out on the White Sands road," he said.

"Then I am going out to Alexander Abraham Bennett's on the White Sands road to see why Jimmy Spencer doesn't come to Sunday school," I said firmly.

Mr. Allan's eye twinkled ever so slightly. I have always insisted that if that man were not a minister he would have a sense of humour.

"Possibly Mr. Bennett will not appreciate your kind interest! He has—ah—a singular aversion to your sex, I understand. No woman has ever been known to get inside of Mr. Bennett's house since his sister died twenty years ago."

"Oh, he is the one, is he?" I said, remembering. "He is the woman-hater who threatens that if a woman comes into his yard he'll chase her out with a pitchfork. Well, he will not chase *me* out!"

Mr. Allan gave a chuckle—a ministerial chuckle, but still a chuckle. It irritated me slightly, because it seemed to imply that he thought Alexander Abraham Bennett would be one too many for me. But I did not show Mr. Allan that he annoyed me. It is always a great mistake to let a man see that he can vex you.

The next afternoon I harnessed my sorrel pony to the buggy and drove down to Alexander Abraham Bennett's. As usual, I took William Adolphus with me for company. William Adolphus is my favourite among my six cats. He is black, with a white dicky and beautiful white paws. He sat up on the seat beside me and looked far more like a gentleman than many a man I've seen in a similar position.

Alexander Abraham's place was about three miles along the White Sands road. I knew the house as soon as I came to it by its neglected appearance. It needed paint badly; the blinds were crooked and torn; weeds grew up to the very door. Plainly, there was no woman about *that* place. Still, it was a nice house, and the barns were splendid. My father always said that when a man's barns were bigger than his house, it was a sign that his income exceeded his expenditure. So it was all right that they should be bigger; but it was all wrong that they should be trimmer and better painted. Still, thought I, what else could you expect of a woman-hater?

"But Alexander Abraham evidently knows how to run a farm, even if he is a woman-hater," I remarked to William Adolphus as I got out and tied the pony to the railing.

I had driven up to the house from the back way and now I was opposite a side door opening on the veranda. I thought I might as well go to it, so I tucked William Adolphus under my arm and marched up the path. Just as I was half-way up, a dog swooped around the front corner and made straight for me. He was the ugliest dog I had ever seen; and he didn't even bark—just came silently and speedily on, with a business-like eye.

I never stop to argue matters with a dog that doesn't bark. I know when discretion is the better part of valour. Firmly clasping William Adolphus, I ran—not to the door, because the dog was between me and it, but to a big, low-branching cherry tree at the back corner of the house. I reached it in time and no more. First thrusting William Adolphus on to a limb above my head, I scrambled up into that blessed tree without stopping to think how it might look to Alexander Abraham if he happened to be watching.

My time for reflection came when I found myself perched half-way up the tree with William Adolphus beside me. William Adolphus was quite calm and unruffled. I can hardly say with truthfulness that I was. On the contrary, I admit that I felt considerably upset.

The dog was sitting on his haunches on the ground

below, watching us, and it was quite plain to be seen, from his leisurely manner, that it was not his busy day. He bared his teeth and growled when he caught my eye.

"You *look* like a woman-hater's dog," I told him. I meant it for an insult; but the beast took it for a compliment.

Then I set myself to solving the question, "How am I to get out of this predicament?"

It did not seem easy to solve it.

"Shall I scream, William Adolphus?" I demanded of that intelligent animal. William Adolphus shook his head. This is a fact. And I agreed with him.

"No, I shall not scream, William Adolphus," I said. "There is probably no one to hear me except Alexander Abraham, and I have my painful doubts about his tender mercies. Now, it is impossible to go down. Is it, then, William Adolphus, possible to go up?"

I looked up. Just above my head was an open window with a tolerably stout branch extending right across it.

"Shall we try that way, William Adolphus?" I asked.

William Adolphus, wasting no words, began to climb the tree. I followed his example. The dog ran in circles about the tree and looked things not lawful to be uttered. It probably would have been a relief to him to bark, if it hadn't been so against his principles.

I got in by the window easily enough, and found myself in a bedroom the like of which for disorder and dust and general awfulness I had never seen in all my life. But I did not pause to take in details. With William Adolphus under my arm, I marched downstairs, fervently hoping I should meet no one on the way.

I did not. The hall below was empty and dusty. I opened the first door I came to and walked boldly in. A man was sitting by the window, looking moodily out. I should have known him for Alexander Abraham anywhere. He had just the same uncared-for, ragged appearance that the house had; and yet, like the house, it seemed that he would not be bad looking if he were trimmed up a little. His hair looked as if it had never been combed, and his whiskers were wild in the extreme.

He looked at me with blank amazement in his countenance.

"Where is Jimmy Spencer?" I demanded. "I have come to see him."

"How did he ever let you in?" asked the man, staring at me.

"He didn't let me in," I retorted. "He chased me all over the lawn, and I only saved myself from being torn piecemeal by scrambling up a tree. You ought to be prosecuted for keeping such a dog! Where is Jimmy?"

Instead of answering, Alexander Abraham began to laugh in a most unpleasant fashion.

"Trust a woman for getting into a man's house if she has made up her mind to," he said disagreeably.

Seeing that it was his intention to vex me, I remained cool and collected.

"Oh, I wasn't particular about getting into your house, Mr. Bennett," I said calmly. "I had but little choice in the matter. It was get in lest a worse fate befall me. It was not you or your house I wanted to see—although I admit that it is worth seeing if a person is anxious to find out how dirty a place *can* be. It was Jimmy. For the third and last time—where is Jimmy?"

"Jimmy is not here," said Mr. Bennett gruffly—but not quite so assuredly. "He left last week and hired with a man over at Newbridge."

"In that case," I said, picking up William Adolphus, who had been exploring the room with a disdainful air, "I won't disturb you any longer. I shall go."

"Yes, I think it would be the wisest thing," said Alexander Abraham—not disagreeably this time, but reflectively, as if there was some doubt about the matter. "I'll let you out by the back door. Then the—ahem!—the dog will not interfere with you. Please go away quietly and quickly."

I wondered if Alexander Abraham thought I would go away with a whoop. But I said nothing, thinking this the most dignified course of conduct, and I followed him out to the kitchen as quickly and quietly as he could have wished. Such a kitchen!

Alexander Abraham opened the door—which was locked—just as a buggy containing two men drove into the yard.

"Too late!" he exclaimed in a tragic tone. I understood that something dreadful must have happened, but I did not care, since, as I fondly supposed, it did not concern me. I pushed out past Alexander Abraham—who was looking as guilty as if he had been caught burglarizing—and came face to face with the man who had sprung from the buggy. It was old Dr. Blair, from Carmody, and he was looking at me as if he had found me shoplifting.

"My dear Peter," he said gravely, "I am *very* sorry to see you here—very sorry indeed."

I admit that this exasperated me. Besides, no man on earth, not even my old family doctor, has any right to "My dear Peter" me!

"There is no loud call for sorrow, doctor," I said loftily. "If a woman, forty-eight years of age, a member of the Presbyterian church in good and regular standing, cannot call upon one of her Sunday School scholars without wrecking all the proprieties, how old must she be before she can?"

The doctor did not answer my question. Instead, he looked reproachfully at Alexander Abraham.

"Is this how you keep your word, Mr. Bennett?" he said. "I thought that you promised me that you would not let anyone into the house."

"I didn't let her in," growled Mr. Bennett. "Good heavens, man, she climbed in at an upstairs window, despite the presence on my grounds of a policeman and a dog! What is to be done with a woman like that?"

"I do not understand what all this means," I said, addressing myself to the doctor and ignoring Alexander Abraham entirely, "but if my presence here is so extremely inconvenient to all concerned, you can soon be relieved of it. I am going at once."

"I am very sorry, my dear Peter," said the doctor impressively, "but that is just what I cannot allow you to do. This house is under quarantine for smallpox. You will have to stay here."

Smallpox! For the first and last time in my life, I openly lost my temper with a man. I wheeled furiously upon Alexander Abraham.

"Why didn't you tell me?" I cried.

"Tell you!" he said, glaring at me. "When I first saw you it was too late to tell you. I thought the kindest thing I could do was to hold my tongue and let you get away in happy ignorance. This will teach you to take a man's house by storm, madam!"

"Now, now, don't quarrel, my good people," interposed the doctor seriously—but I saw a twinkle in his eye. "You'll have to spend some time together under the same roof, and you won't improve the situation by disagreeing. You see, Peter, it was this way. Mr. Bennett was in town yesterday—where, as you are aware, there is a bad outbreak of smallpox—and took dinner in a boarding-house where one of the maids was ill. Last night she developed unmistakable symptoms of smallpox. The Board of Health at once got after all the people who were in the house yesterday, so far as they could locate them, and put them under quarantine. I came down here this morning and explained the matter to Mr. Bennett. I brought Jeremiah Jeffries to guard the front of the house, and Mr. Bennett gave me his word of honour that he would not let anyone in by the back way, while I went to get another policeman and make all the necessary arrangements. I have brought Thomas Wright and have secured the services of another man to attend to Mr. Bennett's barn work and bring provisions to the house. Jacob Green and Cleophas Lee will watch at night. I don't think there is much danger of Mr. Bennett's taking the smallpox, but until we are sure, you must remain here, Peter."

While listening to the doctor I had been thinking. It was the most distressing predicament I had ever got into in my life, but there was no sense in making it worse.

"Very well, doctor," I said calmly. "Yes, I was vaccinated a month ago, when the news of the smallpox first came. When you go back through Avonlea, kindly go to Sarah Pye and ask her to live in my house during my absence and look after things, especially the cats. Tell her to give them new milk twice a day and a square inch of butter apiece once a week. Get her to put my two dark print wrappers, some aprons, and some changes of underclothing in my third-best valise and have it sent down to me. My pony is tied out there to the fence. Please take him home. That is all, I think."

"No, it isn't all," said Alexander Abraham grumpily. "Send that cat home, too. I won't have a cat around the place—I'd rather have the smallpox."

I looked Alexander Abraham over gradually, in a way I have, beginning at his feet and traveling up to his head. I took my time over it; and then I said, very quietly,

"You may have both. Anyway, you'll have to have William Adolphus. He is under quarantine as well as you and I. Do you suppose I am going to have my cat ranging at large through Avonlea, scattering smallpox germs among innocent people? I'll have to put up with that dog of yours. You will have to endure William Adolphus."

Alexander Abraham groaned, but I could see that the way I had looked him over had chastened him considerably.

The doctor drove away, and I went into the house, not choosing to linger outside and be grinned at by Thomas Wright. I hung my coat up in the hall and laid my bonnet carefully on the sitting-room table, having first dusted a clean place for it with my handkerchief. I longed to fall upon that house at once and clean it up, but I had to wait until the doctor came back with my wrapper. I could not clean house in my new suit and a silk shirtwaist.

Alexander Abraham was sitting on a chair looking at me. Presently he said,

"I am *not* curious—but will you kindly tell me why the doctor called you Peter?"

"Because that is my name, I suppose," I answered, shaking up a cushion for William Adolphus and thereby disturbing the dust of years.

Alexander Abraham coughed gently.

"Isn't that—ahem!—rather a peculiar name for a woman?"

"It is," I said, wondering how much soap, if any, there was in the house.

"I am *not* curious," said Alexander Abraham, "but would you mind telling me how you came to be called Peter?"

"If I had been a boy, my parents intended to call me Peter in honour of a rich uncle. When I—fortunately—

turned out to be a girl, my mother insisted that I should be called Angelina. They gave me both names and called me Angelina, but as soon as I grew old enough, I decided to be called Peter. It was bad enough, but not so bad as Angelina."

"I should say it was more appropriate," said Alexander Abraham, intending, as I perceived, to be disagreeable.

"Precisely," I agreed calmly. "My last name is Mac-Pherson, and I live in Avonlea. As you are *not* curious, that will be all the information you will need about me."

"Oh!" Alexander Abraham looked as if a light had broken in on him. "I've heard of you. You—ah—pretend to dislike men."

Pretend! Goodness only knows what would have happened to Alexander Abraham just then if a diversion had not taken place. But the door opened and a dog came in—*the* dog. I suppose he had got tired waiting under the cherry tree for William Adolphus and me to come down. He was even uglier indoors than out.

"Oh, Mr. Riley, Mr. Riley, see what you have let me in for," said Alexander Abraham reproachfully.

But Mr. Riley—since that was the brute's name—paid no attention to Alexander Abraham. He had caught sight of William Adolphus curled up on the cushion, and he started across the room to investigate him. William Adolphus sat up and began to take notice.

"Call off that dog," I said warningly to Alexander Abraham.

"Call him off yourself," he retorted. "Since you've brought that cat here, you can protect him."

"Oh, it wasn't for William Adolphus' sake I spoke," I said pleasantly. "William Adolphus can protect himself."

William Adolphus could and did. He humped his back, flattened his ears, swore once, and then made a flying leap for Mr. Riley. William Adolphus landed squarely on Mr. Riley's brindled back and promptly took fast hold, spitting and clawing and caterwauling.

You never saw a more astonished dog than Mr. Riley. With a yell of terror he bolted out to the kitchen, out of the kitchen into the hall, through the hall into the room, and so into the kitchen and round again. With each circuit he went faster and faster, until he looked like a brindled streak with a dash of black and white on top. Such a racket and commotion I never heard, and I laughed until the tears came into my eyes. Mr. Riley flew around and around, and William Adolphus held on grimly and clawed. Alexander Abraham turned purple with rage.

"Woman, call off that infernal cat before he kills my dog," he shouted above the din of yelps and yowls.

"Oh, he won't kill him," I said reassuringly, "and he's going too fast to hear me if I did call him. If you can stop the dog, Mr. Bennett, I'll guarantee to make William Adolphus listen to reason, but there's no use trying to argue with a lightning flash."

Alexander Abraham made a frantic lunge at the brindled streak as it whirled past him, with the result that he overbalanced himself and went sprawling on the floor with a crash. I ran to help him up, which only seemed to enrage him further.

"Woman," he sputtered viciously, "I wish you and your fiend of a cat were in—in—"

"In Avonlea," I finished quickly, to save Alexander Abraham from committing profanity. "So do I, Mr. Bennett, with all my heart. But since we are not, let us make the best of it like sensible people. And in future, you will kindly remember that my name is Miss MacPherson, *not* Woman!"

With this the end came, and I was thankful, for the noise those two animals made was so terrific that I expected the policeman would be rushing in, smallpox or no smallpox, to see if Alexander Abraham and I were trying to murder each other. Mr. Riley suddenly veered in his mad career and bolted into a dark corner between the stove and the wood-box. William Adolphus let go just in time.

There never was any more trouble with Mr. Riley after that. A meeker, more thoroughly chastened dog you could not find. William Adolphus had the best of it and he kept it.

Seeing that things had calmed down, and that it was five o'clock, I decided to get tea. I told Alexander Abraham that I would prepare it, if he would show me where the eatables were.

"You needn't mind," said Alexander Abraham. "I've been in the habit of getting my own tea for twenty years."

"I daresay. But you haven't been in the habit of getting mine," I said firmly. "I wouldn't eat anything you cooked if I starved to death. If you want some occupation, you'd better get some salve and anoint the scratches on that poor dog's back."

Alexander Abraham said something that I prudently did not hear. Seeing that he had no information to hand out, I went on an exploring expedition into the pantry. The place was awful beyond description, and for the first time a vague sentiment of pity for Alexander Abraham glimmered in my breast. When a man had to live in such surroundings the wonder was, not that he hated women, but that he didn't hate the whole human race.

But I got up a supper somehow. I am noted for getting up suppers. The bread was from the Carmody bakery, and I made good tea and excellent toast; besides, I found a can of peaches in the pantry which, as they were bought, I wasn't afraid to eat.

That tea and toast mellowed Alexander Abraham in spite of himself. He ate the last crust, and didn't growl when I gave William Adolphus all the cream that was left. Mr. Riley did not seem to want anything. He had no appetite.

By this time the doctor's boy had arrived with my valise. Alexander Abraham gave me quite civilly to understand that there was a spare room across the hall and that I might take possession of it. I went to it and put on a wrapper. There was a set of fine furniture in the room, and a comfortable bed. But the dust! William Adolphus had followed me in, and his paws left marks everywhere he walked.

"Now," I said briskly, returning to the kitchen, "I'm going to clean up and I shall begin with this kitchen. You'd better betake yourself to the sitting-room, Mr. Bennett, so as to be out of the way."

Alexander Abraham glared at me.

"I'm not going to have my house meddled with," he snapped. "It suits me. If you don't like it, you can leave it."

"No, I can't. That is just the trouble," I said pleasantly. "If I could leave it, I shouldn't be here for a minute. Since I can't, it simply has to be cleaned. I can tolerate men and dogs when I am compelled to, but I cannot and will not tolerate dirt and disorder. Go into the sitting-room."

Alexander Abraham went. As he closed the door, I heard him say, in capitals, "WHAT AN AWFUL WOMAN!"

I cleaned that kitchen and the pantry adjoining. It was ten o'clock when I got through, and Alexander Abraham had gone to bed without deigning further speech. I locked Mr. Riley in one room and William Adolphus in another and went to bed, too. I had never felt so dead tired in my life before. It had been a hard day.

But I got up bright and early the next morning and got a tiptop breakfast, which Alexander Abraham condescended to eat. When the provision man came into the yard, I called to him from the window to bring me a box of soap in the afternoon, and then I tackled the sitting-room.

It took me the best part of a week to get that house in order, but I did it thoroughly. I am noted for doing things thoroughly. At the end of the time it was clean from garret to cellar. Alexander Abraham made no comments on my operations, though he groaned loud and often, and said caustic things to poor Mr. Riley, who hadn't the spirit to answer back after his drubbing by William Adolphus. I made allowances for Alexander Abraham because his vaccination had taken and his arm was real sore; and I cooked elegant meals, not having much else to do, once I had got things scoured up. The house was full of provisions— Alexander Abraham wasn't mean about such things, I will say that for him. Altogether, I was more comfortable than I had expected to be. When Alexander Abraham wouldn't talk, I let him alone; and when he would, I just said as sarcastic things as he did, only I said them smiling and pleasant. I could see he had a wholesome awe of me. But now and then he seemed to forget his disposition and talked like a human being. We had one or two real interesting conversations. Alexander Abraham was an intelligent man, though he had got terribly warped. I told him once I thought he must have been nice when he was a boy.

One day he astonished me by appearing at the dinner

table with his hair brushed and a white collar on. We had a tiptop dinner that day, and I had made a pudding that was far too good for a woman-hater. When Alexander Abraham had disposed of two large platefuls of it, he sighed and said,

"You can certainly cook. It's a pity you are such a detestable crank in other respects."

"It's kind of convenient being a crank," I said. "People are careful how they meddle with you. Haven't you found that out in your own experience?"

"I am *not* a crank," growled Alexander Abraham resentfully. "All I ask is to be let alone."

"That's the very crankiest kind of crank," I said. "A person who wants to be let alone flies in the face of Providence, who decreed that folks, for their own good, were not to be let alone. But cheer up, Mr. Bennett. The quarantine will be up on Tuesday and then you'll certainly be let alone for the rest of your natural life, as far as William Adolphus and I are concerned. You may then return to your wallowing in the mire and be as dirty and comfortable as of yore."

Alexander Abraham growled again. The prospect didn't seem to cheer him up as much as I should have expected. Then he did an amazing thing. He poured some cream into a saucer and set it down before William Adolphus. William Adolphus lapped it up, keeping one eye on Alexander Abraham lest the latter should change his mind. Not to be outdone, I handed Mr. Riley a bone.

Neither Alexander Abraham nor I had worried much about the smallpox. We didn't believe he would take it, for he hadn't even seen the girl who was sick. But the very next morning I heard him calling me from the upstairs landing.

"Miss MacPherson," he said, in a voice so uncommonly mild that it gave me an uncanny feeling, "what are the symptoms of smallpox?"

"Chills and flushes, pain in the limbs and back, nausea and vomiting," I answered promptly, for I had been reading them up in a patent medicine almanac.

"I've got them all," said Alexander Abraham hollowly. I didn't feel as much scared as I should have expected. After enduring a woman-hater and a brindled dog and the early disorder of that house—and coming off best with all three—smallpox seemed rather insignificant. I went to the window and called to Thomas Wright to send for the doctor.

The doctor came down from Alexander Abraham's room looking grave.

"It's impossible to pronounce on the disease yet," he said. "There is no certainty until the eruption appears. But, of course, there is every likelihood that it is the smallpox. It is very unfortunate. I am afraid that it will be difficult to get a nurse. All the nurses in town who will take smallpox cases are overbusy now, for the epidemic is still raging there. However, I'll go into town to-night and do my best. Meanwhile, as Mr. Bennett does not require any attendance at present, you must not go near him, Peter."

I wasn't going to take orders from any man, and as soon as the doctor had gone I marched straight up to Alexander Abraham's room with some dinner for him on a tray. There was a lemon cream I thought he could eat even if he had the smallpox.

"You shouldn't come near me," he growled. "You are risking your life."

"I am not going to see a fellow creature starve to death, even if he is a man," I retorted.

"The worst of it all," groaned Alexander Abraham, between mouthfuls of lemon cream, "is that the doctor says I've got to have a nurse. I've got so kind of used to you being in the house that I don't mind you, but the thought of another woman coming here is too much. Did you give my poor dog anything to eat?"

"He has had a better dinner than many a Christian," I said severely.

Alexander Abraham need not have worried about another woman coming in. The doctor came back that night with care on his brow.

"I don't know what is to be done," he said. "I can't get a soul to come here."

"*I* shall nurse Mr. Bennett," I said with dignity. "It is my duty and I never shirk my duty. I am noted for that.

He is a man, and he has smallpox, and he keeps a vile dog; but I am not going to see him die for lack of care for all that."

"You're a good soul, Peter," said the doctor, looking relieved, manlike, as soon as he found a woman to shoulder the responsibility.

I nursed Alexander Abraham through the smallpox, and I didn't mind it much. He was much more amiable sick than well, and he had the disease in a very mild form. Below stairs I reigned supreme, and Mr. Riley and William Adolphus lay down together like the lion and the lamb. I fed Mr. Riley regularly, and once, seeing him looking lonesome, I patted him gingerly. It was nicer than I thought it would be. Mr. Riley lifted his head and looked at me with an expression in his eyes which cured me of wondering why on earth Alexander Abraham was so fond of the beast.

When Alexander Abraham was able to sit up, he began to make up for the time he'd lost being pleasant. Anything more sarcastic than that man in his convalescence you couldn't imagine. I just laughed at him, having found out that that could be depended on to irritate him. To irritate him still further, I cleaned the house all over again. But what vexed him most of all was that Mr. Riley took to following me about and wagging what he had of a tail at me.

"It wasn't enough that you should come into my peaceful home and turn it upside down, but you have to alienate the affections of my dog," complained Alexander Abraham.

"He'll get fond of you again when I go home," I said comfortingly. "Dogs aren't very particular that way. What they want is bones. Cats now, they love disinterestedly. William Adolphus has never swerved in his allegiance to me, although you do give him cream in the pantry on the sly."

Alexander Abraham looked foolish. He hadn't thought I knew that.

I didn't take the smallpox, and in another week the doctor came out and sent the policeman home. I was disinfected and William Adolphus was fumigated, and then we were free to go.

"Good-bye, Mr. Bennett," I said, offering to shake hands in a forgiving spirit. "I've no doubt that you are glad to be rid of me, but you are no gladder than I am to go. I suppose this house will be dirtier than ever in a month's time, and Mr. Riley will have discarded the little polish his manners have taken on. Reformation with men and dogs never goes very deep."

With this Parthian shaft I walked out of the house, supposing that I had seen the last of it and Alexander Abraham.

I was glad to get back home, of course; but it did seem queer and lonesome. The cats hardly knew me, and William Adolphus roamed about forlornly and appeared to feel like an exile. I didn't take as much pleasure in cooking as usual, for it seemed kind of foolish to be fussing over oneself. The sight of a bone made me think of poor Mr. Riley. The neighbours avoided me pointedly, for they couldn't get rid of the fear that I might erupt into smallpox at any moment. My Sunday-School class had been given to another woman, and altogether I felt as if I didn't belong anywhere.

I had existed like this for a fortnight when Alexander Abraham suddenly appeared. He walked in one evening at dusk, but at first sight I didn't know him, he was so spruced and barbered up. But William Adolphus knew him. Will you believe it, William Adolphus, my own William Adolphus, rubbed up against that man's trouser leg with an undisguised purr of satisfaction.

"I had to come, Angelina," said Alexander Abraham. "I couldn't stand it any longer."

"My name is Peter," I said coldly, although I was feeling ridiculously glad about something.

"It isn't," said Alexander Abraham stubbornly. "It is Angelina for me, and always will be. I shall never call you Peter. Angelina just suits you exactly; and Angelina Bennett would suit you still better. You must come back, Angelina. Mr. Riley is moping for you, and I can't get along without somebody to appreciate my sarcasms, now that you have accustomed me to the luxury."

"What about the other five cats?" I demanded.

Alexander Abraham sighed.

"I suppose they'll have to come too," he sighed, "though no doubt they'll chase poor Mr. Riley clean off the premises. But I can live without him, and I can't without you. How soon can you be ready to marry me?"

"I haven't said that I was going to marry you at all, have I?" I said tartly, just to be consistent. For I wasn't feeling tart.

"No, but you will, won't you?" said Alexander Abraham anxiously. "Because if you won't, I wish you'd let me die of the smallpox. Do, dear Angelina."

To think that a man should dare to call me his "dear Angelina"! And to think that I shouldn't mind!

"Where I go, William Adolphus goes," I said, "but I shall give away the other five cats for—for the sake of Mr. Riley."

9

Pa Sloane's Purchase

"I GUESS the molasses is getting low, ain't it?" said Pa Sloane insinuatingly. "S'pose I'd better drive up to Carmody this afternoon and get some more."

"There's a good half-gallon of molasses in the jug yet," said Ma Sloane ruthlessly.

"That so? Well, I noticed the kerosene demijohn wasn't very hefty the last time I filled the can. Reckon it needs replenishing."

"We have kerosene enough to do for a fortnight yet." Ma continued to eat her dinner with an impassive face, but a twinkle made itself apparent in her eye. Lest Pa should see it, and feel encouraged thereby, she looked immovably at her plate.

Pa Sloane sighed. His invention was giving out.

"Didn't I hear you say day before yesterday that you were out of nutmegs?" he queried, after a few moments' severe reflection.

"I got a supply of them from the egg-pedlar yesterday," responded Ma, by a great effort preventing the twinkle from spreading over her entire face. She wondered if this third failure would squelch Pa. But Pa was not to be squelched.

"Well, anyway," he said, brightening up under the influence of a sudden saving inspiration, "I'll have to go up to get the sorrel mare shod. So, if you've any little errands you want done at the store, Ma, just make a memo of them while I hitch up."

The matter of shoeing the sorrel mare was beyond Ma's province, although she had her own suspicions about the sorrel mare's need of shoes.

"Why can't you give up beating about the bush, Pa?" she demanded, with contemptuous pity. "You might as well own up what's taking you to Carmody. *I* can see through your design. You want to get away to the Garland auction. That is what is troubling you, Pa Sloane."

"I dunno but what I might step over, seeing it's so handy. But the sorrel mare really does need shoeing, Ma," protested Pa.

"There's always something needing to be done if it's convenient," retorted Ma. "Your mania for auctions will be the ruin of you yet, Pa. A man of fifty-five ought to have grown out of such a hankering. But the older you get, the worse you get. Anyway, if *I* wanted to go to auctions, I'd select them as was something like, and not waste my time on little one-horse affairs like this of Garland's."

"One might pick up something real cheap at Garland's," said Pa defensively.

"Well, you are not going to pick up anything, cheap or otherwise, Pa Sloane, because I'm going with you to see that you don't. I know I can't stop you from going. I might as well try to stop the wind from blowing. But I shall go, too, out of self-defence. This house is so full now of old clutter and truck that you've brought home from auctions that I feel as if I was made up out of pieces and left-overs."

Pa Sloane sighed again. It was not exhilarating to attend an auction with Ma. She would never let him bid on anything. But he realized that Ma's mind was made up beyond the power of mortal man's persuasion to alter it; so he went out to hitch up.

Pa Sloane's dissipation was going to auctions and buying things that nobody else would buy. Ma Sloane's patient endeavours of over thirty years had been able to effect only a partial reform. Sometimes Pa heroically refrained from going to an auction for six months at a time; then he would break out worse than ever, go to all that took place for miles around, and come home with a wagonful of misfits. His last exploit had been to bid on an old dasher churn for five dollars—the boys "ran things up" on Pa Sloane for the fun of it—and bring it home to outraged Ma, who had made her butter for fifteen years in the very latest, most up-to-date barrel churn. To add insult to injury, this was the second dasher churn Pa had bought at auction. That settled it. Ma decreed that henceforth she would chaperon Pa when he went to auctions.

But this was the day of Pa's good angel. When he drove up to the door where Ma was waiting, a breathless, hatless imp of ten flew into the yard, and hurled himself between Ma and the wagon-step.

"Oh, Mrs. Sloane, won't you come over to our house at once?" he gasped. "The baby, he's got colic, and ma's just wild, and he's all black in the face."

Ma went, feeling that the stars in their courses fought against a woman who was trying to do her duty by her husband. But first she admonished Pa.

"I shall have to let you go alone. But I charge you, Pa, not to bid on anything—on *anything*, do you hear?"

Pa heard and promised to heed, with every intention of keeping his promise. Then he drove away joyfully. On any other occasion Ma would have been a welcome companion. But she certainly spoiled the flavour of an auction.

When Pa arrived at the Carmody store, he saw that the little yard of the Garland place below the hill was already full of people. The auction had evidently begun; so, not to miss any more of it, Pa hurried down. The sorrel mare could wait for her shoes until afterwards.

Ma had been within bounds when she called the Garland auction a "one-horse affair." It certainly was very paltry, especially when compared to the big Donaldson auction of a month ago, which Pa still lived over in happy dreams.

Horace Garland and his wife had been poor. When they died within six weeks of each other, one of consumption and one of pneumonia, they left nothing but debts and a little furniture. The house had been a rented one.

The bidding on the various poor articles of household gear put up for sale was not brisk, but had an element of resigned determination. Carmody people knew that these things had to be sold to pay the debts, and they could not be sold unless they were bought. Still, it was a very tame affair.

A woman came out of the house carrying a baby of

about eighteen months in her arms, and sat down on the bench beneath the window.

"There's Marthy Blair with the Garland baby," said Robert Lawson to Pa. "I'd like to know what's to become of that poor young one!"

"Ain't there any of the father's or mother's folks to take him?" asked Pa.

"No. Horace had no relatives that anybody ever heard of. Mrs. Horace had a brother; but he went to Manitoba years ago, and nobody knows where he is now. Somebody'll have to take the baby, and nobody seems anxious to. I've got eight myself, or I'd think about it. He's a fine little chap."

Pa, with Ma's parting admonition ringing in his ears, did not bid on anything, although it will never be known how great was the heroic self-restraint he put on himself, until just at the last, when he did bid on a collection of flower-pots, thinking he might indulge himself to that small extent. But Josiah Sloane had been commissioned by his wife to bring those flower-pots home to her; so Pa lost them.

"There, that's all," said the auctioneer, wiping his face, for the day was very warm for October.

"There's nothing more unless we sell the baby."

A laugh went through the crowd. The sale had been a dull affair, and they were ready for some fun. Someone called out, "Put him up, Jacob." The joke found favour, and the call was repeated hilariously.

Jacob Blair took little Teddy Garland out of Martha's arms and stood him up on the table by the door, steadying the small chap with one big brown hand. The baby had a mop of yellow curls, a pink and white face, and big blue eyes. He laughed out at the men before him and waved his hands in delight. Pa Sloane thought he had never seen so pretty a baby.

"Here's a baby for sale," shouted the auctioneer. "A genuine article, pretty near as good as brand-new. A real live baby, warranted to walk and talk a little. Who bids? A dollar? Did I hear anyone mean enough to bid a dollar? No, sir, babies don't come as cheap as that, especially the curly-headed brand."

The crowd laughed again. Pa Sloane, by way of keeping on the joke, cried, "Four dollars!"

Everybody looked at him. The impression flashed through the crowd that Pa was in earnest, and meant thus to signify his intention of giving the baby a home. He was well-to-do, and his only son was grown up and married.

"Six," cried out John Clarke from the other side of the yard. John Clarke lived at White Sands, and he and his wife were childless.

That bid of John Clarke's was Pa's undoing. Pa Sloane could not have an enemy; but a rival he had, and that rival was John Clarke. Everywhere at auctions, John Clarke was wont to bid against Pa. At the last auction he had outbid Pa in everything, not having the fear of his wife before his eyes. Pa's fighting blood was up in a moment; he forgot Ma Sloane; he forgot what he was bidding for; he forgot everything except a determination that John Clarke should not be victor again.

"Ten," he called shrilly.

"Fifteen," shouted Clarke.

"Twenty," vociferated Pa.

"Twenty-five," bellowed Clarke.

"Thirty," shrieked Pa. He nearly burst a blood-vessel in his shrieking, but he had won. Clarke turned off with a laugh and a shrug, and the baby was knocked down to Pa Sloane by the auctioneer, who had meanwhile been keeping the crowd in roars of laughter by a quick fire of witticisms. There had not been such fun at an auction in Carmody for many a long day.

Pa Sloane came, or was pushed, forward. The baby was put into his arms; he realized that he was expected to keep it, and he was too dazed to refuse; besides, his heart went out to the child.

The auctioneer looked doubtfully at the money which Pa laid mutely down.

"I s'pose that part was only a joke," he said.

"Not a bit of it," said Robert Lawson. "All the money won't be too much to pay the debts. There's a doctor's bill, and this will just about pay it."

Pa Sloane drove back home, with the sorrel mare still unshod, the baby, and the baby's meager bundle of clothes. The baby did not trouble him much; it had become well used to strangers in the past two months, and promptly fell asleep on his arm; but Pa Sloane did not enjoy that drive; at the end of it, he mentally saw Ma Sloane.

Ma was there, too, waiting for him on the back doorstep as he drove into the yard at sunset. Her face, when she saw the baby, expressed the last degree of amazement.

"Pa Sloane," she demanded, "whose is that young one, and where did you get it?"

"I—I—bought it at the auction, Ma," said Pa feebly. Then he waited for the explosion. None came. This last exploit of Pa's was too much for Ma.

With a gasp, she snatched the baby from Pa's arms, and ordered him to go out and put the mare in. When Pa returned to the kitchen, Ma had set the baby on the sofa, fenced him around with chairs so that he couldn't fall off, and given him a molasses cooky.

"Now, Pa Sloane, you can explain," she said.

Pa explained. Ma listened in grim silence until he had finished. Then she said sternly:

"Do you reckon we're going to keep this baby?"

"I—I—dunno," said Pa. And he didn't.

"Well, we're *not*. I brought up one boy and that's enough. I don't calculate to be pestered with any more. I never was much struck on children *as* children, anyhow. You say that Mary Garland had a brother out in Manitoba? Well, we shall just write to him and tell him he's got to look out for his nephew."

"But how can you do that, Ma, when nobody knows his address?" objected Pa, with a wistful look at that delicious, laughing baby.

"I'll find out his address if I have to advertise in the papers for him," retorted Ma. "As for you, Pa Sloane, you're not fit to be out of a lunatic asylum. The next auction you'll be buying a wife, I s'pose?"

Pa, quite crushed by Ma's sarcasm, pulled his chair in to supper. Ma picked up the baby and sat down at the head of the table. Little Teddy laughed and pinched her face—Ma's face! Ma looked very grim, but she fed him his supper as skillfully as if it had not been thirty years since she had done such a thing. But then, the woman who once learns the mother knack never forgets it.

After tea, Ma despatched Pa over to William Alexander's to borrow a high chair. When Pa returned in the twilight, the baby was fenced in on the sofa again, and Ma was stepping briskly about the garret. She was bringing down the little cot bed her own boy had once occupied, and setting it up in their room for Teddy. Then she undressed the baby and rocked him to sleep, crooning an old lullaby over him. Pa Sloane sat quietly and listened, with very sweet memories of the long ago, when he and Ma had been young and proud, and the bewhiskered William Alexander had been a curly-headed little fellow like this one.

Ma was not driven to advertising for Mrs. Garland's brother. That personage saw the notice of his sister's death in a home paper and wrote to the Carmody postmaster for full information. The letter was referred to Ma, and Ma answered it.

She wrote that they had taken in the baby, pending further arrangements, but had no intention of keeping it; and she calmly demanded of its uncle what was to be done with it. Then she sealed and addressed the letter with an unfaltering hand; but, when it was done, she looked across the table at Pa Sloane, who was sitting in the armchair with the baby on his knee. They were having a royal good time together. Pa had always been dreadfully foolish about babies. He looked ten years younger. Ma's keen eyes softened a little as she watched them.

A prompt answer came to her letter. Teddy's uncle wrote that he had six children of his own, but was nevertheless willing and glad to give his little nephew a home. But he could not come after him. Josiah Spencer, of White Sands, was going out to Manitoba in the spring. If Mr. and Mrs. Sloane could only keep the baby till then, he could be sent out with the Spencers. Perhaps they could see a chance sooner.

"There'll be no chance sooner," said Pa Sloane in a tone of satisfaction.

"No, worse luck!" retorted Ma crisply.

The winter passed by. Little Teddy grew and throve,

and Pa Sloane worshipped him. Ma was very good to him, too, and Teddy was just as fond of her as of Pa.

Nevertheless, as the spring drew near, Pa became depressed. Sometimes he sighed heavily, especially when he heard casual references to the Josiah Spencer emigration.

One warm afternoon in early May, Josiah Spencer arrived. He found Ma knitting placidly in the kitchen, while Pa nodded over his newspaper and the baby played with the cat on the floor.

"Good afternoon, Mrs. Sloane," said Josiah with a flourish. "I just dropped in to see about this young man here. We are going to leave next Wednesday; so you'd better send him down to our place Monday or Tuesday, so that he can get used to us, and—"

"Oh, Ma," began Pa, rising imploringly to his feet.

Ma transfixed him with her eye.

"Sit down, Pa," she commanded.

Unhappy Pa sat.

Then Ma glared at the smiling Josiah, who instantly felt as guilty as if he had been caught steeling sheep red-handed.

"We are much obliged to you, Mr. Spencer," said Ma icily, "but this baby is *ours*. We bought him, and we paid for him. A bargain is a bargain. When I pay cash down for babies, I propose to get my money's worth. We are going to keep this baby, in spite of any number of uncles in Manitoba. Have I made this sufficiently clear to your understanding, Mr. Spencer?"

"Certainly, certainly," stammered the unfortunate man, feeling guiltier than ever, "but I thought you didn't want him—I thought you'd written to his uncle—I thought—"

"I really wouldn't think quite so much if I were you," said Ma kindly. "It must be hard on you. Won't you stay and have tea with us?"

But, no, Josiah would not stay. He was thankful to make his escape with such rags of self-respect as remained to him.

Pa Sloane arose and came around to Ma's chair. He laid a trembling hand on her shoulder.

"Ma, you're a good woman," he said softly.

"Go 'long, Pa," said Ma.

10

The Courting of Prissy Strong

I WASN'T able to go to prayer meeting that evening because I had neuralgia in my face; but Thomas went, and the minute he came home I knew by the twinkle in his eye that he had some news.

"Who do you s'pose Stephen Clark went home with from meeting to-night?" he said, chuckling.

"Jane Miranda Blair," I said promptly. Stephen Clark's wife had been dead for two years and he hadn't taken much notice of anybody, so far as was known. But Carmody had Jane Miranda all ready for him, and really, I don't know why she didn't suit him, except for the reason that a man never does what he is expected to do when it comes to marrying.

Thomas chuckled again.

"Wrong. He stepped up to Prissy Strong and walked off with her. Cold soup warmed over."

"Prissy Strong!" I just held up my hands. Then I laughed. "He needn't try for Prissy," I said. "Emmeline nipped that in the bud twenty years ago, and she'll do it again."

"Em'line is an old crank," growled Thomas. He detests Emmeline Strong, and always did.

"She's that, all right," I agreed, "and that is just the reason she can turn poor Prissy any way she likes. You mark my words, she'll put her foot right down on this as soon as she finds it out."

Thomas said that I was probably right. I lay awake for a long time after I went to bed that night, thinking of Prissy and Stephen. As a general rule, I don't concern my

148

head about other people's affairs, but Prissy was such a helpless creature I couldn't get her off my mind.

Twenty years ago Stephen Clark had tried to go with Prissy Strong. That was pretty soon after Prissy's father had died. She and Emmeline were living alone together. Emmeline was thirty, ten years older than Prissy, and if ever there were two sisters totally different from each other in every way, those two were Emmeline and Prissy Strong.

Emmeline took after her father; she was big and dark and homely, and she was the most domineering creature that ever stepped on shoe leather. She simply ruled poor Prissy with a rod of iron.

Prissy herself was a pretty girl—at least most people thought so. I can't honestly say I ever admired her style much myself. I like something with more vim and snap to it. Prissy was slim and pink, with soft, appealing blue eyes, and pale gold hair all clinging in baby rings around her face. She was just as meek and timid as she looked and there wasn't a bit of harm in her. I always liked Prissy, even if I didn't admire her looks as much as some people did.

Anyway, it was plain her style suited Stephen Clark. He began to drive her, and there wasn't a speck of doubt that Prissy liked him. Then Emmeline just put a stopper on the affair. It was pure cantankerousness in her. Stephen was a good match and nothing could be said against him. But Emmeline was just determined that Prissy shouldn't marry. She couldn't get married herself, and she was sore enough about it.

Of course, if Prissy had had a spark of spirit she wouldn't have given in. But she hadn't a mite; I believe she would have cut off her nose if Emmeline had ordered her to do it. She was just her mother over again. If ever a girl belied her name, Prissy Strong did. There wasn't anything strong about her.

One night, when prayer meeting came out, Stephen stepped up to Prissy as usual and asked if he might see her home. Thomas and I were just behind—we weren't married ourselves then—and we heard it all. Prissy gave one scared, appealing look at Emmeline and then said, "No, thank you, not to-night."

Stephen just turned on his heel and went. He was a high-spirited fellow, and I knew he would never overlook a public slight like that. If he had had as much sense as he ought to have had, he would have known that Emmeline was at the bottom of it; but he didn't, and he began going to see Althea Gillis, and they were married the next year. Althea was a rather nice girl, though giddy, and I think she and Stephen were happy enough together. In real life things are often like that.

Nobody ever tried to go with Prissy again. I suppose they were afraid of Emmeline. Prissy's beauty soon faded. She was always kind of sweet looking, but her bloom went, and she got shyer and limper every year of her life. She wouldn't have dared put on her second best dress without asking Emmeline's permission. She was real fond of cats and Emmeline wouldn't let her keep one. Emmeline even cut the serial out of the religious weekly she took before she would give it to Prissy, because she didn't believe in reading novels. It used to make me furious to see it all. They were my next door neighbours after I married Thomas, and I was often in and out. Sometimes I'd feel real vexed at Prissy for giving in the way she did; but, after all, she couldn't help it—she was born that way.

And now Stephen was going to try his luck again. It certainly did seem funny.

Stephen walked home with Prissy from prayer meeting four nights before Emmeline found it out. Emmeline hadn't been going to prayer meeting all that summer because she was mad at Mr. Leonard. She had expressed her disapproval to him because he had buried old Naomi Clark at the harbour "just as if she was a Christian," and Mr. Leonard had said something to her she couldn't get over for a while. I don't know what it was, but I know that when Mr. Leonard *was* roused to rebuke anyone, the person so rebuked remembered it for a spell.

All at once I knew she must have discovered about Stephen and Prissy, for Prissy stopped going to prayer meeting.

I felt real worried about it, someway, and although Thomas said for goodness' sake not to go poking my fingers into other people's pies, I felt as if I ought to do something. Stephen Clark was a good man, and Prissy would have a beautiful home; and those two little boys of Althea's needed a mother if ever boys did. Besides, I knew quite well that Prissy, in her secret soul, was hankering to be married. So was Emmeline, too—but nobody wanted to help *her* to a husband.

The upshot of my meditations was that I asked Stephen down to dinner with us from church one day. I had heard a rumour that he was going to see Lizzie Pye over at Avonlea, and I knew it was time to be stirring, if anything were to be done. If it had been Jane Miranda, I don't know that I'd have bothered; but Lizzie Pye wouldn't have done for a stepmother for Althea's boys at all. She was too bad-tempered, and as mean as second skimmings besides.

Stephen came. He seemed dull and moody, and not much inclined to talk. After dinner I gave Thomas a hint. I said,

"You go to bed and have your nap. I want to talk to Stephen."

Thomas shrugged his shoulders and went. He probably thought I was brewing up lots of trouble for myself, but he didn't say anything. As soon as he was out of the way, I casually remarked to Stephen that I understood that he was going to take one of my neighbours away and that I couldn't be sorry, though she was an excellent neighbour and I would miss her a great deal.

"You won't have to miss her much, I reckon," said Stephen grimly. "I've been told I'm not wanted there."

I was surprised to hear Stephen come out so plump and plain about it, for I hadn't expected to get at the root of the matter so easily. Stephen wasn't the confidential kind. But it really seemed to be a relief to him to talk about it; I never saw a man feeling so sore about anything. He told me the whole story.

Prissy had written him a letter—he fished it out of his pocket and gave it to me to read. It was in Prissy's prim, pretty little writing, sure enough, and it just said that his attentions were "unwelcome," and would he be "kind enough to refrain from offering them." Not much wonder the poor man went to see Lizzie Pye!

"Stephen, I'm surprised at you for thinking that Prissy Strong wrote that letter," I said.

"It's in her handwriting," he said stubbornly.

"Of course it is. 'The hand is the hand of Esau, but the voice is the voice of Jacob,'" I said, though I wasn't sure whether the quotation was exactly appropriate. "Emmeline composed that letter and made Prissy copy it out. I know that as well as if I'd seen her do it, and you ought to have known it, too."

"If I thought that, I'd show Emmeline I could get Prissy in spite of her," said Stephen savagely. "But if Prissy doesn't want me I'm not going to force my attentions on her."

Well, we talked it over a bit, and in the end I agreed to sound Prissy, and find out what she really thought about it. I didn't think it would be hard to do; and it wasn't. I went over the very next day because I saw Emmeline driving off to the store. I found Prissy alone, sewing carpet rags. Emmeline kept her constantly at that— because Prissy hated it, I suppose. Prissy was crying when I went in, and in a few minutes I had the whole story.

Prissy wanted to get married—and she wanted to get married to Stephen—and Emmeline wouldn't let her.

"Prissy Strong," I said in exasperation, "you haven't the spirit of a mouse! Why on earth did you write him such a letter?"

"Why, Emmeline made me," said Prissy, as if there couldn't be any appeal from that; and I knew there couldn't—for Prissy. I also knew that if Stephen wanted to see Prissy again, Emmeline must know nothing of it, and I told him so when he came down the next evening—to borrow a hoe, he said. It was a long way to come for a hoe.

"Then what am I to do?" he said. "It wouldn't be any use to write, for it would likely fall into Emmeline's hands. She won't let Prissy go anywhere alone after this, and how am I to know when the old cat is away?"

"Please don't insult cats," I said. "I'll tell you what we'll do. You can see the ventilator on our barn from your place, can't you? You'd be able to make out a flag or something tied to it, wouldn't you, through that spy-glass of yours?"

Stephen thought he could.

"Well, you take a squint at it every now and then," I said. "Just as soon as Emmeline leaves Prissy alone, I'll hoist the signal."

The chance didn't come for a whole fortnight. Then, one evening, I saw Emmeline striding over the field below our house. As soon as she was out of sight I ran through the birch grove to Prissy.

"Yes, Em'line's gone to sit up with Jane Lawson to-night," said Prissy, all fluttered and trembling.

"Then you put on your muslin dress and fix your hair," I said. "I'm going home to get Thomas to tie something to that ventilator."

But do you think Thomas would do it? Not he. He said he owed something to his position as elder in the church. In the end I had to do it myself, though I don't like climbing ladders. I tied Thomas' long red woolen scarf to the ventilator, and prayed that Stephen would see it. He did, for in less than an hour he drove down our lane and put his horse in our barn. He was all spruced up, and as nervous and excited as a schoolboy. He went right over to Prissy, and I began to tuft my new comfort with a clear conscience. I shall never know why it suddenly came into my head to go up to the garret and make sure that the moths hadn't got into my box of blankets; but I always believed that it was a special interposition of Providence. I went up and happened to look out of the east window; and there I saw Emmeline Strong coming home across our pond field.

I just flew down those garret stairs and out through the birches. I burst into the Strong kitchen, where Stephen and Prissy were sitting as cozy as you please.

"Stephen, come quick! Emmeline's nearly here," I cried.

Prissy looked out of the window and wrung her hands.

"Oh, she's in the lane now," she gasped. "He can't get out of the house without her seeing him. Oh, Rosanna, what shall we do?"

I really don't know what would have become of those two people if I hadn't been in existence to find ideas for them.

"Take Stephen up to the garret and hide him there, Prissy," I said firmly, "and take him quick."

Prissy took him quick, but she had barely time to get back to the kitchen before Emmeline marched in—mad as a wet hen because somebody had been ahead of her offering to sit up with Jane Lawson, and so she lost the chance of poking and prying into things while Jane was asleep. The minute she clapped eyes on Prissy she suspected something. It wasn't any wonder, for there was Prissy, all dressed up, with flushed cheeks and shining eyes. She was all in a quiver of excitement, and looked ten years younger.

"Priscilla Strong, you've been expecting Stephen Clark here this evening!" burst out Emmeline. "You wicked, deceitful, underhanded, ungrateful creature!"

And she went on storming at Prissy, who began to cry, and looked so weak and babyish that I was frightened she would betray the whole thing.

"This is between you and Prissy, Emmeline," I struck in, "and I'm not going to interfere. But I want to get you to come over and show me how to tuft my comfort that new pattern you learned in Avonlea, and as it had better be done before dark I wish you'd come right away."

"I s'pose I'll go," said Emmeline ungraciously, "but Priscilla shall come, too, for I see that she isn't to be trusted out of my sight after this."

I hoped Stephen would see us from the garret window and make good his escape. But I didn't dare trust to chance, so when I got Emmeline safely to work on my comfort, I excused myself and slipped out. Luckily my kitchen was on the off side of the house, but I was a nervous woman as I rushed across to the Strong place and dashed up Emmeline's garret stairs to Stephen. It was fortunate I had come, for he didn't know we had gone. Prissy had hidden him behind the loom, and he didn't dare move for fear Emmeline would hear him on that creaky floor. He was a sight with cobwebs.

I got him down and smuggled him into our barn, and he stayed there until it was dark and the Strong girls had gone home. Emmeline began to rage at Prissy the moment they were outside my door.

Then Stephen came in and we talked things over. He and Prissy had made good use of their time, short as it had been. Prissy had promised to marry him, and all that remained was to get the ceremony performed.

"And that will be no easy matter," I warned him. "Now that Emmeline's suspicions are aroused she'll never let Prissy out of her sight until you're married to another woman, if it's years. I know Emmeline Strong. And I know Prissy. If it was any other girl in the world, she'd run away, or manage it somehow, but Prissy never will. She's too much in the habit of obeying Emmeline. You'll have an obedient wife, Stephen—if you ever get her."

Stephen looked as if he thought that wouldn't be any drawback. Gossip said that Althea had been pretty bossy. I don't know. Maybe it was so.

"Can't you suggest something, Rosanna?" he implored. "You've helped us so far, and I'll never forget it."

"The only thing I can think of is for you to have the license ready, and speak to Mr. Leonard, and keep an eye on our ventilator," I said. "I'll watch here and signal whenever there's an opening."

Well, I watched and Stephen watched, and Mr. Leonard was in the plot, too. Prissy was always a favourite of his, and he would have been more than human, saint as he is, if he'd had any love for Emmeline, after the way she was always trying to brew up strife in the church.

But Emmeline was a match for us all. She never let Prissy out of her sight. Everywhere she went, she toted Prissy, too. When a month had gone by, I was almost in despair. Mr. Leonard had to leave for the Assembly in another week and Stephen's neighbours were beginning to talk about him. They said that a man who spent all his time hanging around the yard with a spyglass, and trusting everything to a hired boy, couldn't be altogether right in his mind.

I could hardly believe my eyes when I saw Emmeline driving away one day alone. As soon as she was out of sight I whisked over, and Anne Shirley and Diana Barry went with me.

They were visiting me that afternoon. Diana's mother was my second cousin, and, as we visited back and forth frequently, I'd often seen Diana. But I'd never seen her chum, Anne Shirley, although I'd heard enough about her to drive anyone frantic with curiosity. So when she came home from Redmond College that summer, I asked Diana to take pity on me and bring her over some afternoon.

I wasn't disappointed in her. I considered her a beauty, though some people couldn't see it. She had the most magnificent red hair and the biggest, shiningest eyes I ever saw in a girl's head. As for her laugh, it made me feel young again to hear it. She and Diana both laughed enough that afternoon, for I told them, under solemn promise of secrecy, all about poor Prissy's love affair. So nothing would do them but they must go over with me.

The appearance of the house amazed me. All the shutters were closed and the door locked. I knocked and knocked, but there was no answer. Then I walked around the house to the only window that hadn't shutters—a tiny one upstairs. I knew it was the window in the closet off the room where the girls slept. I stopped under it and called Prissy. Before long Prissy came and opened it. She was so pale and woe-begone looking that I pitied her with all my heart.

"Prissy, where has Emmeline gone?" I asked.

"Down to Avonlea to see the Roger Pyes. They're sick with measles, and Emmeline couldn't take me because I've never had the measles."

Poor Prissy! She had never had anything a body ought to have.

"Then you just come and unfasten a shutter, and come right over to my house," I said exultantly. "We'll have Stephen and the minister here in no time."

"I can't—Em'line has locked me in here," said Prissy woefully.

I was posed. No living mortal bigger than a baby could have got in or out of that closet window.

"Well," I said finally, "I'll put the signal up for Stephen anyhow, and we'll see what can be done when he gets here."

I didn't know how I was ever to get the signal up on that ventilator, for it was one of the days I take dizzy spells; and if I took one up on the ladder there'd probably be a funeral instead of a wedding. But Anne Shirley said she'd put it up for me, and she did. I had never seen that girl before, and I've never seen her since, but it's my opinion that there wasn't much she couldn't do if she made up her mind to do it.

Stephen wasn't long in getting there, and he brought the minister with him. Then we all, including Thomas—who was beginning to get interested in the affair in spite of himself—went over and held council of war beneath the closet window.

Thomas suggested breaking in doors and carrying Prissy off boldly, but I could see that Mr. Leonard looked very dubious over that, and even Stephen said he thought it could only be done as a last resort. I agreed with him. I knew Emmeline Strong would bring an action against him for housebreaking as likely as not. She'd be so furious she'd stick at nothing if we gave her any excuse. Then Anne Shirley, who couldn't have been more excited if she was getting married herself, came to the rescue again.

"Couldn't you put a ladder up to the closet window," she said, "and Mr. Clark can go up it and they can be married there. Can't they, Mr. Leonard?"

Mr. Leonard agreed that they could. He was always the most saintly looking man, but I know I saw a twinkle in his eye.

"Thomas, go over and bring our little ladder over here," I said.

Thomas forgot he was an elder, and he brought the ladder as quick as it was possible for a fat man to do it. After all, it was too short to reach the window, but there was no time to go for another. Stephen went up to the top of it, and he reached up and Prissy reached down, and they could just barely clasp hands so. I shall never forget the look of Prissy. The window was so small she could only get her head and one arm out of it. Besides, she was almost frightened to death.

Mr. Leonard stood at the foot of the ladder and married them. As a rule, he makes a very long and solemn thing of the marriage ceremony, but this time he cut out everything that wasn't absolutely necessary; and it was well that he did, for just as he pronounced them man and wife, Emmeline drove into the lane.

She knew perfectly well what had happened when

she saw the minister with his blue book in his hand. Never a word said she. She marched to the front door, unlocked it, and strode upstairs. I've always been convinced it was a mercy that closet window was so small, or I believe that she would have thrown Prissy out of it. As it was, she walked her downstairs by the arm and actually flung her at Stephen.

"There, take your wife," she said, "and I'll pack up every stitch she owns and send it after her; and I never want to see her or you again as long as I live."

Then she turned to me and Thomas.

"As for you that have aided and abetted that weak-minded fool in this, take yourselves out of my yard and never darken my door again."

"Goodness, who wants to, you old spitfire!" said Thomas.

It wasn't just the thing for him to say, perhaps, but we are all human, even elders.

The girls didn't escape. Emmeline looked daggers at them.

"This will be something for you to carry back to Avonlea," she said. "You gossips down there will have enough to talk about for a spell. That's all you ever go out of Avonlea for—just to fetch and carry tales."

Finally she finished up with the minister.

"I'm going to the Baptist church in Spencervale after this," she said. Her tone and look said a hundred other things. She whirled into the house and slammed the door.

Mr. Leonard looked around on us with a pitying smile as Stephen put poor, half-fainting Prissy into the buggy.

"I am very sorry," he said in that gentle, saintly way of his, "for the Baptists."

11

The Miracle at Carmody

SALOME looked out of the kitchen window and a pucker of distress appeared on her smooth forehead.

"Dear, dear, what has Lionel Hezekiah been doing now?" she murmured anxiously.

Involuntarily, she reached out for her crutch; but it was a little beyond her reach, having fallen on the floor, and without it Salome could not move a step.

"Well, anyway, Judith is bringing him in as fast as she can," she reflected. "He must have been up to something terrible this time; for she looks very cross, and she never walks like that unless she is angry clear through. Dear me, I am sometimes tempted to think that Judith and I made a mistake in adopting the child. I suppose two old maids don't know much about bringing up a boy properly. But he is *not* a bad child, and it really seems to me that there must be some way of making him behave better if we only knew what it was."

Salome's monologue was cut short by the entrance of her sister Judith, holding Lionel Hezekiah by his chubby wrist with a determined grip.

Judith Marsh was ten years older than Salome, and the two women were as different in appearance as night and day. Salome, in spite of her thirty-five years, looked almost girlish. She was small and pink and flower-like, with little rings of pale golden hair clustering all over her head in a most unspinster-like fashion, and her eyes were big and blue, and mild as a dove's. Her face was perhaps a weak one, but it was very sweet and appealing.

Judith Marsh was tall and dark, with a plain, tragic

face and iron-gray hair. Her eyes were black and sombre, and every feature bespoke unyielding will and determination. Just now she looked, as Salome had said, "angry clear through," and the baleful glances she cast on the small mortal she held would have withered a more hardened criminal than six happy-go-lucky years had made of Lionel Hezekiah.

Lionel Hezekiah, whatever his shortcomings, did not look bad. Indeed, he was as engaging an urchin as ever beamed out on a jolly good world through a pair of big, velvet-brown eyes. He was chubby and firm-limbed, with a mop of beautiful golden curls, which were the despair of his heart and the pride and joy of Salome's; and his round face was usually a lurking-place for dimples and smiles and sunshine.

But just now Lionel Hezekiah was under a blight; he had been caught red-handed in guilt, and was feeling much ashamed of himself. He hung his head and squirmed his toes under the mournful reproach in Salome's eyes. When Salome looked at him like that, Lionel Hezekiah always felt that he was paying more for his fun than it was worth.

"What do you suppose I caught him doing this time?" demanded Judith.

"I—I don't know," faltered Salome.

"Firing—at—a—mark—on—the—henhouse—door—with—new-laid—eggs," said Judith with measured distinctness. "He has broken every egg that was laid to-day except three. And as for the state of that henhouse door—"

Judith paused, with an indignant gesture meant to convey that the state of the henhouse door must be left to Salome's imagination, since the English language was not capable of depicting it.

"O Lionel Hezekiah, why will you do such things?" said Salome miserably.

"I—didn't know it was wrong," said Lionel Hezekiah, bursting into prompt tears. "I—I thought it would be bully fun. Seems's if everything what's fun 's wrong."

Salome's heart was not proof against tears, as Lionel Hezekiah very well knew. She put her arm about the sobbing culprit, and drew him to her side.

"He didn't know it was wrong," she said defiantly to Judith.

"He's got to be taught, then," was Judith's retort. "No, you needn't try to beg him off, Salome. He shall go right to bed without any supper, and stay there till tomorrow morning."

"Oh! not without his supper," entreated Salome. "You—you won't improve the child's morals by injuring his stomach, Judith."

"Without his supper, I say," repeated Judith inexorably. "Lionel Hezekiah, go up-stairs to the south room, and go to bed at once."

Lionel Hezekiah went up-stairs, and went to bed at once. He was never sulky or disobedient. Salome listened to him as he stumped patiently up-stairs with a sob at every step, and her own eyes filled with tears.

"Now, don't for pity's sake go crying, Salome," said Judith irritably. "I think I've let him off very easily. He is enough to try the patience of a saint, and I never was that," she added with entire truth.

"But he isn't bad," pleaded Salome. "You know he never does anything the second time after he has been told it was wrong, never."

"What good does that do when he is certain to do something new and twice as bad? I never saw anything like him for originating ideas of mischief. Just look at what he has done in the past fortnight—in one fortnight, Salome. He brought in a live snake, and nearly frightened you into fits; he drank up a bottle of liniment, and almost poisoned himself; he took three toads to bed with him; he climbed into the henhouse loft, and fell through on a hen and killed her; he painted his face all over with your watercolours; and now comes *this* exploit. And eggs at twenty-eight cents a dozen! I tell you, Salome, Lionel Hezekiah is an expensive luxury."

"But we couldn't do without him," protested Salome.

"*I* could. But as you can't, or think you can't, we'll have to keep him, I suppose. But the only way to secure any peace of mind for ourselves, as far as I can see, is to tether him in the yard, and hire somebody to watch him."

"There must be some way of managing him," said

Salome desperately. She thought Judith was in earnest about the tethering. Judith was generally so terribly in earnest in all she said. "Perhaps it is because he has no other employment that he invents so many unheard-of things. If he had anything to occupy himself with—perhaps if we sent him to school—"

"He's too young to go to school. Father always said that no child should go to school until it was seven, and I don't mean Lionel Hezekiah shall. Well, I'm going to take a pail of hot water and a brush, and see what I can do to that henhouse door. I've got my afternoon's work cut out for me."

Judith stood Salome's crutch up beside her, and departed to purify the henhouse door. As soon as she was safely out of the way, Salome took her crutch, and limped slowly and painfully to the foot of the stairs. She could not go up and comfort Lionel Hezekiah as she yearned to do, which was the reason Judith had sent him up-stairs. Salome had not been up-stairs for fifteen years. Neither did she dare to call him out on the landing, lest Judith return. Besides, of course he must be punished; he had been very naughty.

"But I wish I could smuggle a bit of supper up to him," she mused, sitting down on the lowest step and listening. "I don't hear a sound. I suppose he has cried himself to sleep, poor, dear baby. He certainly is dreadfully mischievous, but it seems to me that it shows an investigating turn of mind, and if it could only be directed into the proper channels—I wish Judith would let me have a talk with Mr. Leonard about Lionel Hezekiah. I wish Judith didn't hate ministers so. I don't mind so much her not letting me go to church, because I'm so lame that it would be painful anyhow; but I'd like to talk with Mr. Leonard now and then about some things. I can never believe that Judith and father were right; I am sure they were not. There is a God, and I'm afraid it's terribly wicked not to go to church. But there, nothing short of a miracle would convince Judith; so there is no use in thinking about it. Yes, Lionel Hezekiah must have gone to sleep."

Salome pictured him so, with his long, curling lashes

brushing his rosy, tear-stained cheek and his chubby fists clasped tightly over his breast as was his habit; her heart grew warm and thrilling with the maternity the picture provoked.

A year previously, Lionel Hezekiah's parents, Abner and Martha Smith, had died, leaving a houseful of children and very little else. The children were adopted into various Carmody families, and Salome Marsh had amazed Judith by asking to be allowed to take the five-year-old "baby." At first Judith had laughed at the idea; but, when she found that Salome was in earnest, she yielded. Judith always gave Salome her own way except on one point.

"If you want the child, I suppose you must have him," she said finally. "I wish he had a civilized name, though. Hezekiah is bad, and Lionel is worse; but the two in combination, and tacked on to Smith at that, is something that only Martha Smith could have invented. Her judgment was the same clear through, from selecting husbands to names."

So Lionel Hezekiah came into Judith's home and Salome's heart. The latter was permitted to love him all she pleased, but Judith overlooked his training with a critical eye. Possibly it was just as well, for Salome might otherwise have ruined him with indulgence. Salome, who always adopted Judith's opinions, no matter how ill they fitted her, deferred to the former's decrees meekly, and suffered far more than Lionel Hezekiah when he was punished.

She sat on the stairs until she fell asleep herself, her head pillowed on her arm. Judith found her there when she came in, severe and triumphant, from her bout with the henhouse door. Her face softened into marvelous tenderness as she looked at Salome.

"She's nothing but a child herself in spite of her age," she thought pityingly. "A child that's had her whole life thwarted and spoiled through no fault of her own. And yet folks say there is a God who is kind and good! If there is a God, He is a cruel, jealous tyrant, and I hate Him!"

Judith's eyes were bitter and vindictive. She thought she had many grievances against the great Power that rules the universe, but the most intense was Salome's

164   *Chronicles of Avonlea*

helplessness—Salome, who fifteen years before had been the brightest, happiest of maidens, light of heart and foot, bubbling over with harmless, sparkling mirth and life. If Salome could only walk like other women, Judith told herself that she would not hate the great tyrannical Power.

Lionel Hezekiah was subdued and angelic for four days after that affair of the henhouse door. Then he broke out in a new place. One afternoon he came in sobbing, with his golden curls full of burrs. Judith was not in, but Salome dropped her crochet-work and gazed at him in dismay.

"Oh, Lionel Hezekiah, what have you gone and done now?"

"I—I just stuck the burrs in 'cause I was playing I was a heathen chief," sobbed Lionel Hezekiah. "It was great fun while it lasted; but, when I tried to take them out, it hurt awful."

Neither Salome nor Lionel Hezekiah ever forgot the harrowing hour that followed. With the aid of comb and scissors, Salome eventually got the burrs out of Lionel Hezekiah's crop of curls. It would be impossible to decide which of them suffered more in the process. Salome cried as hard as Lionel Hezekiah did, and every snip of the scissors or tug at the silken floss cut into her heart. She was almost exhausted when the performance was over; but she took the tired Lionel Hezekiah on her knee, and laid her wet cheek against his shining head.

"Oh, Lionel Hezekiah, what does make you get into mischief so constantly?" she sighed.

Lionel Hezekiah frowned reflectively.

"I don't know," he finally announced, "unless it's because you don't send me to Sunday school."

Salome started as if an electric shock had passed through her frail body.

"Why, Lionel Hezekiah," she stammered, "what put such an idea into your head?"

"Well, all the other boys go," said Lionel Hezekiah defiantly; "and they're all better'n me; so I guess that must be the reason. Teddy Markham says that all little boys should go to Sunday school, and that if they don't they're sure to go to the bad place. I don't see how you can 'spect me to behave well when you won't send me to Sunday school."

"Would you like to go?" asked Salome, almost in a whisper.

"I'd like it bully," said Lionel Hezekiah frankly and succinctly.

"Oh, don't use such dreadful words," sighed Salome helplessly. "I'll see what can be done. Perhaps you can go. I'll ask your Aunt Judith."

"Oh, Aunt Judith won't let me go," said Lionel Hezekiah despondingly. "Aunt Judith doesn't believe there is any God or any bad place. Teddy Markham says she doesn't. He says she's an awful wicked woman 'cause she never goes to church. So you must be wicked too, Aunt Salome, 'cause you never go. Why don't you?"

"Your—your Aunt Judith won't let me go," faltered Salome, more perplexed than she had ever been before in her life.

"Well, it doesn't seem to me that you have much fun on Sundays," remarked Lionel Hezekiah ponderingly. "I'd have more if I was you. But I s'pose you can't 'cause you're ladies. I'm glad I'm a man. Look at Abel Blair, what splendid times he has on Sundays. He never goes to church, but he goes fishing, and has cock-fights, and gets drunk. When I grow up, I'm going to do that on Sundays too, since I won't be going to church. I don't want to go to church, but I'd like to go to Sunday school."

Salome listened in agony. Every word of Lionel Hezekiah's stung her conscience unbearably. So this was the result of her weak yielding to Judith; this innocent child looked upon her as a wicked woman, and, worse still, regarded old, depraved Abel Blair as a model to be imitated. Oh! was it too late to undo the evil? When Judith returned, Salome blurted out the whole story. "Lionel Hezekiah must go to Sunday school," she concluded appealingly.

Judith's face hardened until it was as if cut in stone.

"No, he shall not," she said stubbornly. "No one living in my household shall ever go to church or Sunday school. I gave in to you when you wanted to teach him to say his prayers, though I knew it was only foolish superstition, but I shan't yield another inch. You know exactly how I feel on this subject, Salome; I believe just as father did. You know he hated churches and churchgoing. And was there ever a better, kinder, more lovable man?"

"Mother believed in God; mother always went to church," pleaded Salome.

"Mother was weak and superstitious, just as you are," retorted Judith inflexibly. "I tell you, Salome, I don't believe there is a God. But, if there is, He is cruel and unjust, and I hate Him."

"Judith!" gasped Salome, aghast at the impiety. She half-expected to see her sister struck dead at her feet.

"Don't 'Judith' me!" said Judith passionately, in the strange anger that any discussion of the subject always roused in her. "I mean every word I say. Before you got lame, I didn't feel much about it one way or another; I'd just as soon have gone with mother as with father. But when you were struck down like that, I knew father was right."

For a moment Salome quailed. She felt that she could not, dare not, stand out against Judith. For her own sake she could not have done so, but the thought of Lionel Hezekiah nerved her to desperation. She struck her thin, bleached little hands wildly together.

"Judith, I'm going to church to-morrow," she cried. "I tell you I am; I won't set Lionel Hezekiah a bad example one day longer. I'll not take him; I won't go against you in that, for it is your bounty feeds and clothes him; but I'm going myself."

"If you do, Salome Marsh, I'll never forgive you," said Judith, her harsh face dark with anger; and then, not trusting herself to discuss the subject any longer, she went out.

Salome dissolved into her ready tears, and cried most of the night. But her resolution did not fail. Go to church she would, for that dear baby's sake.

Judith would not speak to her at breakfast, and this almost broke Salome's heart; but she dared not yield. After breakfast, she limped painfully into her room, and still more painfully dressed herself. When she was ready, she took a little old worn Bible out of her box. It had been her mother's, and Salome read a chapter in it every night, although she never dared to let Judith see her doing it.

When she limped out into the kitchen, Judith looked up with a hard face. A flame of sullen anger glowed in her dark eyes, and she went into the sitting-room and shut the door, as if by that act she were shutting her sister for evermore out of her heart and life. Salome, strung up to the last pitch of nervous tension, felt intuitively the significance of that closed door. For a moment she wavered—oh, she could not go against Judith! She was all but turning back to her room when Lionel Hezekiah came running in, and paused to look at her admiringly.

"You look just bully, Aunt Salome," he said. "Where are you going?"

"Don't use that word, Lionel Hezekiah," pleaded Salome. "I'm going to church."

"Take me with you," said Lionel Hezekiah promptly. Salome shook her head.

"I can't, dear. Your Aunt Judith wouldn't like it. Perhaps she will let you go after a while. Now, do be a good boy while I am away, won't you? Don't do any naughty things."

"I won't do them if I know they're naughty," conceded Lionel Hezekiah. "But that's just the trouble; I don't know what's naughty and what ain't. Prob'ly if I went to Sunday school I'd find out."

Salome limped out of the yard and down the lane bordered by its asters and goldenrod. Fortunately, the church was just outside the lane, across the main road; but Salome found it hard to cover even that short distance. She felt almost exhausted when she reached the church and toiled painfully up the aisle to her mother's old pew. She laid her crutch on the seat, and sank into the corner by the window with a sigh of relief.

She had elected to come early so that she might get there before the rest of the people. The church was as yet empty, save for a class of Sunday school children and their teacher in a remote corner, who paused midway in their lesson to stare with amazement at the astonishing sight of Salome Marsh limping into church.

The big building, shadowy from the great elms around

it, was very still. A faint murmur came from the closed
room behind the pulpit where the rest of the Sunday
school was assembled. In front of the pulpit was a stand
bearing tall white geraniums in luxuriant blossom. The
light fell through the stained-glass window in a soft tangle
of hues upon the floor. Salome felt a sense of peace and
happiness fill her heart. Even Judith's anger lost its importance. She leaned her head against the window-sill, and
gave herself up to the flood of tender old recollections that
swept over her.

Memory went back to the years of her childhood
when she had sat in this pew every Sunday with her
mother. Judith had come then, too, always seeming grown
up to Salome by reason of her ten years' seniority. Her
tall, dark, reserved father never came. Salome knew that
the Carmody people called him an infidel, and looked
upon him as a very wicked man. But he had not been
wicked: he had been good and kind in his own odd way.

The gentle little mother had died when Salome was
ten years old, but so loving and tender was Judith's care
that the child did not miss anything out of her life. Judith
Marsh loved her little sister with an intensity that was
maternal. She herself was a plain, repellent girl, liked by
few, sought after by no man; but she was determined that
Salome should have everything that she had missed—
admiration, friendship, love. She would have a vicarious
youth in Salome's.

All went according to Judith's planning until Salome
was eighteen, and then trouble after trouble came. Their
father, whom Judith had understood and passionately loved,
died; Salome's young lover was killed in a railroad accident; and finally Salome herself developed symptoms of
the hip-disease which, springing from a trifling injury,
eventually left her a cripple. Everything possible was done
for her. Judith, falling heir to a snug little fortune by the
death of the old aunt for whom she was named, spared
nothing to obtain the best medical skill, and in vain. One
and all, the great doctors failed.

Judith had borne her father's death bravely enough in
spite of her agony of grief; she had watched her sister
pining and fading with the pain of her broken heart with-

out growing bitter; but when she knew at last that Salome would never walk again save as she hobbled painfully about on her crutch, the smouldering revolt in her soul broke its bounds, and overflowed her nature in a passionate rebellion against the Being who had sent, or had failed to prevent, these calamities. She did not rave or denounce wildly; that was not Judith's way; but she never went to church again, and it soon became an accepted fact in Carmody that Judith Marsh was as rank an infidel as her father had been before her; nay, worse, since she would not even allow Salome to go to church, and shut the door in the minister's face when he went to see her.

"I should have stood out against her for conscience' sake," reflected Salome in her pew self-reproachfully. "But, O dear, I'm afraid she'll never forgive me, and how can I live if she doesn't? But I must endure it for Lionel Hezekiah's sake; my weakness has perhaps done him great harm already. They say that what a child learns in the first seven years never leaves him; so Lionel Hezekiah has only another year to get set right about these things. Oh, if I've left it till too late!"

When the people began to come in, Salone felt painfully the curious glances directed at her. Look where she would, she met them, unless she looked out of the window; so out of the window she did look unswervingly, her delicate little face burning crimson with self-consciousness. She could see her home and its back yard plainly, with Lionel Hezekiah making mud-pies joyfully in the corner. Presently, she saw Judith come out of the house and stride away to the pine wood behind it. Judith always betook herself to the pines in time of mental stress and strain.

Salome could see the sunlight on Lionel Hezekiah's bare head as he mixed his pies. In the pleasure of watching him, she forgot where she was and the curious eyes turned on her.

Suddenly Lionel Hezekiah ceased concocting pies, and betook himself to the corner of the summer kitchen, where he proceeded to climb up to the top of the storm-fence and from there to mount the sloping kitchen roof. Salome clasped her hands in agony. What if the child should fall? Oh! why had Judith gone away and left him alone? What if—what if—and then, while her brain with lightning-like rapidity pictured forth a dozen possible catastrophes, something really did happen. Lionel Hezekiah slipped, sprawled wildly, slid down, and fell off the roof, in a bewildering whirl of arms and legs, plump into the big rain-water hogshead under the spout, which was generally full to the brim with rain-water, a hogshead big and deep enough to swallow up half a dozen small boys who went climbing kitchen roofs on a Sunday.

Then something took place that is talked of in Carmody to this day, and even fiercely wrangled over, so many and conflicting are the opinions on the subject. Salome Marsh, who had not walked a step without assistance for fifteen years, suddenly sprang to her feet with a shriek, ran down the aisle, and out of the door!

Every man, woman, and child in the Carmody church followed her, even to the minister, who had just announced his text. When they got out, Salome was already half-way up her lane, running wildly. In her heart was room for but one agonized thought. Would Lionel Hezekiah be drowned before she reached him?

She opened the gate of the yard, and panted across it just as a tall, grim-faced woman came around the corner of the house and stood rooted to the ground in astonishment at the sight that met her eyes.

But Salome saw nobody. She flung herself against the hogshead and looked in, sick with terror at what she might see. What she did see was Lionel Hezekiah sitting on the bottom of the hogshead in water that came only to his waist. He was looking rather dazed and bewildered, but was apparently quite uninjured.

The yard was full of people, but nobody had as yet said a word; awe and wonder held everybody in spellbound silence. Judith was the first to speak. She pushed through the crowd to Salome. Her face was blanched to a deadly whiteness; and her eyes, as Mrs. William Blair afterwards declared, were enough to give a body the creeps.

"Salome," she said in a high, shrill, unnatural voice, "where is your crutch?"

Salome came to herself at the question. For the first time, she realized that she had walked, nay, run, all that distance from the church alone and unaided. She turned pale, swayed, and would have fallen if Judith had not caught her.

Old Dr. Blair came forward briskly.

"Carry her in," he said, "and don't all of you come crowding in, either. She wants quiet and rest for a spell."

Most of the people obediently returned to the church, their suddenly loosened tongues clattering in voluble excitement. A few women assisted Judith to carry Salome in and lay her on the kitchen lounge, followed by the doctor and the dripping Lionel Hezekiah, whom the minister had lifted out of the hogshead and to whom nobody now paid the slightest attention.

Salome faltered out her story, and her hearers listened with varying emotions.

"It's a miracle," said Sam Lawson in an awed voice.

Dr. Blair shrugged his shoulders.

"There is no miracle about it," he said bluntly. "It's all perfectly natural. The disease in the hip has evidently been quite well for a long time; Nature does sometimes work cures like that when she is let alone. The trouble was that the muscles were paralyzed by long disuse. That paralysis was overcome by the force of a strong and instinctive effort. Salome, get up and walk across the kitchen."

Salome obeyed. She walked across the kitchen and back, slowly, stiffly, falteringly, now that the stimulus of frantic fear was spent; but still she walked. The doctor nodded his satisfaction.

"Keep that up every day. Walk as much as you can without tiring yourself, and you'll soon be as spry as ever. No more need of crutches for you, but there's no miracle in the case."

Judith Marsh turned to him. She had not spoken a word since her question concerning Salome's crutch. Now she said passionately:

"It *was* a miracle. God has worked it to prove His existence to me, and I accept the proof."

The old doctor shrugged his shoulders again. Being a wise man, he knew when to hold his tongue.

"Well, put Salome to bed, and let her sleep the rest of the day. She's worn out. And for pity's sake, let some one take that poor child and put some dry clothes on him before he catches his death of cold."

That evening, as Salome Marsh lay in her bed in a glory of sunset light, her heart filled with unutterable gratitude and happiness, Judith came into the room. She wore her best hat and dress, and she held Lionel Hezekiah by the hand. Lionel Hezekiah's beaming face was scrubbed clean, and his curls fell in beautiful sleekness over the lace collar of his velvet suit.

"How do you feel now, Salome?" asked Judith gently.

"Better. I've had a lovely sleep. But where are you going, Judith?"

"I am going to church," said Judith firmly, "and I am going to take Lionel Hezekiah with me."

12

The End Of a Quarrel

NANCY ROGERSON sat down on Louisa Shaw's front doorstep and looked about her, drawing a long breath of delight that seemed tinged with pain. Everything was very much the same; the square garden was as square as ever, and as disorderly, with the same old charming hodge-podge of fruit and flowers, and gooseberry bushes and tiger lilies, a gnarled old apple tree sticking up here and there, and a thick cherry copse at the foot. Behind was a row of pointed firs, coming out darkly against the swimming pink sunset sky, not looking a day older than they had looked twenty years ago, when Nancy had been a young girl walking and dreaming in their shadows. The old willow to the left was as big and sweeping and, Nancy thought with a little shudder, probably as caterpillary, as ever. Nancy had learned many things in her twenty years of exile from Avonlea, but she had never learned to conquer her dread of caterpillars.

"Nothing is much changed, Louisa," she said, propping her chin on her plump white hands, and sniffing at the delectable odour of the bruised mint upon which Louisa was trampling. "I'm glad; I was afraid to come back for fear you would have improved the old garden out of existence, or else into some prim, orderly lawn, which would have been worse. It's as magnificently untidy as ever, and the fence still wobbles. It *can't* be the same fence, but it looks exactly like it. No, nothing is much changed. Thank you, Louisa."

Louisa had not the faintest idea what Nancy was thanking her for, but then she had never been able to fathom Nancy, much as she had always liked her in the old girlhood days that now seemed much further away to Louisa than they did to Nancy. Louisa was separated from them by the fulness of wifehood and motherhood, while Nancy looked back only over the narrow gap that empty years make.

"You haven't changed much yourself, Nancy," she said, looking admiringly at Nancy's trim figure, in the nurse's uniform she had donned to show Louisa what it was like, her firm, pink-and-white face and the glossy waves of her golden brown hair. "You've held your own wonderfully well."

"Haven't I?" said Nancy complacently. "Modern methods of massage and cold cream have kept away the crowsfeet, and, fortunately, I had the Rogerson complexion to start with. You wouldn't think I was really thirty-eight, would you? Thirty-eight! Twenty years ago I thought anybody who was thirty-eight was a perfect female Methuselah. And now I feel so horribly, ridiculously young, Louisa. Every morning when I get up, I have to say solemnly to myself three times, 'You're an old maid, Nancy Rogerson,' to tone myself down to anything like a becoming attitude for the day."

"I guess you don't mind being an old maid much," said Louisa, shrugging her shoulders. She would not have been an old maid herself for anything; yet she inconsistently envied Nancy her freedom, her wide life in the world, her unlined brow, and care-free lightness of spirit.

"Oh, but I do mind," said Nancy frankly. "I hate being an old maid."

"Why don't you get married, then?" asked Louisa, paying an unconscious tribute to Nancy's perennial chance by her use of the present tense.

Nancy shook her head.

"No, that wouldn't suit me either. I don't want to be married. Do you remember that story Anne Shirley used to tell long ago of the pupil who wanted to be a widow because 'if you were married your husband bossed you and if you weren't married people called you an old maid?' Well, that is precisely my opinion. I'd like to be a widow. Then I'd have the freedom of the unmarried, with the kudos of the married. I could eat my cake and have it, too. Oh, to be a widow!"

"Nancy!" said Louisa in a shocked tone.

Nancy laughed, a mellow gurgle that rippled through the garden like a brook.

"Oh, Louisa, I can shock you yet. That was just how you used to say 'Nancy' long ago, as if I'd broken all the commandments at once."

"You do say such queer things," protested Louisa, "and half the time I don't know what you mean."

"Bless you, dear coz, half the time I don't myself. Perhaps the joy of coming back to the old spot has slightly turned my brain. I've found my lost girlhood here. I'm *not* thirty-eight in this garden—it is a flat impossibility. I'm sweet eighteen, with a waist line two inches smaller. Look, the sun is just setting. I see he has still his old trick of throwing his last beams over the Wright farmhouse. By the way, Louisa, is Peter Wright still living there?"

"Yes." Louisa threw a sudden interested glance at the apparently placid Nancy.

"Married, I suppose, with half a dozen children?" said Nancy indifferently, pulling up some more sprigs of mint and pinning them on her breast. Perhaps the exertion of leaning over to do it flushed her face. There was more than the Rogerson colour in it, anyhow, and Louisa, slow though her mental processes might be in some respects, thought she understood the meaning of a blush as well as the next one. All the instinct of the matchmaker flamed up in her.

"Indeed he isn't," she said promptly. "Peter Wright has never married. He has been faithful to your memory, Nancy."

"Ugh! You make me feel as if I were buried up there in the Avonlea cemetery and had a monument over me with a weeping willow carved on it," shivered Nancy. "When it is said that a man has been faithful to a woman's memory, it generally means that he couldn't get anyone else to take him."

"That isn't the case with Peter," protested Louisa. "He is a good match, and many a woman would have been glad to take him, and would yet. He's only forty-three.

But he's never taken the slightest interest in anyone since you threw him over, Nancy."

"But I didn't. He threw me over," said Nancy, plaintively, looking afar over the low-lying fields and a feathery young spruce valley to the white buildings of the Wright farm, glowing rosily in the sunset light when all the rest of Avonlea was scarfing itself in shadows. There was laughter in her eyes. Louisa could not pierce beneath that laughter to find if there were anything under it.

"Fudge!" said Louisa. "What on earth did you and Peter quarrel about?" she added, curiously.

"I've often wondered," parried Nancy.

"And you've never seen him since?" reflected Louisa.

"No. Has he changed much?"

"Well, some. He is gray and kind of tired-looking. But it isn't to be wondered at—living the life he does. He hasn't had a housekeeper for two years—not since his old aunt died. He just lives there alone and cooks his own meals. I've never been in the house, but folks say the disorder is something awful."

"Yes, I shouldn't think Peter was cut out for a tidy housekeeper," said Nancy lightly, dragging up more mint. "Just think, Louisa, if it hadn't been for that old quarrel, I might be Mrs. Peter Wright at this very moment, mother to the aforesaid supposed half-dozen, and vexing my soul over Peter's meals and socks and cows."

"I guess you are better off as you are," said Louisa.

"Oh, I don't know." Nancy looked up at the white house on the hill again. "I have an awfully good time out of life, but it doesn't seem to satisfy, somehow. To be candid—and oh, Louisa, candour is a rare thing among women when it comes to talking of the men—I believe I'd rather be cooking Peter's meals and dusting his house. I wouldn't mind his bad grammar now. I've learned one or two valuable little things out yonder, and one is that it doesn't matter if a man's grammar is askew, so long as he doesn't swear at you. By the way, is Peter as ungrammatical as ever?"

"I—I don't know," said Louisa helplessly. "I never knew he *was* ungrammatical."

"Does he still say, 'I seen,' and 'them things'?" demanded Nancy.

"I never noticed," confessed Louisa.

"Enviable Louisa! Would that I had been born with that blessed faculty of never noticing! It stands a woman in better stead than beauty or brains. *I* used to notice Peter's mistakes. When he said 'I seen,' it jarred on me in my salad days. I tried, oh, so tactfully, to reform him in that respect. Peter didn't like being reformed—the Wrights always had a fairly good opinion of themselves, you know. It was really over a question of syntax we quarreled. Peter told me I'd have to take him as he was, grammar and all, or go without him. I went without him—and ever since I've been wondering if I were really sorry, or if it were merely a pleasantly sentimental regret I was hugging to my heart. I daresay it's the latter. Now, Louisa, I see the beginning of the plot far down in those placid eyes of yours. Strangle it at birth, dear Louisa. There is no use in your trying to make up a match between Peter and me now—no, nor in slyly inviting him up here to tea some evening, as you are even this moment thinking of doing."

"Well, I must go and milk the cows," gasped Louisa, rather glad to make her escape. Nancy's power of thought-reading struck her as uncanny. She felt afraid to remain with her cousin any longer, lest Nancy should drag to light all the secrets of her being.

Nancy sat long on the steps after Louisa had gone—sat until the night came down, darkly and sweetly, over the garden, and the stars twinkled out above the firs. This had been her home in girlhood. Here she had lived and kept house for her father. When he died, Curtis Shaw, newly married to her cousin Louisa, bought the farm from her and moved in. Nancy stayed on with them, expecting soon to go to a home of her own. She and Peter Wright were engaged.

Then came their mysterious quarrel, concerning the cause of which kith and kin on both sides were left in annoying ignorance. Of the results they were not ignorant. Nancy promptly packed up and left Avonlea seven hundred miles behind her. She went to a hospital in Montreal and studied nursing. In the twenty years that had followed, she had never even revisited Avonlea. Her sudden descent on it this summer was a whim born of a moment's homesick longing for this same old garden. She had not thought about Peter. In very truth, she had thought little about Peter for the last fifteen years. She supposed that she had forgotten him. But now, sitting on the old doorstep, where she had often sat in her courting days, with Peter lounging on a broad stone at her feet, something tugged at her heartstrings. She looked over the valley to the light in the kitchen of the Wright farmhouse, and pictured Peter sitting there, lonely and uncared for, with naught but the cold comfort of his own providing.

"Well, he should have got married," she said snappishly. "I am not going to worry because he is a lonely old bachelor, when all these years I have supposed him a comfy Benedict. Why doesn't he hire him a housekeeper, at least? He can afford it; the place looks prosperous. Ugh! I've a fat bank account, and I've seen almost everything in the world worth seeing; but I've got several carefully hidden gray hairs and a horrible conviction that grammar isn't one of the essential things in life after all. Well, I'm not going to moon out here in the dew any longer. I'm going in to read the smartest, frilliest, frothiest society novel in my trunk."

In the week that followed, Nancy enjoyed herself after her own fashion. She read and swung in the garden, having a hammock hung under the firs. She went far afield, in rambles to woods and lonely uplands.

"I like it much better than meeting people," she said, when Louisa suggested going to see this one and that one, "especially the Avonlea people. All my old chums are gone, or hopelessly married and changed, and the young set who have come up know not Joseph, and make me feel uncomfortably middle-aged. It's far worse to feel middle-aged than old, you know. Away there in the woods, I feel as eternally young as Nature herself. And oh, it's so nice not having to fuss with thermometers and temperatures and other people's whims. Let me indulge my own whims, Louisa dear, and punish me with a cold bite when I come in late for meals. I'm not even going to church again. It was horrible there yesterday. The church is so offensively spick-and-span brand new and modern."

"It's thought to be the prettiest church in these parts," protested Louisa, a little sorely.

"Churches shouldn't be pretty—they should at least be fifty years old and mellowed into beauty. New churches are an abomination."

"Did you see Peter Wright in church?" asked Louisa. She had been bursting to ask it.

Nancy nodded.

"Verily, yes. He sat right across from me in the corner pew. I didn't think him painfully changed. Iron-gray hair becomes him. But I was horribly disappointed in myself. I had expected to feel at least a romantic thrill, but all I felt was a comfortable interest, such as I might have taken in any old friend. Do my utmost, Louisa, I couldn't compass a thrill."

"Did he come to speak to you?" asked Louisa, who hadn't any idea what Nancy meant by her thrills.

"Alas, no. It wasn't my fault. I stood at the door outside with the most amiable expression I could assume, but Peter merely sauntered away without a glance in my direction. It would be some comfort to my vanity if I could believe it was on account of rankling spite or pride. But the honest truth, dear Weezy, is that it looked to me exactly as if he never thought of it. He was more interested in talking about the hay crop with Oliver Sloane—who, by the way, is more Oliver Sloaneish than ever."

"If you feel as you said you did the other night, why didn't you go and speak to him?" Louisa wanted to know.

"But I don't feel that way now. That was just a mood. You don't know anything about moods, dearie. You don't know what it is to yearn desperately one hour for something you wouldn't take if it were offered you the next."

"But that is foolishness," protested Louisa.

"To be sure it is—rank foolishness. But oh, it is so delightful to be foolish after being compelled to be unbrokenly sensible for twenty years. Well, I'm going picking strawberries this afternoon, Lou. Don't wait tea for me. I probably won't be back till dark. I've only four more days to stay, and I want to make the most of them."

Nancy wandered far and wide in her rambles that afternoon. When she had filled her jug, she still roamed about with delicious aimlessness. Once she found herself in a wood lane skirting a field wherein a man was mowing hay. The man was Peter Wright. Nancy walked faster when she discovered this, with never a roving glance, and presently the green, ferny depths of the maple woods swallowed her up.

From old recollections, she knew that she was on Peter Morrison's land, and calculated that if she kept straight on she would come out where the old Morrison house used to be. Her calculations proved correct, with a trifling variation. She came out fifty yards south of the old deserted Morrison house, and found herself in the yard of the Wright farm!

Passing the house—the house where she had once dreamed of reigning as mistress—Nancy's curiosity overcame her. The place was not in view of any other near house. She deliberately went up to it, intending—low be it spoken—to peep in at the kitchen window. But, seeing the door wide open, she went to it instead and halted on the step, looking about her keenly.

The kitchen was certainly pitiful in its disorder. The floor had apparently not been swept for a fortnight. On the bare deal table were the remnants of Peter's dinner, a meal that could not have been very tempting at its best.

"What a miserable place for a human being to live in!" groaned Nancy. "Look at the ashes on that stove! And that table! Is it any wonder that Peter has got gray? He'll work hard haymaking all the afternoon—and then come home to *this!*"

An idea suddenly darted into Nancy's brain. At first she looked aghast. Then she laughed and glanced at her watch.

"I'll do it—just for fun and a little pity. It's half-past two, and Peter won't be home till four at the earliest. I'll have a good hour to do it in, and still make my escape in good time. Nobody will ever know; nobody can see me here."

Nancy went in, threw off her hat, and seized a broom. The first thing she did was to give the kitchen a thorough sweeping. Then she kindled a fire, put a kettle full of water on to heat, and attacked the dishes. From the number of them, she rightly concluded that Peter hadn't washed any for at least a week.

"I suppose he just uses the clean ones as long as they hold out, and then has a grand wash-up," she laughed. "I wonder where he keeps his dish-towels, if he has any."

Evidently Peter hadn't any. At least, Nancy couldn't find any. She marched boldly into the dusty sitting-room and explored the drawers of an old-fashioned sideboard, confiscating a towel she found there. As she worked, she hummed a song; her steps were light and her eyes bright with excitement. Nancy was enjoying herself thoroughly, there was no doubt of that. The spice of mischief in the adventure pleased her mightily.

The dishes washed, she hunted up a clean, but yellow and evidently long unused, tablecloth out of the sideboard, and proceeded to set the table and get Peter's tea. She found bread and butter in the pantry, a trip to the cellar furnished a pitcher of cream, and Nancy recklessly heaped the contents of her strawberry jug on Peter's plate. The tea was made and set back to keep warm. And, as a finishing touch, Nancy ravaged the old neglected garden and set a huge bowl of crimson roses in the centre of the table.

"Now I must go," she said aloud. "Wouldn't it be fun to see Peter's face when he comes in, though? Ha-hum! I've enjoyed doing this—but why? Nancy Rogerson, don't be asking yourself conundrums. Put on your hat and proceed homeward, constructing on your way some reliable fib to account to Louisa for the absence of your strawberries."

Nancy paused a moment and looked around wistfully. She had made the place look cheery and neat and homelike. She felt that queer tugging at her heartstrings again. Suppose she belonged here, and was waiting for Peter to come home to tea. Suppose—Nancy whirled around with a sudden horrible prescience of what she was going to see! Peter Wright was standing in the doorway.

Nancy's face went crimson. For the first time in her

life she had not a word to say for herself. Peter looked at her and then at the table, with its fruit and flowers.

"Thank you," he said politely.

Nancy recovered herself. With a shame-faced laugh, she held out her hand.

"Don't have me arrested for trespass, Peter. I came and looked in at your kitchen out of impertinent curiosity, and, just for fun, I thought I'd come in and get your tea. I thought you'd be so surprised—and I meant to go before you came home, of course."

"I wouldn't have been surprised," said Peter, shaking hands. "I saw you go past the field and I tied the horses and followed you down through the woods. I've been sitting on the fence back yonder, watching your comings and goings."

"Why didn't you come and speak to me at church yesterday, Peter?" demanded Nancy boldly.

"I was afraid I would say something ungrammatical," answered Peter drily.

The crimson flamed over Nancy's face again. She pulled her hand away.

"That's cruel of you, Peter."

Peter suddenly laughed. There was a note of boyishness in the laughter.

"So it is," he said, "but I had to get rid of the accumulated malice and spite of twenty years somehow. It's all gone now, and I'll be as amiable as I know how. But since you have gone to the trouble of getting my supper for me, Nancy, you must stay and help me eat it. Them strawberries look good. I haven't had any this summer— been too busy to pick them."

Nancy stayed. She sat at the head of Peter's table and poured his tea for him. She talked to him wittily of the Avonlea people and the changes in their old set. Peter followed her lead with an apparent absence of self-consciousness, eating his supper like a man whose heart and mind were alike on good terms with him. Nancy felt wretched—and, at the same time, ridiculously happy. It seemed the most grotesque thing in the world that she should be presiding there at Peter's table, and yet the most natural. There were moments when she felt like crying—other moments when her laughter was as ready and spontaneous as a girl's. Sentiment and humour had always waged an equal contest in Nancy's nature.

When Peter had finished his strawberries, he folded his arms on the table and looked admiringly at Nancy.

"You look well at the head of a table, Nancy," he said critically. "How is it that you haven't been presiding at one of your own long before this? I thought you'd meet with lots of men out in the world that you'd like—men who talked good grammar."

"Peter, don't!" said Nancy, wincing. "I was a goose."

"No, you were quite right. I was a tetchy fool. If I'd had any sense, I'd have felt thankful you thought enough of me to want to improve me, and I'd have tried to kerrect my mistakes instead of getting mad. It's too late now, I suppose."

"Too late for what?" said Nancy, plucking up heart of grace at something in Peter's tone and look.

"For—kerrecting mistakes."

"Grammatical ones?"

"Not exactly. I guess them mistakes are past kerrecting in an old fellow like me. Worse mistakes, Nancy. I wonder what you would say if I asked you to forgive me, and have me after all."

"I'd snap you up before you'd have time to change your mind," said Nancy brazenly. She tried to look Peter in the face, but her blue eyes, where tears and mirth were blending, faltered down before his gray ones.

Peter stood up, knocking over his chair, and strode around the table to her.

"Nancy, my girl!" he said.

ABOUT THE AUTHOR

L. M. MONTGOMERY's fascinating accounts of the lives and romances of Anne, Emily, and other well-loved characters have achieved long-lasting popularity the world over. Born in 1874 in Prince Edward Island, Canada, Lucy Maud showed an early flair for storytelling. She soon began to have her writing published in papers and magazines, and when she died in Toronto in 1942, she had written more than twenty novels and a large number of short stories. Most of her books are set in Prince Edward Island, which she loved very much and wrote of most beautifully. *Anne of Green Gables*, her most popular work, has been translated into thirty-six languages, made into a film twice, and has had continuing success as a stage play. Lucy Maud Montgomery's early home at Cavendish, P.E.I., where she is buried, is a much-visited historic site.